MORE THAN A PROMISE

The author is happy to receive feedback from readers.
She can be contacted via her website
http://members.iinet.net.au/~woods
or by post
PO Box 2099
Kardinya 6163
Western Australia

MORE THAN A PROMISE

Janet Woods

This first world edition published in Great Britain 2006 by
SEVERN HOUSE PUBLISHERS LTD of
9–15 High Street, Sutton, Surrey SM1 1DF.
This first world edition published in the USA 2006 by
SEVERN HOUSE PUBLISHERS INC of
595 Madison Avenue, New York, N.Y. 10022.

British Library Cataloguing in Publication Data

Woods, Janet, 1939-
   More than a promise
   1.   Women singers - Ireland - Fiction
   2.   Ireland - Social conditions - Fiction
   3.   Love stories
   I.   Title
   823.9'14 [F]

   ISBN-10: 0-7278-6330-4

For my sister, Daphne Wallis, with love.

Typeset by Palimpsest Book Production Ltd.,
Polmont, Stirlingshire, Scotland.
Printed and bound in Great Britain by
MPG Books Ltd., Bodmin, Cornwall.

Prologue

County Kilkenny, 1900

There were no rainbows with pots of gold waiting for the arrival of Erin Maguire. After a long, dry summer, a wind roared in from the Atlantic Ocean pushing eighty miles of churning clouds across the October sky. The rain was an icy torrent, so the Callacrea midwife was forced to shoulder into the gale and wade through ankle-deep mud to get to the Maguires' home.

Situated in an acre where dark sheets of slate poked sharply though the sod, the building was little more than a two-roomed cottage cowering into the side of the hill, though its walls were thick and solid.

Whichever way a visitor came to it, they had to cross Lord Sanders' land, so the acre wasn't worth much to the casual eye. The peppercorn tenure had been a wedding present from Lord Sanders when one of his maids, Cliona Kelly, had wed his foreman, Dermot Maguire, and the arrangement had been agreed to on a handshake.

The gift had not brought the mismatched pair any joy, and the village tongues had wagged, especially when the infant was born.

'A difficult birth, to be sure,' the midwife told the village women. 'Though hardly a groan did Cliona Maguire make. The infant's skin has the sheen of pearls, her eyes are the colour of bluebells in spring and her hair is as dark as the devil's beard.'

'And a handsome devil that Colby fellow was too,' one of the women said.

The midwife gave a sly cackle. 'The infant is large for one come seven months into the marriage, and the daughter,

1

though holding more than a passing resemblance to her mother, has no pretence to Dermot hisself.

'Cliona whispered, "*A ghrá mo chroi*," when I placed the child in her arms, but so quietly that the blessing was meant for the ears of herself and the babe alone. "Love of my heart," she repeated in English, loud enough for her man to hear.' The midwife lowered her voice. 'God help the infant with Dermot Maguire for a father, for he stared down at Cliona with those cold, slate eyes of his, and he says, "A girl is of no bloody use to man or cause."'

'What did Cliona call her little shame?'

'Erin Grace she was named, after God's own country.' The midwife smoothed her apron down over her skirt, muttering, 'May the good Lord help Cliona if she fails to produce a son for her man in the future.'

One of the village women crossed herself. 'And may the devil help her if she does, for the pair who came with Dermot Maguire to the marriage are as mean as rats.'

One

Callacrea, 1910

The girl was a small, pinch-faced little thing, with dark braids dangling over her ears on both sides of her head. Her eyes were a startling blue and reflected the emotion of the song she was singing.

> Mellow the moonlight to shine is beginning,
> Close by the window young Eileen is spinning.
> Bent o'er the fire her blind grandmother sitting,
> Crooning and moaning and drowsily knitting
> Merrily, cheerily . . .

Tears came to Sister Agnes's eyes as Erin Maguire completed the verse with dreamy-eyed emotion. 'You're blessed with a rare voice,' she said, when the last trembling note died away. 'If you pass the scholarship exam, I'll teach you to play the harp. Your voice blends quite beautifully with it.'

The promise proved to be an incentive to the girl, for the marks she achieved in the exam were outstanding.

'But she and her mother are not of the faith, and if she's anything like her brothers . . .' Father Brian sighed. 'Those boys were a pair of rogues.'

'They're nothing less than thugs, Father. They'll come to no good.' Sister Agnes settled herself on a chair, folded her hands into her sleeves and prepared to do battle. Nearly seventy years old, she could have been Father Brian's mother twice over.

'It's not fair to judge Erin Maguire by the behaviour of her brothers. The girl gained outstanding marks in the exam and seems to be a well-behaved child.'

3

'But what if the place is needed by a Catholic child?'

'Which child, pray? All the parishioners' children are placed. Where is your charity, Father? If we don't accept her she'll receive no further education. It won't be the first time we've educated a stray.'

Noting the indecision in his face, Sister Agnes pressed home her advantage. 'Didn't you hear her sing? She could win the prize for us at the Fleadh Ceoil in a year or two. It's about time the proddies lost it, and wouldn't it be ironic if one of their own won it for us?'

A grin spread across Father Brian's face. 'Shame on you, Sister. And here was me thinking you'd captured an Irish nightingale in your study. It's sticking the devil's fork into the backsides of the opposition you're after doing, not educating their little heathens.'

'This one already has a cross to bear,' she gently reminded him.

'The sins of the father,' the priest murmured almost to himself. He exchanged a glance with the old woman and nodded. 'With Dermot Maguire for a father, let's not add to her troubles then. We'll accept her.'

Two years later, Erin's mouth curved in a smile as she skipped along the lane humming to herself, her school bag swinging from her shoulder. She couldn't wait to sing to her mammy the song she'd learned.

Putting up with the teasing of the other children wasn't hard, since she was used to it now and wasn't afraid to hit back. Being the only Protestant educated on a scholarship at a Catholic school was more difficult. But having a father who was the foreman of the Callacrea House estate made life easier, because everyone was scared of Dermot Maguire. Erin didn't have any friends though.

'Dirty proddy,' someone yelled when she reached the top of the hill, and a clod of earth hit her in the middle of the back.

It was Liam O'Connor, who lived on the estate with a half dozen scruffy sisters and a scrap of a brother. 'Dirty caffler, yourself,' she yelled and, picking up a stone, took aim.

There came a scuffling noise from behind the dry stone

wall, then fingers closed around her wrist and squeezed hard. "Drop it,' her brother Patrick said.

Squealing with pain, Erin dropped the stone.

Patrick gazed down at her. 'Dirty caffler is it? Wait till I tell our dad you're causing trouble.'

'I'm not so. He called me a dirty proddy, first.'

'Only because you are one.'

Michael came to stand in front of her, buttoning up the front of his trousers. She squealed when he pinched her ear and he laughed. 'You sound like a pig.'

The pair were twins, but not exactly alike, for Patrick was bigger and had grey eyes, whilst Michael's were pale blue. Large for fifteen, they both had greasy light-brown hair, and their eyebrows met in the middle. She wondered why they weren't at work, for they had jobs in the canning factory.

Erin's eyes widened when she saw the eldest of the O'Connor sisters climbing over the wall. 'If you tell on me I'm telling on you.'

'Will you now?' Annie O'Connor said, swaying forward, her blouse open. 'And what is it you'll be telling your daddy, pray?'

'That you were behind the wall with my brothers.'

'So?'

'And you were showing them yourself.'

'Showing them myself? Like this, you mean.' Annie's hands grabbed her blouse and jerked. Erin clutched the torn pieces together as the buttons popped, but her brothers pulled her arms aside.

'Would you look at that then,' Michael taunted. 'A chest as flat as a pancake. D'you want a feel of her, Liam?'

'There's not a ha'penny worth there to feel. Perhaps I can make them bigger for her.' As Erin struggled between her brothers, Liam took her nipples between his fingers and thumbs and pulled.

The scream of pain she gave made her brothers laugh. Sobbing with the agony of the act, and the shame of being exposed, she gathered her torn blouse together and picked up her bag.

'We haven't said you can go yet.' Annie grabbed her school satchel and tipped it out. The boys scuffed their feet all over the contents.

5

Catching her by her pigtails, Patrick jerked her head back and hissed into her face. 'Next time you give us lip you'll get a taste of my fist. Understand?'

Dumbly, she nodded. Letting her go, Patrick pulled Annie O'Connor against him, rubbing her private part through her skirt. 'Right you. You've had my shilling, but me and my brother haven't had the worth of it yet. Get back behind the wall.'

'You make sure you don't get me in the family way, else you'll have to marry me.'

'Not much chance of that. Every man from here to Dublin has done you, from what I hear.'

'Can I watch?' Liam asked.

'No, you can keep a fecking lookout, like I told you.'

Whilst gathering up the contents of her bag she could hear Annie O'Connor giggling and her brother grunting behind the wall, and could see Michael, his hand fiddling inside his pocket as he sat and watched. She hated her brothers with everything that was in her. Her father, too. She was scared of his bad temper, of his pinches and slaps if she got in his way. Her body was covered in bruises from them all.

'I'll give you a toffee if you let me feel inside your drawers,' Liam said to her.

Erin felt sick. Coming upright, she slapped his face and hissed, 'Dirty caffler, you should wash out your mouth with soap.' She began to run, but was sent sprawling by a stone as it hit her in the middle of her back. She scrambled upright, her knees stinging and bleeding from the gravel.

'It's you that's dirty. I know something about you,' Liam shouted. 'I heard my father tell my mother.'

She stared at him. 'What is it?'

'It's a secret. I'm going to tell the others though.'

'I don't care. You're bog-brained, and you can keep your secret.'

When Liam bent to pick up another stone Erin began to run. She didn't stop until she was in sight of the cottage. Her mammy was in the garden, her skirt and apron blowing in the wind as she fought to take down the washing flapping on the line.

'Mammy,' Erin shouted, and the woman turned round.

Erin threw herself into her arms and hugged her tight.

'Why, whatever's the matter, my love?' Cliona Maguire said.

Erin's heart slowed its rapid beating. She felt safe now. 'Nothing. I was in a hurry to get home so you could hear the song I learned, and I fell on the road and hurt myself.'

Leaving the washing, Cliona Maguire took her indoors and washed the gravel from her knees. As bright beads of blood welled from the scratches, her mother sighed and wrapped some clean rags around them. 'I think I got all the dirt out. In a day or two it will scab over and start to heal. How did your blouse get ripped?'

Erin reddened, hung her head and said nothing.

'Ah, well, it must have happened when you fell then,' her mother said lightly, 'for if any lad was rude with my daughter, she'd tell her mammy, wouldn't she?'

Erin nodded.

'That's a good girl. Your brothers are in trouble again. The polis were here looking for them this morning.'

Erin's head jerked up. 'What for?'

'They were seen breaking into a house in Dublin to steal money last night. They hit an old man and left him unconscious. It was a miracle he didn't die.'

'Wouldn't they have been working night shift at the factory?'

'They would, had they still a job to go to. The pair were sacked for skiving off when they should've been working, and they didn't come home this morning. Have you seen them anywhere? There'll be hell to pay when their father finds out.'

There would probably be hell to pay anyway. There usually was on a Friday, for it was pay-day. Her daddy went to the pub after work, usually staying there until closing time, when he came home after a skinful. He was a mean drunk, and Erin was frightened of him then.

'I saw Pat and Mick up the road with Liam and Annie O'Connor,' she admitted.

Her mother gave her a hug. 'Then I must be after speaking with their mammy, for her boy's bog-brained, and they'll be after leading him astray.'

7

'Their Annie . . .' Erin hesitated.

'You keep away from that one, else trouble is what you'll get. What of her, anyway?'

Through the window Erin saw her brothers come swaggering down from the road, punching each other on a shoulder and laughing as they slogged through the boggy patch. Her heart fell, for it meant she wouldn't be able to spend time alone with her mother. 'Oh, nothing . . . here come the boys.'

'Not a word about what I told you, now. Their father can handle it. Go and get the rest of the washing in, like I asked you. You can iron it if you like. We'll leave your song till later, for they're bound to go out again.'

'Dirty proddy,' Michael hissed as they passed each other in the doorway.

Patrick elbowed her in the stomach, so she doubled over. 'What's to eat?' he shouted at Cliona, the pair of them not bothering to wipe their boots as they clumped muck across the floor.

'Nothing till dinner.'

Michael lifted the lid from a blackened pot of mutton broth, releasing a cloud of aromatic steam. 'I'm hungry now,' Patrick said, picking up the ladle.

Her mother pushed between Patrick and the pot. 'It's not cooked yet, you greedy lump of nothing. You can wait, the same as the rest of us. Get yourself some bread and scrape, for 'tis the end of the week and your father won't thank you for eating his share.'

'It would be your share I'd be eating, you skinny crow. Yours, and that bastard of Charles Colby's.' His head jerked in Erin's direction. 'It's him who should be paying for her dinner.'

Her mother's face paled as she glanced her way. 'I told you to fetch the washing in, our Erin.'

But Erin's feet seemed to have rooted themselves to the spot. What did her brother mean?

'You didn't think we knew about that, did you? You with your airs and graces. So what have you got to be so proud about? The girl isn't even our sister. Liam O'Connor overheard his parents talking about it. Wait till our dad finds out.'

'While you're about it, tell him about the house you robbed in Dublin the night before last, and the old man you hit over the head,' Cliona retorted.

Patrick took Erin's mother by the throat. 'What are you talking about, you fecking liar?'

'You know very well what I'm talking about. Weren't the polis here this very morning, looking for the pair of you.'

'Let's get the hell out of here,' Michael shouted in panic.

'Shut your trap for a minute and let me think.' For a moment, Patrick stared hard at his stepmother. 'What did you tell the polis?'

'What was there to tell that they don't already know?'

Patrick smiled. 'Where do you keep your savings?'

'Don't be daft, where would I get money to save from? 'Tis little enough I get to feed us all with.' Cliona began to struggle when Patrick applied pressure to her throat.

'Come on,' Michael urged, as she began to gasp for air. 'They might be watching the place.'

Finding courage, Erin grabbed the poker and whacked Patrick across the knees. He gave a howl as he let her mother go and hopped from one foot to the other, his cussing turning the air blue. Michael knocked a chair aside and headed towards them.

Taking Erin's hand Cliona retreated, pulling her into the other room. 'Quick, the dresser,' she panted and, between them, they dragged it across the door.

From outside came a crash, then the boys began to hammer on the door. After a while it stopped and Michael's voice said against the door panel, 'If we get in there we'll kill the pair of you.'

'Feck off, you dirty cafflers,' Erin said under her breath, and got a swift clip around her ear for her trouble.

'Say that word again and I'll scour the skin from your tongue with the scrubbing brush,' her mother warned, then to Michael, 'Is it murder you'll be adding to your sins? I just hope you enjoy swinging from the end of a rope, then.'

'Now,' Patrick said and there was the crash of combined shoulders against the door. The dresser shifted.

Through the window Erin saw a man gazing over the wall at the cottage. Wondering what the shouting was all about, no doubt! It would be all over Callacrea by nightfall. 'The polis are up on the road, they're hiding behind the wall,' she shouted.

'You're lying,' Patrick said, but uneasily.

There came the sound of a whistle.

'Fecking hell!' Michael shouted. 'I'm off! If we get away over the fields and swim across the river, we can hide out till dark then get away to Dublin.'

When Erin and her mother emerged from their hiding place it was to find the contents of the stew pot thrown all over the floor. From the doorway, they watched the boys tearing down across the field as fast as their legs could carry them. The chickens cackled and squawked in alarm. Her mother gazed around her. 'Where's the polis? The only person I can see is Donny Flynn with his dog and a flock of sheep.'

Erin managed a grin, but her heart was beating fit to bust after their narrow escape. 'Can't a body make a mistake, then?'

When Donny whistled at his dog and the Maguire boys picked up speed, her mother began to laugh. 'That pair won't stop till they reach Dublin Town, and good riddance to them.'

'What are we going to give my daddy for his dinner?'

Her mother's smile faded. 'I'll scrape the stew up off the floor. What he can't see won't hurt him. You and me will have bread and scrape, and a fresh egg the hens laid this morning. Now, go and get the washing in, there's a good girl.'

'Mammy,' she said, lingering in the doorway. 'What did Patrick mean when he said I wasn't his sister? Who's Charles Colby?'

Three strides brought her mother across the room to kiss the top of her head. 'Damn Patrick and his mischievous tongue. It's true, *alanah*. You're no blood kin to the Maguires, but you're a cut above, and the better you are for it, too. Special, you are, and I love you dearly because of it. But now's not the time to tell you, for you're not old enough to understand, and I don't want you to think the worst of your mammy.' Her gaze wandered to the far end of the field. 'See that stone in the corner?'

'The one like a praying angel, with its wings folded down its back.'

Her mother smiled at that. 'I've never seen an angel leaning

10

like that one before. She must have been at the poteen before she started praying. Between herself and the wall I've buried a tin under a flat stone. I've wrapped it in oilcloth to keep the damp out and its contents will tell you all you'll need to know, if anything happens to me. 'Tis my secret, but now I'm sharing it with you, so it's our secret now.'

Erin was pleased to be sharing a secret with her mother, but not quite sure about the other bit. It was a bit frightening to learn that her brothers weren't really her brothers, and her daddy wasn't her daddy. There was also a tickle of relief. She tugged at her mother's skirt, worry replacing the relief. 'You *are* my mammy, though?'

'Do you think I found you under the gooseberry bush, then? Didn't I love you something fierce from the moment God saw fit to put you inside me?'

Erin's hand went to her mother's stomach. 'Like the one inside you now.'

'You don't miss much, do you? The Lord didn't bless me with this one, but Dermot Maguire himself in a fit of drunken rage. Don't be surprised if God takes it away from me, same as the others.' Her mother ruffled her hair, saying gently, 'Go and fetch that washing in now, Erin. How many more time do I have to tell you?'

Erin puzzled over what her brother had said as she fought with the wind for possession of the washing. What was a bastard? Her glance kept going to the stone angel and nerves tingled up her spine. Her mother had said she was special, that God had put her inside of her. Did that mean Charles Colby was God, then?

She shook her head and put the matter from her mind. It was best not to puzzle about religious matters for there was no figuring them out, else why would everyone argue about them all the time? But still, now she knew she was special, the rock seemed to take on a holy glow. Plucking some daisies from the lawn, Erin swiftly fashioned them into a garland and placed it on the angel's head.

From the doorway, Cliona Maguire watched her daughter, tears brimming in her eyes. The girl was growing up too soon. Life was terrible hard sometimes, and she prayed it would treat Erin more kindly than it had her.

Two

The public bar of the Lucky Shamrock resembled any other public house on a Friday evening. The men stood elbow to elbow, shifting aside as their companions moved through with empty pint pots held over their heads, returning from the bar with full ones, dripping with froth. The crowd swayed this way and that with each passage, taking on the movement of a carefully-rehearsed male ritual dance.

There was a pleasant burr of voices, an occasional raucous laugh rising above it as if it was trying to escape, only to be pulled back in. As the evening grew older the crowd would thin and the noise increase, for the hard drinkers would progress from mellow to mean as the alcohol robbed their muscles of strength and pumped false courage into their brains.

The place stank of unwashed bodies, spilled ale and the smoke drifting up to the yellow ceiling. There was also a faint odour of manure, for most of the Callacrea men worked on Lord Sanders' estate. Dermot Maguire, who was the foreman of Sanders' labour force, was seated on a stool by the bar enjoying his second pint. None would challenge him for the seat, and it remained empty even when he was absent.

A fiddler struck up and everyone groaned when Malachy Magee began to sing.

'Shut that fecking noise up,' Dermot yelled, and the singing stopped.

Dermot turned and glared when somebody jogged his elbow, spilling some of his ale on to the bar. 'Watch yourself, O'Toole.'

'Sorry, Dermot. Someone pushed me. Sure, but wouldn't it be nice to have a fine singer to listen to instead of paying old Malachy, though his fiddle scraping is worth the pennies.'

O'Toole threw a coin on to the bar as he slid in between Dermot and the occupant of the next stool. He lowered his voice. 'Have the next one on me, Dermot. I heard the polis were looking for your boys, earlier.'

Dermot subjected the informer to a hard, sideways stare. 'What are they supposed to have done?'

'They hit an old man in Dublin and robbed him.'

'And when was this supposed to have happened?'

'Last night.'

'It couldn't have been my lads then, they were working the night shift.'

O'Toole shrugged. 'I heard the cannery laid them off a couple of days ago.'

Dermot downed his bitter in several noisy gulps, and then wiped the back of his hand across his mouth before pocketing the coin O'Toole had left there. 'So they were. My boys were safe at home with me last night, and anyone who says different is a bloody liar. My woman can back me up on that. I'd best get home and warn her to expect a visit from the law.'

'The polis were at your house this morning, so Donny Flynn told me. And your lads were there a couple of hours ago. He heard them shouting at your missus, then watched them take off across the field towards the river, as if the devil hisself was after them.'

Dermot cursed, then fisted O'Toole's jacket and pulled him almost nose to nose. 'You saw my boys when you dropped in for a game of cards last night, remember?'

'Wasn't that last Tues—?' The man's expression suddenly became wary under the scrutiny of the flat, slaty eyes. He began to perspire. 'Sure, I remember it clearly now, Dermot. Yesterday, it was. I was thinking to mesself just a minute ago, you still owe me the shilling or two I won.'

'Do I hell.' Releasing the man's coat and giving him a scowl, Dermot turned on his heels, pushing his way through the crush of men. They parted before him like the Red Sea and closed just as quickly behind him. As the door slammed, O'Toole spat into the sawdust on the floor.

'Dermot Maguire is a bad bugger to cross,' the man on the next stool murmured into his ale.

'And I'll not be the one to do it.' Taking up his glass, O'Toole swigged the contents down in one gulp and set it back down on the bar. 'I'll have me another, and a drop of the pure to go with it,' he said to the landlord.

Red-faced from her efforts, Cliona couldn't stop laughing as she sprawled in a chair by the stove and fanned her face with her apron.

'That was a fancy jig you played. I thought my feet would dance me all the way into Tipperary. Sing me the song you learned whilst I catch my breath a bit.'

It was grand to see her mother merry and laughing. Erin slipped the penny whistle into her pocket, picked up the harp and plucked a few plaintive notes from it.

> I'll take you home again, Kathleen,
> Across the ocean wild and wide . . .

When she finished singing her mother had tears in her eyes. 'If you don't win a medal I'll skin the cat.'

'We haven't got a cat.'

'Then the cat doesn't know how lucky it is, does it?' Cliona reached over to give the remains of the stew a stir to prevent it from sticking to the pot. 'I was trying to think of something you could wear for the competition, and I remembered that velvet dress of mine.'

'But, Mammy, that was given to you by Lady Sanders to wear on your wedding day.'

'And a right show of mesself I made by thinking I was a cut above and wearing it,' she scorned. 'It was old-fashioned even then with those leg-o'-mutton sleeves. And I put it on again when King Edward visited County Kilkenny. That must have been all of five years ago. But the King didn't come to Callacrea at all. It was old Murphy who started the rumour, and he rode through the town on his donkey, as drunk as a lord. He was weaving all over the place, a painted cardboard crown on his head, smiling and waving at everyone as if it was the biggest joke in the world.'

When Erin giggled her mother gave her an amused look.

'Sure, and didn't you encourage the fool by laughing louder than anyone else.'

'We had some times then.'

'Aye, we had some times, but not enough of them. I was thinking that there's some good material in the skirt of that dress. I could make a little jacket from the embroidered bodice. I picked the lace off, to keep it separate, and stretched it into shape. It's as good as the day it was made, for the gentry only buy quality that lasts.' She smiled as she touched her daughter's face gently with her finger. 'The lace will make a pretty collar, and the colour will look well with those bonny blue eyes of yours.' Opening her sewing basket, Cliona began to darn a hole in a black stocking.

Erin set the flat irons to heat on the stove top. She wrapped the harp in an old sheet so the draughts coming under the door wouldn't set it singing in the dead of the night. When the harp played its own eerie melody it seemed to be alive.

''Tis only the spirit of Ireland whispering to you,' her mother had told her once. 'You mustn't be afraid of it.'

But Erin admitted to herself that it made her uneasy. The spirit seemed to warn her of sorrow, and of changes. She placed the instrument on its side under her bed, which was set into a curtained alcove in the wall.

The cottage had two sleeping areas. The loft space was shared by Michael and Patrick, the adjoining room by her parents. Though Dermot Maguire wasn't her daddy after all, she reminded herself, a thrill running through her as she wondered what her real daddy was like. But as bad as he was to take, Erin felt slightly insecure now she knew, as if the rug was about to be pulled out from under her feet.

Laying an old, singed blanket on the table, Erin picked up the flat iron with the kettle-holder and spat on to the plate. It didn't spit back: it needed another minute or two to heat.

Crossing to the window she gazed down over the field while she waited. The wind still displayed some strength in the way it flattened the grass. The washing line was weighed down in the middle, captured by the cleft stick used as a clothes-prop. The prop swayed gently to and fro.

Everything moved in constant harmony, the river, landscape and sky with its sun, moon and stars, and all of the creatures on earth. A hawk hovered over the field. Her mother's needle threaded in and out of the stocking. Her own heart beat a path to the life which lay ahead of her. Why shouldn't the harp sing its own tune, too? she thought. She would remove its covering, listen to its whispers. Perhaps she would learn something.

Streaked with bands of purple, pink and grey, the sky was taking on the misty appearance of dusk. Long shadows stretched over the land. On the horizon, rain drifted down from the sky to the earth in grey moving bands.

The few moments of peace slid into her memory as she turned away. She hoped she had time for the ironing before the light went altogether.

'I'm glad Patrick and Michael are not my real brothers,' Erin remarked to nobody in particular.

Biting through the end of her darning wool, Cliona said, as she folded the stocking, 'The way that pair were running, they'll be halfway to Dublin by now.'

Erin bit her lip. 'Did you love him?'

'Who, Dermot Maguire?' And the scorn in her mother's eyes told its own story.

'No, no, not Dermot Maguire. My father.'

Their glances met, her mother's eyes became dark and soft, her voice almost a sigh. 'I'd have laid my life down for him. Looking at you is like looking at him. Handsome he was, with dark hair and eyes like hyacinths. He had a way of talking, of looking, and his hands were so tender a woman's senses could drown in the sweet touch of him.'

'Why didn't you wed him?'

'The matter didn't come up. He was engaged to another at the time,' her mother said flatly, and her lips pressed into a thin line. 'We'll talk no more of him now. Be careful with that flat iron, it's getting too hot and if you burn that shirt there'll be hell to pay.'

There was hell to pay anyway. Dermot, knowing the working of his sons' minds as easily as he knew his own, intercepted them as they emerged from the river to collapse upon the bank.

Taking the two drenched youths by the scruff of their necks, he banged their heads together. 'You bloody fools, what did you run off for? Not only is it a sure sign of guilt, you could have drowned in the river. There's a bridge up around the bend.'

'The polis are after us and we didn't want to be seen.'

'They'll be waiting for you on the road to Dublin, no doubt. Listen to me, you idiots. All we have to tell them is that you were home last night. It will be your word against mine. O'Toole will back me up if he knows what's good for him. And he does.'

'What about our stepmother?'

'Cliona and the brat will say what I tell them. I'm going up to the cottage now. Hide yourself until it's dark, then come home. I heard there was an argument with your step-mother earlier. Is there anything I should be knowing?'

The Maguire boys gazed at each other and shuffled their feet.

'Well?' Dermot roared. 'Is there or isn't there?'

'There was a rumour about Erin,' Patrick answered finally, staring at his feet.

'And when we told Cliona we'd tell you, she took to us,' Michael added.

'Is that it?' Dermot smashed a fist against his palm and both of them cowered away from him. 'Well, 'tis only the truth you heard, I suppose.'

'You mean you know?'

'Of course. Why d'you think I wed her? Lord Sanders hisself offered me the cottage in exchange for a name for the brat. It suited me fine, seeing as I had two motherless boys to raise, though sometimes I wonder why I bothered as you haven't got a brain between you. The only thing you two are good at is lying.'

'Erin is Lord Sanders' daughter, then? Annie O'Connor said it was someone else.'

His eyes narrowed at that. 'If Erin was Sanders' spawn I'd have got more out of him than a bit of cash for my pocket and an acre of rent-free land covered in slate. There's hardly enough soil on it to grow a row of tatties. Charles Colby it was. Him who is Lord Sanders' brother-in-law. He ploughed Cliona's furrow when she was a maid at the house.' Dermot laughed when Patrick's jaw dropped. 'Sure, but I'm surprised you haven't heard the tittle-tattle before now.'

There was a touch of the braggart in Patrick's voice. 'Nobody

17

says anything to our faces. They're all frightened of you.'

Dermot's eyes hardened. 'They have reason to be. I'll be having words with O'Connor.' Turning his back, he undid his trousers and pissed into the grass, sighing with relief as he buttoned up his fly. 'I'll away home now. I'll catch the woman with her feet up, for she'll not be expecting me yet. Keep out of sight until after dark, you two. I'll hang a rag on the line if it's safe to come home.'

Cliona was surprised when her husband walked in, and him still in a state of sobriety. He brought an atmosphere of tension in with him, so her nerves vibrated like a bowstring and the hairs on the back of her neck prickled. Folding the blouse she was turning the collar on, she placed it on top of her sewing box and stood up. 'You're home early, Dermot.'

He didn't answer, but swung his forearm across the table in an arc, sending the neatly folded ironing to the floor. He took his place at the table while Erin scrambled to pick the clothes up.

'I'll be having my dinner now, woman.'

Cliona felt no guilt as she ladled the mutton stew on to a plate, for if she could have got away with feeding the man poison, she would have. She'd thinned the stew down with water, reckoning the mud she'd picked up with it from the floor would disguise its thinness. She'd added dumplings for bulk, mixing some wild sage into the dough to give it a stronger flavour.

Dermot picked up a shank and noisily sucked the meat from the bone. The gravy slid down his chin and dripped back on to the plate. A slab of bread was torn into chunks, then slopped into the gravy to soak. He wolfed it down in a couple of minutes, using his spoon to shovel it into his mouth. Smacking his lips he leaned back on his chair and belched. 'That tasted odd.'

'What d'you expect? 'Tis the end of the week, we have to make do.'

As she reached to take the empty plate his fingers came around her wrist, the heel of his hand flattening hers to the table. 'I expect my wife to keep a civil tongue in her head, that's what I expect. Have you seen the boys?'

18

Cliona knew better than to try and pull her hand from his grip. She also knew when to lie and when not to. 'Of course I've seen them. Didn't the pair go slinking off like a couple of mangy curs with their tails between their legs no more than an hour or so ago? The polis are after them, too. They came pushing through the door this morning, all arrogance and orders, searching under the bed and tossing everything about.'

'And what did you tell the polis?'

'Nothing. There was nothing to tell.'

His fingers tightened around her wrist. 'What did you tell them, Cliona?'

'That I hadn't seen them.'

'But you did see them, last night.'

'They didn't come home last—' The next moment she flew backwards as he backhanded her. Giving a scared little yelp Erin rushed to where she lay. The chair scraped as Dermot stood up.

Feeling dazed, Cliona called breathlessly, 'For God's sake, get out of his way, Erin.'

But Dermot got to Erin first, gripping her by the pigtails and dragging her over to the chair by them. 'Listen to what I have to say, you stinking little by-blow, and learn it good. Your mother's wrong. Patrick and Michael did come home last night. If the polis come again, you're to swear on the Bible they were here last night. Got it?'

'Yes,' Erin whispered.

'Then say it.'

'Patrick and Michael were here last night. I saw them with my own eyes.'

'Louder, unless you want a good thrashing!'

Staggering to her feet, Cliona spat at him. 'Let go of her, you coward. It's those lads of yours who need a thrashing. They're nothing but trouble. Good riddance to them. I hope they don't come back.'

'Coward, is it?' Dermot said softly, and doubling his fist, hit her in the stomach.

As she doubled over in agony, gasping to take in a breath, Erin began to sob, 'Don't hurt her any more, Daddy, please don't hurt her.'

Dermot squatted on his haunches by her side. 'Now, Cliona,

19

tell me the truth. Did you see the boys last night?'

'Yes. They were here with us, all night.'

He pulled her to her feet. 'So you lied to the polis then?'

She couldn't bring herself to admit defeat completely, but the lout wouldn't know the difference. 'Not exactly. I'd forgotten they came in for dinner and went up to their beds early, that's all.'

She flinched when he roughly patted her cheek. 'Just don't forget it again then,' he grunted, and his glance hardened in on Erin. 'After all, neither of us would want anything bad to happen to our children, now, would we?'

He pulled Erin's jacket from the hook on the back of the door and threw it at her. 'Put that on.'

Erin glanced from one to the other, fright in her eyes. 'Where are you taking her?'

'To sing at the pub. She can start earning a few coppers to help towards her keep. It'll be a good experience for her.'

'Erin's too young to go into public bars.'

'Just mind your own business, woman. She'll come to no harm with me.' Taking Erin by the arm Dermot led her towards the door and pushed it open.

Cliona rushed after them, alarm in her eyes. 'Did you hear what I said? I don't want her in a pub with a lot of drunken, swearing men.'

'Shuddup, woman.' Dermot shoved her back inside and closed the door in her face.

'You look after her, Dermot Maguire,' she shouted against the panel, unease and rage filling her heart. She didn't want her daughter exposed to such rough places at her young age. 'And mind you don't you keep her out too late.'

As the pair moved off sickness filled Cliona's stomach. Staggering outside she began to retch.

Erin had a job to keep up with her father's long stride as they headed for the village, but a fist clutching at her collar kept her skipping along at top speed.

'I've got a stone in my boot,' she screeched at him, feeling it rubbing at the tender arch of her foot through her sock. As it was, the boots pinched her toes and rubbed blisters on her heels.

'Stop your whining.'

She was soon out of breath and dug her heels into the dirt, gasping, 'I won't have any breath left to sing with if you don't slow down.'

He came to a halt and stared at her. 'Get the stone out, girl. I'll wait.'

He sighed impatiently as she began to fumble at the laces, then squatted down in front of her and thrust her hand aside. He nearly twisted her foot off at the ankle to remove the boot. She gave a muted cry when he brushed the stone aside and forced her foot back into it. 'That hurt.'

'It's about time you toughened up. Your mammy goes too easy on you.' Tying a knot in the lace he pulled her to her feet. 'Get a move on now, else there won't be any money left to earn.'

The public bar was hot, noisy and full of smoke. The crowd fell quiet as her father marched her through the crowd and set her on the bar. 'This is Erin Maguire,' he shouted. 'She'll sing a song for a penny from each of you, and a damned better job she'll make of it than old Malachy, though he can play the tunes for her.'

'The girl's under age, she shouldn't be in here,' the land-lord protested.

'Aw, shut your trap if you know what's good for you. Right, who's going to be first to pay up?'

'Does she know "Irish Lullaby"?' somebody shouted out.

'Sure she does. Let's see the colour of your money, first.' Dermot snatched the work cap from his head and set it on the bar. 'If she doesn't earn a couple of shillings a song, she sings no more.'

The fiddler came to stand beside her and played the intro-duction. Erin sucked in a deep breath and began to sing the first verse.

> Over in Killarney,
> Many years ago,
> Me mither sang a song to me
> In tones so sweet and low . . .

A hush came over the room as her voice rang out sweet and true.

21

'Will you listen to that, now,' someone said quietly, then as the chorus began the crowd began to sway and sing as one.

Too-ra-loo-ra-loo-ra, too-ra-loo-ra-li . . .

And so it went on. By closing time Erin had a headache and her throat was hoarse. Her father's cap was heavy with coins. After he gave Malachy his share, Dermot folded the cap in half and placed it inside his jacket for safekeeping.

'That's a grand voice that little lass of yours has got,' a man said as they left, then patting her on the head he went weaving off down the street.

The night was dark, the clouds having obscured the moon. Rain began to drizzle as they reached the top of the hill. Fighting weariness, Erin trailed after her father, getting soaked through, her feet slipping and sliding on the loose stones. Eventually, she came to a stop. 'I'm tired, don't walk so fast.'

There was no answer. 'Daddy,' she screamed into the dark, and began to run.

She ran slap bang into something solid. 'Boo!' Dermot roared. Frightened, she began to scream, only to receive a sharp slap across her face. 'That'll teach you to lag behind.'

Heart running fast, and with tears trickling down her face, Erin held on to his jacket. They passed the gates to Callacrea House. The house was set back a way, but she could see lights in the upstairs windows blazing into the night. She thought how wonderful it would be to live there, to never go hungry and to dress in satin and silk. Siobhan Kelly, whose mother helped with the laundry, said the Sanders family had several rooms to bathe in, with tubs the length of a man and two taps, one that spouted hot water and one that spouted cold. There was scented soap to wash in, she'd said, and the family took a bath every day when they were there. The linen had the initials of the family embroidered on it and the knives and forks were made of solid silver. Erin couldn't think of anything grander.

Leaving the house behind, the road began to slope down-hill, then took a left turn down to the cottage. A lump came to Erin's throat when she saw the light from the lantern glowing in the window. She wiped her eyes on her sleeve so her mother wouldn't know she'd been crying. Tired to death, she couldn't wait to get into her bed.

Then she heard a long drawn-out groan.

Her breath caught in her throat. 'Mammy,' she cried out and began to run.

Her mother was on her hands and knees when she burst through the door, a bloodied sheet held between her thighs. 'I'm losing the infant,' she whispered. 'Don't be scared, love, 'tis the cramps that are making me cry out. I'll be all right when it's gone.'

Dermot gazed down at her, his teeth chewing at the inside of his cheek. 'I didn't know.'

'What was the point of telling you when I wasn't sure? I lost the others, so expected it, especially after you punched me.' Cliona gritted her teeth as another cramp hit her.

Shifting from one foot to the other, Dermot asked her, 'Have my boys been home yet?'

Cliona shook her head.

Dermot grinned as he remembered he'd forgotten to hang the rag on the line. If they were stupid enough to sleep in the rain, let them. 'Then I'll sleep in the loft.' Scaling the ladder he disappeared into the roof space.

'You'll have to help me, love. Fetch me a bowl of warm water with a tablespoon of vinegar in it. There's a rubber tube in the bottom drawer. Then get me a pail to sit on so I can flush all the muck out of me. Lock the door in case Patrick and Michael come back. I don't need them looking on.'

Upstairs, Dermot Maguire began to loudly snore.

'Pig,' her mother said under her breath. 'Thank God no infant of his will stick to my womb.'

After her mother had completed her ablutions, Erin fetched her some clean linen squares to wad between her legs and to tie to a strip of rag around her waist. She looked pale, Erin thought as she set the sheet to soak in a tub of cold salty water outside. She insisted that her mother go to bed whilst she cleaned up the mess.

It was after midnight when she fell into bed. During the

23

night the wind came up and the harp under the bed began to whisper. Sound asleep, Erin didn't hear its voice.

If she had it might have told her that Patrick and Michael Maguire had been caught by the polis and carted off to Dublin.

By the time Dermot found out, it was too late to lie. The boys had been tried and found guilty on the irrefutable evidence of five people, two of them policemen. They were sentenced to two years in the boys' prison. Dermot decided to keep the knowledge to himself and, although word leaked out, none would mention it to him.

Three

For as long as she could remember, Catherine Sanders had spent her summers at Callacrea House.

She loved the tall building with its sweeping views down over the valley to the Suir, the narrow chimneys pointing to the sky, the stained-glass windows and the long, dim hallways that led from one sunny room to the next. The house had an imposing dignity on the outside. Inside, it glowed in the shadows and warmed in the light.

As the Rolls purred through the gates and made a sweep of the driveway before coming to a stop, excitement built in her. Here, she would have more freedom; there was a pony and trap to take her out and about and Kell to accompany her.

How handsome her brother had grown since she last saw him, she thought. He would be eighteen after Christmas, and going to Cambridge. He looked quite the man now. His face had discarded its adolescent plumpness, to reveal high cheekbones. His dark eyes had a haunting, vulnerable look and the gauche awkwardness he'd once possessed had developed into an endearing charm. Only his hair was the same: a bunch of dark, loose, unruly curls which Kell had inherited from their mother.

It was this hair which was their mamma's despair. 'Gypsy hair,' Dorothea would wail at her reflection in the dressing mirror. 'How can a woman be expected to look elegant when she's cursed with such an abundance.'

Catherine, with her straight mouse-brown hair, and eyes the colour of toffee, longed with all her heart to look like her vivacious and beautiful mother.

25

'You're sweet just as you are,' her mother would say to her, giving her a peck on the cheek.

Beyond her mother's smile Catherine would catch a glimpse of pity, and sometimes impatience. Dorothea Sanders had a natural repugnance to anything less than perfect, and found physical flaws in people a little hard to cope with – especially when attached to a daughter born of perfect parents. Unless her father decided otherwise, which he often did, Catherine was kept hidden away in her room in London if they had visitors, as if something defective and to be ashamed of had risen in the bloodline.

Catherine found both options painful, for visitors rarely treated her as an intelligent person. Conversations were stilted. People talked loudly and slowly to her, and sometimes her mother answered their questions on her behalf.

'Oh yes, Catherine loves studying. She has a tutor three times a week,' or, 'The dear child plays the piano and sings most beautifully. Such a pity.'

Then they'd all go quiet and stare at her, as if they could see her weak muscles through her skirt. After all, it wasn't as if she had two heads and dribbled all over them. Her infirmity had been caused by German measles in infancy; the fever had spread to cause a temporary paralysis. The doctor had told her parents that there would always be a weakness in her limbs, because her nerves had been damaged, but she might improve in time. Not that she could remember being paralysed, thank goodness. It must have been awful not to be able to move.

Kell was the only one who teased her about it. It was Kell who now lifted her from the car, as easily as if she were a baby. He smiled down at her, his eyes alight with mischief. 'Shall I carry you, or would you prefer to walk?'

'I don't think I'd be able to get up the steps without losing my balance. I do wish they'd put a bannister there for me. I asked Mamma last time. It's demeaning to have to be carried up and down.'

'I'll tackle Father about it when he comes. I'll tell him that going up and down the steps might strengthen the muscles a bit. And it will. Don't forget, you promised me the first dance at your debut ball.'

'That's six years away. Besides, what's the point of having

26

a ball? I can't dance, and who would fall in love with a girl who limps, let alone propose marriage to her?'

'I love you, Catherine.'

She punched him lightly on the shoulder. 'You're obliged to love me. I'm your sister.'

'And an awful pest of a sister you are sometimes.'

Kell dumped her at the top of the steps with her crutches, and turned to watch the servants unpack the luggage from the two-year-old convertible. The Rolls would be cleaned and garaged, ready for the return trip. In Callacrea they used horses for transport.

Their father had been detained in the city by urgent business. He would travel up in two weeks' time, followed later by their aunt and her husband, who would join them for a month of hunting and fishing. The Colbys hadn't visited Callacrea House since they'd married over thirteen years ago, and the family thought it would be rather jolly to have them.

The reason why the Colbys had not visited had been revealed to Kell. While he was in London, his father had taken him into the study and, after some throat clearing, had said gruffly, 'You're almost a man now, Kell. Charles has suggested it might be the time to tell you of what happened in the past. It's something that must be kept from the women, of course. The fact is, Kell, my boy, Charles was indiscreet with one of the maids some time back, and she became pregnant. It was taken care of, of course. I arranged for the girl to be respectably married off to the foreman.'

'To Dermot Maguire?'

'He needed a mother for his boys so the union served the two of them. Painful for Charles, since he had feelings towards the girl. But duty is duty and he soon settled down to it. The Anglican church did the deed, and no nonsense from the vicar. He makes a poor living in these parts, so the donation was welcome. Just telling you in case anything crops up. These things happen and there are bound to be rumours. I'd hate you to find out through gossip. Right, that's that sordid business over and done with. I doubt if we'll need to discuss this again, will we, Kell . . . sherry, my boy?'

'That would be nice, Father. Thank you for telling me. I appreciate the confidence and trust you place in me.'

27

While in Ireland, their father would play Lord Sanders to the hilt. He would address the workers, hold a fete in the grounds and put on a dinner for the local dignitaries and their wives. He would also allow selected estate workers to make appointments and put their grievances or requests to him. Usually, they were small, unimportant matters. If someone had been caught trapping a rabbit they would be severely reprimanded. Although it was poaching, his father was inclined to treat such matters with leniency if there was no commerce involved. Or sometimes, it was notification that estate workers wished to be wed. That was a nuisance, because it meant that new staff had to be trained. However, there was no denying nature when men and women were attracted to each other, whatever their status, his father had said.

'As the Irish estate brings in a great deal of our income and the local workers earn that for us by their labour, it's only right and proper that we should make ourselves available to them whilst we're here. Your mamma will visit the local women as a gesture of goodwill,' his father had requested before they left for Callacrea House.

To which Dorothea had wrinkled her nose. 'Must I, Willie? The last time, I was obliged to talk to an old woman with no teeth in her head. I couldn't understand her mumbling, so I just kept nodding. I learned later, that the woman couldn't speak English.'

'Oh, the poor thing!' Catherine had exclaimed. 'If I had no teeth and didn't speak English, I'd hate it if someone like you knocked at my door and expected me to socialize.'

'And what's wrong with me, pray?'

'Nothing, Mamma. It's just . . . the people who live in Callacrea are not used to people like us dropping in on them. They feel . . . awkward. After all, how would you like it if a stranger walked unannounced into your bedroom and expected to be entertained, especially when you had clothes scattered all over the floor?'

'How clever of you, darling. That's exactly what I've been trying to tell your father. Not that my apparel is scattered all over the floor, of course. The maid picks everything up.' She'd gazed at her husband, laughing in a light, appealing way she had with her when she was set on getting her own way. 'See. I shan't do it, Willie. It upsets the natives.'

'Hmmm, a good point,' his father had answered and gazed at Dorothea over his spectacles in a reflective way. He hated his word being overruled in front of his children and a wintery smile had touched his mouth. 'I shall ask my secretary to arrange an itinerary, and tell him to make sure the recipients of your social visits are warned in advance.'

'Oh you!' And although she'd laughed, there had been annoyance in her eyes.

His glance had flicked Catherine's way, and his smile had warmed a trifle. 'You profess to know the minds of the locals, Catherine. You can accompany your mother.'

Far from being annoyed, Catherine had grinned at him, for she was gregarious by nature and loved visiting people, whoever they were.

His father's gaze had then alighted on him. 'You, Kell, will oblige me by acting as escort to your mother and sister.'

'I'll be most happy to,' he said, and meant it.

'There, it is settled then,' his father had said, and then he had continued reading his newspaper.

And settled it was. But sometimes, endings set into motion a whole new circumstance of events. This was one of those times.

The cottage floor was scrubbed, the windows sparkled in the sun and, as an unexpected treat, an apple cake cooled on the rack.

Red-faced from her efforts, Erin's mother smoothed a perfectly ironed tablecloth on to the battered table, then blew an errant piece of hair back from her face. 'It's a ragamuffin you look in that dress. Go and change into your best one.'

'This is the best one.'

'Why didn't you tell me you'd grown out of it before this? The seam has ripped under the sleeve. Go and put on the dress I made you for the Fleadh Ceoil.'

Erin's heart sank. She felt like an idiot in the blue dress with its fancy collar and embroidered jacket. 'This one'll do.'

'Not if we want to make a good impression.'

'Those posh folk will forget what we look like as soon as

the door closes behind them on the way out. It's out of sight, out of mind, with them.'

'Erin Maguire, you will do as you're told.'

Erin grinned from her position at the window. 'No, I won't, I haven't got time, for they're coming down the road. Now, there's a sight. Two women in a trap with a pony, and a man on a great red horse that would win the Irish Grand National.'

'They're early.' Her mother's glance darted in panic around the cottage one last time. She nodded to herself. 'Don't you dare lift your arm up whilst they're here, mind. I don't want you shaming me.' A clean apron came flying across the table. 'Here, put that on, at least it will cover your knees. And fetch a couple more of the plates from the cupboard, ones without chips in them, mind.'

Erin scrambled to obey as a knock came at the door; she curtsied when her mother opened the door.

'You needn't do that, we're not royalty,' a voice said.

When she looked up it was into a pair of eyes so dark and amused they took her breath away. He was laughing at her, was he? 'Well, I didn't think you were that grand. I was just tying up my boot lace.'

'Erin, go and get the cups out. Come in out of the sun, will you.' As a cloud chose that moment to plunge them into shade, her mother said in a slightly flustered voice, 'Come in, anyway. Can I take your hat, Lady Sanders?'

So big was the hat, and so covered in feathers, it resembled the nest of an eagle perched on her head.

'That won't be necessary, Mrs . . . um . . .'

'Maguire,' the man reminded her, bending his head to follow his mother and sister through the door. The girl walked slowly, and with crutches under her arms to support her weight.

Lady Sanders waved a hand vaguely in her children's direction. 'My daughter, Miss Sanders. And this gentleman is my son, Mr Sanders.'

Mr Sanders formed an elegant curve leaning against the door jamb. 'Kell,' he said, 'and who might you be, young lady?'

'Erin Maguire, sir.' She nearly curtsied again. Noticing the involuntary bob of her head, he grinned.

She gave him a bit of a glare as Lady Sanders was being seated on the best chair. The woman sat right on the edge, her back straight, her knees together, her legs trapped inside a long, narrow skirt of blue and beige stripes.

There was an awkward silence, broken only by the noise of the cast-iron kettle singing on the hob, and the occasional rattle of its lid.

'That cake looks delicious, Mrs Maguire,' Kell said, reminding her mother of her manners. Tea was hastily made, the cake sliced.

Erin handed it round, trying not to expose her armpit or knees in case they offended the guests and shamed her mother.

Miss Sanders had taken a seat in the alcove that had once held Erin's bed. It was now occupied by an old wooden settle and her mother's harp. She and Miss Sanders were about the same height and build. Head to one side, the girl smiled at her. 'Have we met before? Your face looks familiar?'

'No, miss.'

'Please call me Catherine.'

'I can't do that, miss. It wouldn't be respectful.'

Catherine sighed gently and touched one of the strings on the harp. 'Who plays this?'

'My mammy does, and myself. But I'm not as good as she is.'

'Erin's going to sing in the Fleadh Ceoil,' her mother said proudly. 'Her teacher thinks she has a good chance of winning a medal.'

'I've entered for that myself. I've been practising all year. I'm singing "I'll Take You Home Again, Kathleen". Which song are you singing?'

Erin gazed at her mother in dismay. 'I . . . um . . . I'm not sure.'

'"Black Is The Colour",' her mother said firmly.

'I don't recall that one. Perhaps you'd care to sing it for us, Miss Maguire.'

'I can't—'

'Sure, you can,' her mother said sharply. 'I sang it to you often enough when you were in your cradle. I'll play the music and the words will soon come back to you.'

Fetching the harp, Cliona struck a few notes of introduction.

31

The song came stealing into Erin's mind like a thief, along with a memory of her mother with tears trickling down her cheeks, her kisses against her hair.

> But black is the colour of my true love's hair.
> His face is like some rosy fair,
> The prettiest face and the neatest hands,
> I love the ground whereon he stands.
> I love my love, as well he knows . . .

Erin forgot the visitors and concentrated on remembering the words of the song: the harp a plaintive sound in the background as she mourned her mother's lost love. For only now did she understand the song. When she faltered, for she couldn't remember all the words of every verse, her mother prompted her.

As the sounds died away there was a hush. Lady Sanders looked slightly annoyed and Catherine had her mouth open. Once again the silence was broken by Kell, who gave a light, incredulous laugh. 'That was absolutely enthralling, Miss Maguire. I'll be very surprised if you don't win.'

Catherine had tears in her eyes. 'You're right, Kell. I shall have to practise harder to match that. Will you be accompanying her on the harp, Mrs Maguire?'

'No. She'll be playing it by herself.'

Erin's heart sank, for it meant she had two weeks to learn the music as well as the lyrics. And that on top of singing at the pub on Friday and at another one on Saturday. Not that she ever saw any of the money she earned, and neither did her mother.

The visit was soon over. Lady Sanders had taken a bite from the cake, and a few sips from the tea. 'Thank you, Mrs Maguire, I'm pleased to find you well. Perhaps we shall see you at the music festival.'

'Delicious cake, Mrs Maguire,' said Kell. 'It's just like my governess used to make. Would you mind if I ate the slice my mother left?'

Gaining permission, he allowed the two women of his family go on ahead. Lady Sanders looked as crippled as her daughter, taking tiny steps in her stupid skirt.

'What's wrong with your legs?' Erin asked Catherine, catching her up.

Kell Sanders' red horse turned its head at the sound of her voice, then lowered its nose comfortably on to her shoulder to be fondled.

Catherine appeared taken aback, as if nobody had asked her such a thing before. 'When I was a baby I caught German measles. For a while I couldn't move and the doctors thought I would die. Then I began to improve, but my leg muscles were left weak.'

Suitably awed by the thought of the wealthy Catherine Sanders being near to death, Erin couldn't imagine not being able to move. 'Do your legs hurt?'

'Sometimes, if I do too much. The doctor said I'll regain some strength if I exercise them. Kell says if they hurt it shows they're being used. He says I'm lazy, and if he was my doctor he'd make me walk a mile and back before breakfast.'

'Would he now? Easy for him to say, him with his strong legs to cart himself around on.'

'He's only teasing me, Erin. Kell's really sweet.'

'I'm not really. I'm an ogre.' Strolling up behind them, Kell bowed over her hand. 'Thank you for an enjoyable visit.'

Snatching her hand away she said tartly, 'You don't have to bow. I'm not royalty.'

'*Touché*,' he said, his laughter ringing out. And as well it might, because she'd never heard the word before, let alone knew what it meant, and it sounded like a sneeze to her. 'You're better than royalty, Erin. You have the voice of an angel and a face to match. But I think there's a fiery temper kept hidden inside you.'

She grinned at that. 'Get away with you, Kell Sanders, you're full of blarney.'

Lady Sanders cried out impatiently, 'Kell, will you please come and help me into the trap. Catherine, you can drive us home.'

Kell gave a quiet chuckle. 'My dear Mamma, I told you that skirt wouldn't do for the country. Nobody gives a damn about fashion in Callacrea.'

'One has to keep up appearances,' she replied.

The split seam in Erin's armpit suddenly took on the proportions of a quarry as the heir of Callacrea House moved off to help his mother and sister into the trap. The red horse whickered moistly and the long hairs on his velvety snout tickled Erin's face.

'Soft in the head, you are. Fancy a grown-up horse like you wanting a cuddle,' Erin scolded him. 'And you're dribbling on my shoulder.' The horse closed his eyes when she began to stroke him again.

Kell gave a soft laugh when he came back. 'Nero seems to have taken to you.'

'Nero is a big baby. And him named after a Roman emperor, and all, he should be ashamed of himself, so he should.' She gave the horse a final pat and moved away from the animal, allowing Kell Sanders to mount.

From the saddle he gazed down at her in reflection. 'Where did you learn about Roman emperors?'

'In school, where else? Did you think I'd been to Rome to have an audience with Pope Pius the tenth himself, with me being a proddy, and all? Thank you for being nice to my mother, Mr Sanders.'

'Why shouldn't I be pleasant to her? She was pleasant to me, which is more than I can say for her daughter. And your mother's cake is the best I've ever eaten. Good day to you, Miss Erin Maguire.' Touching his riding crop against his forehead in farewell he moved off after the pony and trap, leaving her feeling ashamed of her bad manners.

'Come away in now,' her mother said from the doorway. 'I don't want them to see you gawking after them like they're something special. What were you talking to that girl about?'

'Her legs. She said the weakness in them was caused by German measles.'

''Tis not nice to remind crippled folk of their peculiarities.'

'She didn't mind talking about it. Besides, it isn't peculiar. I liked her.'

'Your curiosity will get you into trouble, one day. You don't want to get yourself noticed by her in that silly skirt.' Her mother sniffed. 'You should have seen her face when you were singing. A pity that girl picked the same song as yours. Still, you've got two weeks to learn the other one in, and 'tis a better song anyway.'

'But not so popular. Sister Agnes said that "Kathleen" will touch the hearts of the judges.'

'What does a dried-up caffler nun know about love? It's not the song, *alanah*, 'tis the way you sing it that will touch the heart, like Ireland itself is doing the singing. All the wealth of the Sanders family will not give that girl a better voice than yours.'

'You're being unfair to her, Mammy. We haven't heard Catherine Sanders sing yet, so what are you mithering on about it for?'

'Mithering on, is it?' Her mother flicked a dish rag at her and laughed. 'You're getting to be too pert by far, Erin Maguire. I'll see if I can find a shilling or two and we'll go to the used clothes shop in Tipperary the day after tomorrow, and I'll buy you another dress to replace the one you're wearing. Take that one off so I can repair and wash and iron it. It'll fetch a penny or so towards the newer one.'

The Sanders family were almost home when Dorothea demanded that the trap be brought to a halt.

'That woman,' she said to Kell when he came up along-side her. 'What was her name?'

'Cliona Maguire.'

'She seems familiar. Did she ever work up at the house?'

'She may have. Cliona Maguire is married to the foreman. He taught me to box when I was small.' Kell smiled as he recalled his memories. 'Maguire's sons were about my age and he used to pit me against them for practice. They were a quick tempered pair who forgot the rules and lost control easily. I always managed to beat them, but they gave me a few bruises.'

Dorothea's mouth pursed. 'Your father shouldn't have allowed you to mix with the workers' children. You might have caught something from them.'

'Like head lice,' Catherine broke in, vigourously scratching her head. 'I've been itchy since we left the cottage.'

'Me too,' said Kell, scratching at his leg.

They exchanged a grin when their mother gave a delicate shudder and her hand strayed to the back of her neck. 'Do stop that scratching, Catherine,' she said in sudden annoyance as she realized they were making a joke of it. 'It's as unfeminine as your sense of humour.'

'What did you think of the girl's voice?' Kell asked them. 'I thought it was quite unique.'

'She hasn't learned her song well, she stumbled in a few places,' Dorothea said, slightly scathingly,

'Her voice is wonderful though, Mamma. She's bound to win the medal,' Catherine said. 'I wish I could sing that well.'

To which her mother answered, 'You'll be able to sing better than her by the time the festival comes. I'll send you to a singing teacher in Dublin for tuition every day. It will give the chauffeur something to do. You'll win the medal for your age group, Catherine, I promise.' She gazed around her. 'Why have we stopped? We'll get caught in the rain if we're not careful.'

'Really, Mother, you told her to stop.'

'I can't imagine why. Drive on at once, Catherine.'

It wasn't until they reached home that Dorothea remembered Cliona Maguire again. She decided to ask her husband about the woman when he arrived the following week.

'Cliona Maguire?' William Sanders shook his head. 'I can't recall her.'

'She's married to one of your foremen. The family live on that slate field.'

Had she but known it, William's recall was a moment of instant shock, though he managed to present a credible indifference. Only Kell knew the truth about Cliona Maguire and her daughter. 'Why the interest?'

'Her daughter is a rival for Catherine in the festival. Her voice is good, Willie. Really good.'

'Catherine will have to take her chances.'

'But I so want Catherine to win. She's not very good at anything except singing, and it would be so encouraging for her.'

'Of course it would, but it's just as encouraging for an ordinary Irish girl to win a medal – more encouraging, in fact. You've told me Catherine is having extra tuition, so stop worrying about it. Our daughter is more privileged than most girls of her age, so not winning a medal won't be the end of the world.'

'I seem to know Cliona Maguire's face. I thought the woman might have worked here as a maid, at one time.'

'Perhaps she did. What of it? Half the women in the village have worked here. As soon as they marry, they start having babies and leave, then another maid takes their place. You can't expect me to remember them all. Now, is there anything else? I have to go through the books with the steward.'

'No, nothing.'

He rose from behind his desk and came to where she stood. 'Why don't you start making arrangements for the fete before Elizabeth and Charles arrive? You're really good at it, and it will stop you from worrying about Catherine.'

Dorothea brightened at that. 'I suppose I could make a start. I stored last year's arrangements in the bureau in my sitting room. I'll go and find them.'

He tipped up her chin and kissed her briefly on the mouth. 'That's my girl. You make yourself useful, it will keep you out of mischief.' He'd learned very early in their marriage that, despite Dorothea's strict upbringing, her passionate nature led her into trouble very easily. He could only thank God that she was discreet.

After his wife had gone, William Sanders poured himself a small brandy. Had he been here, she would never have been allowed to visit the Maguire household.

Not that she knew about the affair, or of the bastard child, of course. Women didn't understand such things, and made such a fuss, blowing things up out of all proportion.

So, Cliona had given birth to a daughter all those years ago? William had never enquired, had never really wanted to know. He'd covered up Charles's mistake as best he could by coming to an arrangement with Dermot Maguire to provide for the child and her mother.

As for Charles, he'd reimbursed William for the annual loss of the cottage rent, and without fail. He hadn't given the child much thought in the arrangement. As it was, she'd soon be old enough to work for a living. When that happened, Charles's obligation to him would come to an end – and William's obligation to the Maguires would also come to an end. Whatever the verbal contract between himself and Dermot Maguire had been, William Sanders had plans for that land.

Four

Erin enjoyed sleeping in the loft. It was private. The little window afforded her some fresh air, and the chimney bricks were heated by the cooking range downstairs.

Overhead, the slated roof provided a home for a family of mice. Hearing them squeaking and shuffling at night made her smile. She imagined the mother mouse fussing over her children, making sure their faces and whiskers were clean before she led them down into the dark kitchen below to forage for crumbs for their supper.

On the morning of the music festival her mother woke her before the crack of dawn. The washing tub had been half-filled with some cold water. Now her mother added boiling water from the kettle and handed her a sliver of pink soap.

'Have a good wash and don't worry about anyone coming through the door. Dermot's already on his way to see the boys, and he won't be back tonight. Don't you linger in the tub though, for we've a long walk ahead of us today.'

'How can I linger when the water's only lukewarm. We're not walking all the way, are we? Tipperary is twenty miles or more.'

'Of course not, but we've got to get ourselves over to Holycross to fetch ourselves a ride, and that will take an hour or so. Wash your hair as well.'

'What for, when it's going to be braided?'

'Isn't cleanliness next to godliness? You'll be on public show, my girl. I don't want to be shamed by someone saying the Maguires are fit only for the slums.'

So Erin scrubbed herself until her skin glowed as pink as the soap. Into wide-legged flannel drawers, she went, followed by a calico petticoat which was topped by the despised velvet costume. The lace collar flopped about her

39

shoulders as the embroidered jacket was settled over the top. And a right dog's-dinner she felt, too. But Erin glowered at the dress only when her mother wasn't looking, for it had taken Cliona many hours to make.

The hair braiding was done swiftly and tightly, so it tugged painfully at her scalp in places. White satin ribbons were tied at the ends and double-knotted. They hung heavily downwards, like tulips sodden by rain. A critical gaze was aimed at her boots. 'I wish I could afford you a new pair, Erin.'

'So do I. These pinch my toes, and they have holes in the bottom.'

'Wishing will get us nothing though, will it? I'll cut the toes out. Nobody'll be the wiser with your black stockings on. And I'll see if I can stick some folded paper over the holes. I'll give them a good polish up after, so I will.'

An hour later the pair set out. The hedges were festooned with spider webs, weighed down with quivering pearls of water, as if the spiders had hung out their best suits to dry. The dawn sky was banded with bright pink and yellow, sand-wiched between streaks of grey cloud.

They spied a vixen heading for a thicket.

'Lord Sanders will have that one lined up in his sights once he gets the smell of it in his nostrils,' her mother said under her breath.

The thought of killing such a lovely creature horrified Erin. 'How can he be so mean as to shoot it?'

'Sure, but can't the English shoot anything, including the Irish when they've a mind to?' Her mother sent her a smile to soften the reality of it. ''Tis said foxes are vermin and carry a deadly disease, so 'tis doing us a favour they are.'

'And what would the Sanders know, when they're here for only a few weeks a year?'

'That fox is a greedy old girl who has carried off several of our hens. I'd rather put the meat in our own stomachs than hers and her kits.' Her mother grinned. 'To be sure, I'd shoot it myself if I had a bullet and a gun to put it in.'

'And knew how to fire it. You'd jump a mile into the air when it went off.'

Her mammy's grin widened. 'Now there would be a fine

sight, and me wearing my raggiest britches, and all. But its fur would make me a nice warm hat for winter.'

'And your head would be full of fleas making a meal of you, most like.'

Her mother's stride lengthened. 'Come on now, we're over the hill, stop lagging behind.'

'This harp is heavy.'

'Have pity for the poor angels then, for it'll get heavier before the day is over.'

Her mother hefted the bag she carried from one shoulder to the other. It contained their lunch, a bottle of water and a couple of sacks to cover their shoulders if it rained. Erin had the harp tied to her shoulders and upper back, so it didn't bounce around and so her arms were left free.

Pulling her shawl tighter around her, Cliona gazed at the sky and prophesied, 'It'll rain later.'

There was no need for Erin to comment. Both of them were used to the rain. She just hoped it was light, and not the heavy, relentless stuff that turned the roads into mire and flattened the grass.

They walked on in silence, stopping only to remove the sharp stones that took up residence in Erin's boots at frequent intervals. At least she could tilt her feet and tap the stones back out on to the road now, instead of unlacing her boots. The paper had shredded a few minutes after they started walking, and the stones found their way through one hole and went out of the other.

There was a fresh morning smell to the air as the dew rose from the grass and the flowers opened to the sun. 'It's a grand day, Mammy.'

'And will be a grander day still when you win yourself a medal. I'm going to be so proud of you. Look, there's Sister Agnes and Father Brian waiting for us in the cart.'

They weren't the only passengers. One of the village boys was also going to Tipperary with his mother for the festival. Nevin had a battered violin case hugged firmly against his chest with both hands.

'Hello, Nevin,' she said.

Nevin seemed glad to be noticed. Small for his age, he was wearing a bow tie and a checked coat that looked as if it belonged to his elder brother. When he eyed her costume, Erin shrugged and exchange a grin with him.

'I expect you've met Mrs O'Connor,' Father Brian said, untying the harp from her back and placing it in the cart between them.

Cliona nodded at the woman, but she turned her head away. Mouth pursing, she sniffed and folded her arms over her chest.

'Good morning, Mrs Maguire,' said Sister Agnes. 'Erin, you look lovely.'

'Thank you, Sister.'

As the driver set the horse in motion Father Brian asked, 'How are those two stepsons of yours? I haven't seen them around lately.'

Erin's mother's face reddened. 'They're living in Dublin now.'

'Ah . . . yes, I'd forgotten.'

Mrs O'Connor sniffed again.

'I hope you don't pass on that cold,' Erin's mother said sharply.

Mrs O'Connor gave Cliona a look fit to wither an apple, though it had no effect on her. 'I want to talk to you, Mrs Maguire. It's about our Annie and your boys.'

'Your Annie, is it? And her no better than she ought to be. Perhaps it's my husband you should talk to, for the boys are his.'

'And a no-good pair they are, too. As for our Annie, there's some around here who shouldn't be calling the kettle black.'

To which Father Brian interjected, 'Ladies, if you can't talk politely to one another I'd be obliged if you'd kindly hold your tongues this fine morning.'

This time, both of the women sniffed. They turned their heads away from each other, one looking in the direction they were going to, the other from where they'd been.

Nevin was gazing at Erin's boots. She wriggled her toes at him and he began to laugh. His mother clipped him around the ear and he stopped.

Erin slipped her hand inside her mother's and laid her head against her shoulder. 'I've got a devil's own brew of butterflies in my stomach.'

She watched her mother smile at that. 'It wouldn't be natural if you hadn't.'

''Tis no smiling matter, Mam. What if I'm sick, what then?'

'Then you'll be sick and be done with it, though what there is to be sick with I don't know, since you were so skittish this morning, you ate no breakfast.'

'My Nevin was sick last night,' Mrs O'Connor offered. ''Tis the nerves that get to them.'

Sister Agnes plunged her hand into a bag she was carrying and fished out two apples. 'Here, children, these will settle your stomachs.'

The ice broken, the two women decided to be pleasant to one another and exchanged a couple of remarks before falling silent. After Erin finished her apple she rested her head against her mother's arm. With the sun warm against her back and the gentle rhythm of the wheels over gravel her eyes began to droop and her head nod.

When she woke, she found her head cradled in her mother's lap and her feet on Sister Agnes's.

It was the impatient hooting behind that that had woken her. The cart pulled into the hedge and the Sanders' car swept past. Lady Sanders stared straight ahead, but the men nodded in their direction.

Catherine waved and smiled. 'Good luck, Erin,' she shouted.

'And you,' Erin called back.

Kell caught her eye, winked and tipped his hat, a rather silly-looking straw boater.

'Give it some ribbons and bells and it'll resemble the one Shamus O'Reily's donkey wears to church on Sunday,' Erin whispered to her mother, who laughed.

'Now, now, Mrs Maguire,' Father Brian admonished. 'You shouldn't encourage your daughter to mock her betters. Where would your husband be without the job they provide?'

'Back in Belfast where he belongs, and what a relief that would be,' Cliona said tartly.

The festival was held in a hall, which was crowded with children like herself. They were well down on the list, and by the time they were announced, Erin's dress was crumpled and her mouth was dry.

Erin didn't play a false note and, after a drink of water, had managed to sing with all the emotion her song allowed. Her mother had tears streaming down her face. And tears came to the eyes of some of the judges and they smiled back and forth at each other. Her mother gave her a hug and gazed around the audience, smiling as she basked in her daughter's glory.

Catherine Sanders' turn was straight after Erin. Helped to the stage by her accompanist, she supported herself on her crutches, looking fragile in a gown of cream silk and lace. Lady Sanders smiled graciously at the judges as her daughter's accompanist played the introduction.

There was a sigh when Catherine began to sing 'Kathleen' and worked her magic on the audience. The ladies in the crowd took out their handkerchiefs to dab their eyes with.

'Poor dear,' somebody whispered. 'How brave of the girl to get up on stage and sing, when she can hardly stand.'

Erin exchanged a glance with her mother. Heartsick, both of them knew what the outcome of this particular competition would be without being told.

'The girl can't sing as well as you and she's not Irish, even though she was born here,' her mother said fiercely as they began on the long walk back to the cottage from Holycross, where the cart had dropped them off.

She had held it all in this far, putting up with Mrs O'Connor's crowing over Nevin's win on the earlier part of the journey.

'You were the best one in that competition, that you were, whatever those judges said. They were all peeing their drawers to please her ladyship. Yes, my Lady, no, my Lady . . . well, feck you, my Lady, may the worms eat your tattie crop!'

'*Mammy!*' Erin giggled.

A sack was shoved into Erin's hands. 'Here, put this over you, it's beginning to rain.'

And indeed it was, coming down out of the sky in undulating sheets of heavy drizzle, which soaked the ground and filled the potholes with muddy brown water.

They'd just rounded a bend when they were forced to move quickly when the Sanders' car came sweeping round the bend after them. Jumping to one side, the weight of the harp on her back pulled Erin over backwards. She tripped over a stone and sprawled on to her back. Water sprayed over them.

The car stopped a little further up the road, the gears were engaged and the shining monster flowed smoothly back to where they stood; only a cat's purr under the bonnet telling them it was mechanical. A window was wound down a crack, a man's voice said, 'I'm so sorry. Is everything all right?'

'There's no bones broken,' her mother answered. 'Thanks for asking, though. Get up, our Erin.'

'I can't. The harp's keeping me on my back and I can't lift myself.'

Another window was wound fully down and Catherine gazed out at her. 'I was going to congratulate you on your singing, Erin, but you were gone before I could reach you. You were the much better singer in the competition and should have won the medal.'

Kell's head joined Catherine's. 'My sister wants you to have the medal. Both of us think you deserved to win. Can I give you a hand to stand up?'

'Sure, but we can manage.' Grabbing the edges of the sack, her mother hauled her upright and stood her on her feet. Then she turned towards the car with a determined expression on her face. 'And as for the rest, be that as it may. The judges thought differently, and people don't always get what they deserve. That being said, Erin won't accept what she didn't win fair and square.' Her mother adjusted the sack over her head, sniffed, then muttered, 'It's late, so let's be getting on, our Erin. Sure, but what use is a medal, since it doesn't put food on the table.'

The sky seemed to open and the rain became a deluge.

'Such churlishness doesn't deserve an answer. Close that window, Catherine, my dear, the rain is coming in.' Lady Sanders then instructed the chauffeur. 'Do drive on, man, what are you waiting for?'

The car sped off silently, but then it suddenly came to a halt. Wrapped in a raincoat, Kell got out. He unfolded a large black umbrella, then waved the car on.

When they reached him he bade them stop. Handing her mother the umbrella, he lifted the harp from Erin's back and said, 'Here, let me take that,' then turned to her mother. 'The umbrella should shelter you a bit, Mrs Maguire . . . and Erin too, for she's only a little bit of a thing.'

Her mother said nothing as they trudged along through the mud. Erin was too shy to look at Kell. The cottage was a welcome sight to both of them.

'Are you coming in for a cup of tea?' her mother said, when they reached the gate.

'Thank you, Mrs Maguire, but I must be getting home.'

Her mother nodded. 'That was a kind thing you did. And look at you, like a drowned rat, you are.'

'It was my pleasure.' Kell gave a short bow. 'Get along in now and warm yourself before you catch cold. Goodnight, Mrs Maguire . . . Erin. I truly did enjoy your performance. So did Catherine.'

'Thank you for saying so,' she said quietly, feeling her cheeks colour.

His smile seemed to contain what seemed to be genuine warmth. Then he turned away and was gone, the rain cascading off the umbrella like a waterfall as he strode off up towards the road.

Erin turned to her mother. 'He's nice for a gentleman.'

'Manners is bred into the gentry, my love. Just remember, however nice-mannered they seem to be, they can't be trusted. 'Twas good of him to give us a helping hand, though. Not many would go out of their way for a body, like that. He got himself soaked through, right enough.'

That was the first and the last festival Erin entered – although she continued singing in the public bar, much against her mother's wishes.

That occupation came to an abrupt end when, two years later, the polis came and arrested her father at his place of work. Later in the day, they came to ransack the cottage. Cliona could do nothing but stand there, wringing her hands whilst their worldly goods were tossed around the place.

Erin's mother was in the fifth month of her latest pregnancy, and bewailed the amount of damage being done. 'What are you looking for?' she shouted.

'Your man's plotting against the state, missus. We're looking for evidence.'

They took her mother away for questioning with them.

Cliona didn't return for three days, and she was grey and

exhausted. 'I had to walk from Tipperary. They've taken Dermot Maguire to Dublin.' Slumping into a chair she began to cry. 'What's to become of us now, with no money coming in?'

'You go to bed, Ma. I'll think of something. We should save up and go to London. You can work as a maid, and I can get work singing.'

Her mother managed a smile. 'Sure. And who would want a worn-out old body like me for a maid . . . and with one inside me waiting to see the light of day? And where will we get the fare from?'

'I'll sing in the Shamrock and, with Dermot gone, we can keep the money ourselves.'

'There'll be no singing in bars now, d'you hear? 'Tis too risky for a girl your age, since there's no accounting what men will do when their minds are sodden with ale. We must be thankful for a roof over our heads. We'll sleep on things, Erin love, and decide what to do in the morning. I'm too tired to think straight at the moment.'

That night, when her mother was fast asleep, Erin went out singing again.

'Not tonight,' the landlord told her.

Someone shouted out, 'Hey, let the girl in. I'm in the mood for a song. Malachy, get your fiddle tuned so Erin Maguire can sing us a song. Off you go, Erin.' He dropped a penny on the bar.

The bartender waited until just before closing time, then his hand swept most of the pennies from the bar. 'That should cover what your father owes me.'

'But I need the money, so my mother can have a meal.'

He smiled nastily as he pushed the remaining few coins her way. 'The Maguire family has earned their last meal on my premises. Now, off you go, Erin, and don't come back.'

The night was lit by half a moon, which sailed in and out of the clouds so one moment it was light and the next she was plunged into shadow. It was cold, but fine, and she pulled her shawl around her shoulders as she began the trudge home.

Erin had covered a third of the way when she heard someone coming up behind her.

Turning, she said nervously to the dark shadow, 'Who is it?'

'You needn't be fearful. 'Tis me, Liam O'Connor.'

'Sure, and why should I be fearful, when the sight of you is enough to make a cat laugh.'

'That's not very friendly of you, Erin. What are you doing out at this time of night?'

'I could have asked the same of you if I was the type to stick my nose into another person's business.'

He laughed mockingly. 'I can smell tobacco smoke and ale on you. Been singing down at the Lucky Shamrock, have you? You want to be careful. There's some rough types around and they might get the wrong idea about you if they have had a skinful.'

'What do you mean?'

'Well, you're getting to be a woman now. Before you know it, one of them could take you behind a wall and put his hand up your skirt.'

'Like your Annie, you mean? I hear she sells her wares on the street corners in Dublin now, since your pa turned her out, and her with a chisler inside her. Well, just let anyone try it with me, and see what they get for their trouble.'

His hand closed around her arm and he spun her round to face him. Although Liam had grown into a man, he was thin, and his pasty face was pocked with spots. He worked at the canning factory. 'And who d'you think planted the bastard in our Annie, then?'

'Not my stepbrothers, that's for sure.' She tried to shake him off. 'Let go of my arm.'

'Dermot Maguire got her in the way, that's who.'

She stared unbelievingly at him. 'You're lying!'

'No, I'm not.' Head to one side, he smiled. 'He didn't get away with it though. A word in Lord Sanders' ear about your father and that was that. My pa has been offered his position at the estate . . .'

'And my ma had to walk all the way home from Tipperary because of it, and her in the way, too,' she said indignantly.

'Serves her right.' His smile grew wider. 'You're a pretty thing, Erin. If you were to become my sweetheart I could look after you. We could marry when you turn sixteen.'

She laughed. 'Marry you, Liam O'Connor? That's the daftest idea I've heard of in a long time. Anyway, you're a caffler.'

'If you took instruction you could become one too.'

'I've got plans, and they don't include marrying at sixteen, having one babby after another and spending my life with my hands in the laundry tub. I'm going to have a career singing on the stage.'

'The only stage you're singing on is the public bar.'

'A lot you know. Me and my ma are going to London as soon as I've saved the money for our fare.'

His smile became a sneer. 'You think you're too good for the likes of me, don't you?'

'I rarely think of you at all, Liam O'Connor. Marry you?' She tossed a scornful laugh in his direction. 'I think I'd rather starve.' Jerking her arm away she marched off, head held high.

Catching up with her, he grabbed her arm again and sneered, 'Perhaps you will starve, Miss High and Mighty. And perhaps you'll end up on the street like our Annie, with your skirt up round your neck and a stranger between your legs. I'll give you a taste of what that's like, right now.' A foot behind her ankles saw her spread flat on her back.

Liam knelt with his knees either side of her leg and forced her thighs apart.

She struck out at him, yelling, 'My daddy will kill you when he finds out.'

'Like hell he will,' Liam growled. 'Dermot Maguire is going away for a long, long time, my pa made sure of that. Sides, he's not your daddy. You're a bit of rubbish someone at the big house planted inside your ma.'

She screamed as loudly as she could, knowing that nobody would be able to hear her.

Liam began to breathe heavily and attempted to kiss her. His mouth was slobbery and his breath smelled like rotten fish. Gagging, she bit down on his lip.

He released her with a snarl, but only to slap her face. As he began to loosen his trousers, he relaxed his grip on her, and she saw her chance, for he was as clumsy as an ox. It was when Liam lifted his rear to ease his trousers over his buttocks that she brought up her knee.

The connection sounded solid. An agonized howl rent the air and Liam fell sideways, where he drew up his knees and cursed horribly. His rear hung out of his trousers like a pair of pale flabby moons.

Spots on his arse, too, Erin thought fleetingly. She was on her feet and running like the wind before he could recover, her heartbeat thumping in her ears. But it wasn't long before she heard Liam coming after her.

'Wait, Erin, I mean you no harm,' he called out, his voice breathless from the pain she'd caused him, so it was almost unrecognizable.

Hurdling a wall, she crouched in the shadows and felt around her for a stone, her hand closing around one that fitted comfortably in her palm. Her pursuer was a dark shadow on the road. He stopped to gaze into the darkness, around him. From her position on the sloping ground and gazing upwards towards him, Liam appeared taller, larger, and more threatening.

The moon came out from behind a cloud and there was enough light for her to see that he was staring straight at her. Without thinking, she hurled the stone at him with all her strength. It connected with his forehead. Before he dropped to the ground she saw that it wasn't Liam, at all.

It was Kell Sanders!

Scrambling to where he lay, she gazed down at him. Blood was oozing from a small cut on his temple. Around it, the flesh was already beginning to turn purple and swell.

Bundling her shawl into a pillow she placed it under his head and whispered, 'You'd better have a head as hard as a rock and a disposition like an angel, Kell Sanders, else I'm going to be in trouble. More trouble is not what we need at the moment, what with us not knowing where the next meal is coming from, another mouth to feed on the way, and my mother wearied by it all.'

Relief filled her heart when his eyelids began to flutter. 'That's right, Mr Sanders. You wake up, now. I don't want a dead body on my hands, what with all the explaining I'd have to do.'

His eyes opened and focused on her. He looked puzzled. 'Did I have an accident?'

For a moment Erin was tempted to affirm the notion in his head that he had, but she'd been taught not to lie. 'You could say that, but the truth of the matter is, I thought you were someone else after me, so I threw a stone.'

'Ah . . . yes.' Shakily, he rose to his feet and, wincing, tentatively touched a finger against the swelling. 'I must say, your aim was pretty good.'

'Sure, but 'tis no joking matter, and you'll get dirt into the wound if you do that,' she scolded. 'The cottage is close. I'll clean and bandage your head before you go home. What are you doing out at this time of night, anyway?'

'I could ask you the same thing.'

'And if you were to ask, I'd tell you I was singing for my supper at the pub.'

'At your age. You can't be more than . . . fifteen perhaps? As for me, I'm out walking my dog.'

'I'm fourteen, but some of us have to start earning money as soon as we can, and the best way we can.' Erin gazed around her. 'I can't see any dog.'

He whistled. A few moments later a huge brown dog came hurtling out of the bushes to sit at Kell's feet and gaze adoringly up at him. 'This is Wolf,' he said. 'Wolf, say hello to Miss Erin Maguire.'

The dog lifted its paw.

'There's an idiot creature you are, but such lovely manners for all that,' she said, thinking she must be daft to shake the dog's paw, and even dafter to carry on a conversation with it.

'Did you mean me?'

'Both of you.' She looked at him fondly, pleased he'd remembered her name. 'I'm sorry I hurt you, Mr Sanders. I thought you were someone else, altogether.'

He managed a smile. 'Was the someone else altogether, the poor young man I saw on the road?'

'Don't you go feeling sorry for him . . . didn't he deserve what he got, trying to force himself on some unsuspecting female who was going about her own business at the time?'

'He was trying to force himself on you? He told me you were his sweetheart.'

'Sweetheart, is it? As if I'd become the sweetheart of Liam O'Connor. 'Tis all in his head, and more besides.' She snorted. 'He'll be lucky if I don't call the polis out to him, that he will.'

Kell Sanders fell into step beside her. 'You could charge him, you know.'

'Sure, but who would believe me when there were no witnesses, and the Maguire family is already in the bad books of the polis.'

They stopped at the wall that encircled the cottage grounds, where Kell said soberly, 'Ah yes, I'd forgotten about Dermot Maguire. I'm so very sorry. I'll have a word with Mr O'Connor about young Liam. He shouldn't bother you again. How will you and your mother manage?'

Erin shrugged. 'I'll try and get a job, I suppose.'

He inclined his head. 'One of the maids is getting married soon. I'll tell our housekeeper to let you know when a position becomes available at the house. Will that suit?'

'Very nicely, sir, thank you. Now, we best get that cut seen to.'

He pressed a finger gently against it. 'It seems to have stopped bleeding, so I can manage until I get home. I'm leaving for Cambridge the day after tomorrow, so goodnight, Miss Maguire. Perhaps I'll see you again next summer.'

'Goodnight, sir. And thank you for being so kind. I'd appreciate it if you didn't tell anyone about . . . *anything*. My mother's got more on her plate than she can bear at the moment. And if Liam O'Connor blackens my name over what happened I'll tear his tongue out by the roots.'

Kell chuckled. 'When a man attacks a woman and comes off the worse for it, it's not something he usually brags about.'

He called his dog to his side and the pair strolled off, with Kell whistling a little tune to himself.

The cottage was in darkness. Trying not to disturb her mother, Erin tiptoed up the stairs and slipped into bed. It was a relief to know that Kell Sanders was going to keep quiet about what had happened.

She was woken at dawn by her mother, whose nightdress was saturated in blood.

'I've lost the infant and I'm bleeding badly, Erin. I can't stop it, so get yourself dressed and fetch me the doctor – and as quick as you can.

Erin began to scramble into her clothes.

Five

As soon as he heard of Cliona Maguire's death Kell Sanders delayed his journey back to Cambridge.

He cornered his father in his study. 'The girl has nobody to help her. She must be offered assistance.'

William gazed sharply at his son. 'The church will help her bury her mother, Kell. I pay enough into the funeral fund.'

'I'm not talking about the burial. Erin Maguire is all alone in the world now.'

With the point of a paperknife, his father traced the name Charles Colby on his blotter. 'What do you suggest, Kell, that I employ her here?'

'I don't see why not.'

William hesitated for a moment. 'I've instructed O'Connor to give the girl her notice after the funeral. With her father in prison, and her mother dead, the family no longer needs the cottage. I've plans to mine the field for the slate.'

'You're throwing Erin out?'

'I can't support the girl for ever, and she's old enough to earn a living.' William sighed. 'I'll give her the wages Dermot Maguire worked for before he left, that should keep her until she can find a job. Though she's not entitled to it, since Maguire left without giving proper notice.'

'Hardly planned.'

'Which can't be said for his activities, by all accounts. It was a nuisance though. O'Connor won't be able to control the workers as well as Maguire did.'

Kell shrugged. 'He's not half as handy with his fists, if that's what you mean. Give Erin a job here. One of the maids is getting married soon.'

'Not a good idea, Kell, considering the situation. What if Charles recognizes her?'

53

Kell thought it might be good for his uncle if he did recognize Erin. 'What if he does? It's not very likely that he'd tell your sister about Erin, is it?'

'There's that. Elizabeth would never forgive him, I imagine, for she's never been able to have a child of her own.'

'Aunt Elizabeth has devoted her life to good works. She might have adopted Erin at the time, brought her up as their own. If we don't employ Erin, he might find her a job in London, perhaps. We can't allow the poor girl to starve.'

His father gave him a harsh look. 'You know, Kell, Erin Maguire isn't really our problem. I've been good to her family over the years, and look how her father repaid me.'

Kell gave a faint smile. 'Dermot Maguire isn't her father. Erin has no money and nowhere to go if you turn her out. It's our duty to do something for her.'

'Do something for whom?' Catherine poked her head around the door. Her nose was red and her voice husky from the cold she was recovering from. 'You two look serious. Is this a private conversation? If so, I shall go away.'

'We were discussing Erin Maguire. Father intends to mine the slate from the field her cottage is on. She'll have to find somewhere else to live.'

Catherine frowned. 'How perfectly horrid of you, Father. Poor Erin has just lost her mother and must be in a terrible state. Kell, we must go and see her, we might be able to help.'

'The funeral is tomorrow. I'll be going to that. Then I must return to Cambridge, else the term will start without me.' He turned to his father. 'Shall I offer her employment then, Pa?'

When their father hesitated, Catherine said, 'Oh, please do, Father. I really like Erin, and she'll be company for me, since we're the same age. Besides, you said I could have my own maid when I turned sixteen.'

'That's eighteen months away.'

'In that time, Erin can learn how to be a proper maid and companion. She can learn how to arrange hair from Mother's maid. She'll never be out of work then.'

'She certainly won't,' their father said drily.

Crossing to where he sat, Catherine gently kissed the bald

spot on top of his head. 'Please allow me to have my own way for once. It will be good for your soul.'

'Don't I always? Oh . . . all right, but the Maguire girl comes on a month's trial, and she works in the house as well. Kell, perhaps you'd tell her of the arrangements tomorrow, after the funeral has taken place.'

'She might need a female shoulder to cry on.'

William Sanders smiled at that. 'She probably will, since the Irish have a sentimental attachment to the act of dying. But she'll have to manage without yours, Catherine. You'll stay inside until the doctor says otherwise. Why are you here, anyway? Did you want me for anything in particular?'

'Yes. Mother sent me to tell you that the Colbys have arrived unexpectedly. Uncle Charles said they're having a new bathroom installed in their house, and the noise is giving Aunt Elizabeth a constant headache. She does look rather pale, poor thing. The country air should do her good.'

'Tell your mother I'll be there shortly.'

The two men exchanged a glance after Catherine had gone. William shrugged. 'I can't put off quarrying the slate, since I have contracts to fill. I'll warn Charles of Erin's presence in the house, and we'll try and keep her out of sight. She can be used in the laundry while the Colbys are here.'

There was a bitterness to the day, but not for the want of sunshine, for September had been a month of glowing skies and landscape that would warm even the chilliest of hearts.

The bitterness lay in Erin's heart. Her mother was going into the part of the graveyard reserved for paupers. The ground there was sodden and already filling with water. There were no mourners bar herself, and the two gravediggers were covered in mud and leaning on their shovels. That morning she'd walked the five miles to the church on an empty stomach, following after the parish cart and donkey. There was no food left in the cottage.

'Sit on the coffin if you like,' the driver had said.

But that would have been disrespectful to her mother.

Erin was too tired to cry. She felt as though she was a grey stain within the brightness of life, like a spreading patch of mould. She couldn't even afford a headstone for her mother, she thought, as she gazed down at the oozing hole.

The reverend was a long time coming to say his prayer over the departed. Her mother's coffin, a rough box supported over the hole on a couple of planks, was waiting for the honour – as if it were a ship being launched into the muddy ocean.

Not that she'd ever seen such an event, but Paddy O'Rourke's father had once worked for a shipyard, and Paddy had told her all about it.

She imagined her mother's coffin as a ship taking her on a journey. 'Sure, but you'd laugh at such a notion, Mammy,' she said gently, 'for a burial box has no sails. But when I get home, I'll sing you a song of your very own to take with you.'

She would talk to the reverend afterwards, and see if he could help her. At least, he might give her something to eat.

Footsteps sounded on the gravel path. When somebody stood beside her she glanced up and found herself gazing into a pair of dark eyes.

'I'm so sorry, Erin,' Kell Sanders said. 'Catherine sends her condolences. She would have come herself except she's recovering from a cold.'

'I thought you'd gone back to Cambridge, Mr Sanders.'

'How could I, when you needed someone so badly?' He gave her a little smile as they heard the minister coming along the path. 'We'll talk afterwards.'

How grand that Kell and Catherine Sanders would spare a thought for her in her time of trouble. The English weren't half as bad as Dermot Maguire had said. Tears filled her eyes as she choked out miserably, ''Tis good to me, you are, Kell Sanders, and no mistake. You're a body worth knowing. Despite your fancy English ways, nobody else gives a tinker's cuss . . . and here's me bawling like a babby and without a hanky to my name to dry my tears on.'

He handed his to her: a clean, white square with his initials embroidered on it in blue. By the time the small service was over the white square was dampened all the way through.

'Goodbye, Mammy, darling,' she whispered. 'You deserved a better place to rest and my heart is shattered into a thousand pieces. I don't know how I'll manage without you, but one day I'll earn enough money to buy you a grand headstone.'

Kell took her to one side and pulled a package from inside his waistcoat. 'They're daffodil bulbs. I thought you might like to plant them on her grave, so come what may, your mother will have flowers every spring.'

That started Erin off crying again. He put his arm around her and after a while she laid her head against his chest for the comfort it afforded her. How clean his skin smelt and how warm his body. His heart beat steadily against her ear. After a while she pulled away, feeling awkward.

He smiled. 'Feeling better now, Erin?'

Shyly, she nodded. They waited while the gravediggers shovelled the dirt on to the coffin, and then planted the bulbs. ''Twas a nice thought, Mr Sanders, and I thank you. You'd best be getting on now, for your driver has just come with the car and you won't want to keep him waiting.'

'I have my horse.' Erin noticed for the first time that Kell was wearing his riding outfit. As he gazed towards the road he said, 'It might be my father.'

But when they neared the car she saw another man gazing at them through the partly open window. He was an imposing-looking man, his eyes a blue that matched her own. His hair was dark too, with streaks of iron grey threaded through it.

He opened the door and got out, standing tall in front of them. 'Ah, Kell, your father told me you were here.'

'Uncle Charles? I wasn't expecting you to attend.' Kell gazed at Erin, slightly apologetic. 'May I present Miss Erin Maguire. We've just buried her mother.'

So this was the man who'd fathered her. She looked at him with open curiosity.

'Yes, I've just heard about Cliona . . . I'm so sorry, Miss Maguire.' There was a moment of pain in the intense blue eyes as he looked at her. 'Her loss will be a great blow.'

Her father! Far from being shamed, Erin felt joy trickle through her body. Better him than that bully, Dermot Maguire. Charles Colby was a fine-looking man and her mother had loved him. That was good enough for her.

Black is the colour of my true love's hair, Erin thought, as she watched his hair ruffle in the breeze and remembered her mother's favourite song.

'My condolences. If there's anything I can do . . .'

'Yes, Mr Colby, there is. My mother needs a headstone and I can't afford one.'

'You know my name, then?'

She stared at him, partly defiant, but afraid as well as she moved closer. 'My mother told me who you are.'

A smiled touched his lips but was quickly gone.

'Will you pay for it, then? You needn't fear I'll come knocking on your door in the future, for I'll never ask for anything else from you. My mother suffered for the love of you, and sure, didn't she die with your name on her last breath.'

To which stretch of the truth he raised an elegant eyebrow, so the blood rose to her face. He took her chin in his hand and gazed at her face, his eyes searching it. How soft the skin of his palm was, the nails on his fingers clean and manicured.

The prettiest face and the neatest hands.

'You're beautiful, just like your mother was, Erin Maguire,' he said softly, and then his hand withdrew. 'Cliona will not be forgotten. I'll see to the headstone.'

'Thank you, sir.'

Charles Colby seemed to be about to say something else for he hesitated, then nodded and returned to the car. The window was closed and the car drove off, dust billowing behind it.

Erin stared after it, a little seed of longing growing in her heart. But it was no good hankering after a different life. She dashed away the tears in her eyes and turned, aware that Kell Sanders was talking to her about a job at Callacrea House.

'My father is going to quarry the field, and the cottage will store the equipment and serve as an office, you see,' he told her.

'You're turning me out, then?'

He turned his dark eyes upon her, and gave her all of his attention. 'You'll have a room at the house to sleep in, unless you'd prefer to find lodgings in the village.'

She thought about it for a moment. If she stayed at the house she'd be at the beck and call of the family when they were there. But she didn't know anyone in the village who would be willing to take her in. Most of the inhabitants of Callacrea had more than enough bodies to feed as it was. She nodded. 'I've things to sort out at home, first. I'll have to sell the furniture, for I'll have nowhere to put it. Perhaps the villagers will buy some pieces. I'll come to the house as soon as I'm able.'

Kell untethered his horse. 'How are you going to get home?'

'The same way as I got here, on my own two legs.'

Nero tossed his head and pawed at the ground. His hoof striking at the flinty surface of the road raised sparks.

Mounting, Kell held his arm out to her. 'Step into the stirrup. Get up behind me and hold tight to my waist. Nero will take the pair of us.'

'As long as you don't have him galloping along, else I'll fall off. I'm not used to fancy horses.'

Turning his head, Nero gazed down his nose at her and whickered softly.

Kell laughed. 'See, he remembers you from years ago.'

Taking Kell's arm she was soon mounted behind him, her thighs spread across the horse's broad back. She held on tightly as they moved from a walk to a canter, frightened she'd slip on the animal's silky coat. But no such mishap occurred, and soon they reached the cottage.

To her dismay she saw a cart outside, and two men who were loading the furniture on to it.

Throwing herself from the horse, she fell forward on to her knees, then scrambled upright to cry out accusingly, 'What are you doing with my mother's furniture?'

'I'm the bailiff. 'Tis being seized to pay Dermot Maguire's debts.'

A man came out carrying her harp.

'You can't take that. It belonged to my mother and she gave it to me.'

'We have to take everything.' He held a paper out to her, his voice apologetic. 'See, this is an order issued by the court in Dublin. Every possession in the house is to be collected, it says.'

Erin turned to Kell. 'Can they do this?'

Kell took the paper from her and his eyes skimmed over it. His look was sympathetic. 'I'm afraid so, Erin.'

Sinking to the ground, she held her head in her hands, saying dully, 'The harp belonged to my mother.'

Gently, he caressed her shoulder. 'I'll see if they'll hand it over to me.' She watched Kell cross to the cart, and heard him say, 'My father is Lord Sanders, of Callacrea House.'

The two men whipped off their caps and stood awkwardly.

'The girl wants her harp.' He pointed in her direction then lowered his voice slightly, but Erin still heard every word. 'How much to forget you ever set eyes on it?'

One of the men looked at the other and grinned. 'Did you be hearing that, Magee?'

'What was it the fine gentleman said, five shillings apiece?'

'I thought it was a pound.' The man cupped his hand about his ear. 'I didn't quite hear you, sir?'

Sighing, Kell took out his wallet and extracted a pound note. 'It was a pound between you, gentlemen.'

'That harp is worth more than a pound, and it's not ours to sell.'

'It's not, is it?' To Erin's disappointment, Kell began to slide the note back into his wallet.

'On the other hand, it's not Dermot Maguire's harp either,' the man said hastily, and held out his hand. 'I reckon Magee and myself might go and have a pot of ale for a while. We can finish off later.' The money was slid into his palm and the pair went ambling off down the lane.

Kell said, 'If there's anything else you need you'd better get it now, then come back with me to the house.'

She fetched her threadbare change of clothes, then her glance went to the angel stone in the corner of the field. 'Will you wait a minute, sir?'

Using a piece of slate she scraped around until she found a flat stone, then dug around it.

'What have you got buried there?' Kell said, coming up behind her.

'My mother said she hid a tin here under a flat stone. She said if anything happened to her, it was mine to keep.' But the flat stone was heavy and buried in dirt and she couldn't lift it.

'Let me help.' Kell grasped the edge of the slab and pulled it upright. Underneath was an oilskin cloth wrapped around something hard. It was tied with a string. Erin pulled it out and brushed the dirt from it.

'What's in it?' Kell asked.

'I don't really know. My mother said it was a tin containing personal things, such as her birth certificate, and the medal she won at the music festival when she was a child.' Her fingers stroked over the oilskin as she said angrily, 'It's not much to show for her life of hardship, is it?'

'She had you, Erin Maguire,' he said softly. 'That's something worth having, and don't you believe anyone who tells you otherwise.'

Tears pricked her eyes at that, and her eyes met his. 'For all the hard things they say about the English, it's a lovely man you've grown up to be, Kell Sanders.'

'Thank you, Erin. I'm honoured that I meet with your approval,' he said, and smiled to take the sting from his teasing.

They strolled back to the cottage so she could take a last look around. The place was untidy, as the men had strewn things about the floor. She picked up her mother's purse, an old worn thing made of black leather. There was a halfpenny in it. She tipped it into her palm and stared hard at it.

'Stale bread for tea again, Ma, and my stomach fierce with hunger so the weakness comes upon my limbs and the inside of my head swirls like dust in the wind.' Her hand closed around the coin. She turned to Kell. 'Have you ever been hungry, Mr Sanders?'

'Never,' he said.

'I vow, I'll never spend this halfpenny. I'll work hard, and I'll make something of myself. This will be a reminder of the past, so I'll always be grateful for what I have. One day I'll repay you that pound.'

'There's no need, Erin.'

'Well, didn't I know you'd say that, and mean it. But the poor have their pride and I need to hold my head up, so I won't be beholden to you, Kell Sanders. You shall have your pound, however long it takes me to pay you back.' She stalked off without another word, her childhood put behind her.

Picking up her bundle of clothes she reached out for the harp.

Kell lifted it from the cart before her fingers hooked around it. 'I'll carry it.'

'I'll be grateful, for it's been a long day and I'm so tired my eyes will hardly stay open.' Indeed, she staggered when they reached the road and her head spun. She had to sit and rest. 'I'll be all right in a minute,' she said, pushing his hand away.

'When did you last eat?'

'The day before yesterday . . . sometime.' She passed a shaking hand over her face. 'I can't really remember.'

When she'd recovered a little he lifted her on to his horse, and began to lead her away. When she began to protest he said, almost angrily, 'Do be quiet, Erin. Save your strength.'

By the time they reached Callacrea House she was half asleep. They went through the back door into the kitchen, where Kell seated her on a chair.

'Lordy me, there's a bedraggled-looking sparrow,' the cook said. 'Erin Maguire, isn't it?'

'That's right, Mrs Flynn,' Kell said. 'Erin buried her mother today. In the future she's going to be working here, but she's weak from hunger at the moment. Feed her some of your delicious broth while I go and talk to the housekeeper.'

'You poor little scrap,' Mrs Flynn said, ladling steaming lamb broth into a bowl. She added a chunk of bread and set it in front of Erin. 'There, you get that inside you, my dear.'

Although Erin's mouth watered at the thought of food, the woman's kindly tone made her burst into tears. Mrs Flynn placed an arm around Erin's shoulders and held her head against her rounded waist, which bulged against the snowy white surface of the apron she wore. 'You've had a hard time of it lately, haven't you, my love?'

Erin dumbly nodded.

'Listen to me, then. You've fallen on your feet here, for Lord Sanders and his family are fair employers. If you do your work properly and give them no cheek, you'll have a roof over your head and food in your belly for life.' Mrs Flynn let her go, handing her a piece of rag to blow her nose on. 'Now, get on with your broth before the housekeeper comes to take you away. Are those all the possessions you've got?'

'The bailiff came for the rest.'

'Ah well, them who travel light, travel further, 'tis said. And the housekeeper, her with her English nose in the air, who came down from London with the family to manage us all, will soon give you something to wear around the house. She likes things doing her way, so you mind her while she's here.'

It wasn't long before the housekeeper came for her. The woman was as thin as two sticks tied together with string. 'Maguire,' she said, 'I'm Mrs Baily. Bring your things and follow me.'

Full to bursting with lamb broth, Erin followed the woman up several flights of stairs. She was taken to a narrow room under the eaves. It contained an iron bedstead, a washstand of stained grey marble, and a curtained-off alcove with shelves for her clothes. A pair of patched sheets, a pillow-case and a grey blanket were folded neatly on the end of a striped mattress. A chamber pot with roses on resided under-neath the bed, almost too grand to pee in.

'Are those the only clothes you have?' she asked.

Erin nodded.

'You will answer, yes or no, Mrs Baily.'

'Yes, Mrs Baily.'

The woman's mouth puckered slightly. 'I'll see if I can find something better for you to wear to church on Sundays. You're of the Anglican faith, I understand. We can't have you standing behind the family in those rags. It will offend them.'

'Sure, but they didn't notice my rags before when I attended the service with my mother.'

'You will not pass opinions about your employers,' Mrs Baily said coldly.

'No, Mrs Baily. I'm sorry.'

The woman hesitated and gazed at the harp. 'Do you play that instrument often, Maguire?'

'Surely I do, for my mother told me the noise from the strings are the voices of angels rising in glorious song.'

'I'm afraid those voices must remain mute while the family is in residence. It might cause them nuisance.'

Erin doubted it, but she said dutifully, 'Yes, Mrs Baily. I'll mind your words.'

An expression of approval appeared on the housekeeper's face. 'There are some rules governing the servants which you'll need to learn. You will be issued with one candle a week . . .'

A whole string of instructions came after: where to find the servants' water pump, where to empty the chamber pot, when to rise and when to go to bed. 'You will start off in the laundry,' the woman said. Erin's head was in a whirl by the time Mrs Baily had finished.

She was given two house gowns of blue calico with white aprons to wear over them, and a cap for her head. There was a skirt of thick navy blue cotton and a lighter blue bodice that buttoned up to her neck, for attending church in. With it came a pair of high-buttoned boots, which were polished to a high shine. The soles had been repaired with thick slabs of leather hammered in with nails. They looked to be a perfect fit.

'Sure, but this is a fine outfit,' she said.

'Look after it, for you'll only get one set a year. The hem will need taking up and the waist taking in. There's a needle and thread in the washstand drawer. Dinner will be in the kitchen at eight o'clock. Can you remember how to get there?'

'Yes, Mrs Baily.'

'Good.' Mrs Baily forced a small, tight smile. 'I hope we shall get on, Maguire. I'm sorry your mother died, for that's a hard thing to bear at your age. But bear it you must, and you must make your own way, as I once had to.'

The woman had reached the door when Erin said, 'Was it hard? Did you do what you'd always dreamed of doing?'

Mrs Baily turned, her brown eyes searching Erin's face. 'We can't always have what we want from life, Maguire. Sometimes, we just have to make the best of things, as your mother did.' A nod, and she was gone, her footsteps pattering on the bare boards becoming quieter as she descended the stairs and disappearing into silence as she reached the carpeted lower levels.

Erin's heart ached as she picked up the oilskin-wrapped package. Trapped inside were her mother's hopes and dreams.

With trembling fingers she untied the string and unwrapped the oilskin. The rusting tin had once contained tea and she had to struggle to loosen the lid, for the damp had got to it. The first thing she saw was a letter. She took it out, turning the yellowed, rust-spotted envelope over in her fingers, for it was addressed to her mother and she was reluctant to open it. The sheet of paper inside slid out easily.

Cliona, my dear one,
I will love you always.

Elizabeth is not strong. In all conscience I cannot leave her, and she cannot learn of the child's existence, since she's unable to bear one of her own.

Cherish our blessed unborn child. It's to my shame that I cannot acknowledge the infant. Arrangements have been made with my brother-in-law for you both, and I trust they will prove satisfactory.

Sweet Irish love, though it's probable we shall never meet again, I will cherish your memory every day of my life. If ever it becomes possible, I will come for you.

Remember me with kindness, my Cliona, and accept this small gift as a token of the love we've shared.
Your own,
Charles.

There was a gold locket wrapped in a handkerchief with the initials CC embroidered in dark green. Inside one half was a painted miniature of Charles Colby. The other half held a lock of dark hair, braided and coiled inside a little window. She didn't know whether it was Charles Colby's hair, or her mother's. Or perhaps it was the two entwined, for some was finer than the other. It didn't really matter. What mattered was that Charles Colby – her father – had loved her mother.

As well as the locket was her mother's gold medal, won all those years ago at the music festival. There were also some golden sovereigns, a half dozen of them, and her mother's and her own birth certificate. Dermot Maguire was named as her father.

'Thank goodness Dermot Maguire didn't know about this fortune buried in the bottom of the garden, Ma,' she whispered. 'But why didn't you use them, so we could escape?'

Because her stepfather would have come after them, that's why, she thought. And also, because her mother had lived in hope that the man she loved would one day come to claim her.

Placing the objects back in the tin, Erin added the purse containing the halfpenny that she'd found on the cottage floor. She replaced the fastenings and set the parcel on the shelf in the alcove. It would remain there until she needed it. In the meantime, she would take Mrs Baily's advice and make the best of things – at least until she grew up a little more and figured out the ways of the world.

Six

Erin had been at Callacrea House for over two years and had only seen the Sanders family on a couple of occasions. They had not visited the house for the past eighteen months.

''Tis the war keeping them in London,' Mrs Flynn told her. 'Sure, but the family is making too much profit from the misfortune of others to bother about the likes of us.'

'I thought the family manufactured gas cookers?'

'Well, don't they use gas in the trenches on the front to kill our boys? If the soldiers survive the bullets and shells, the poor buggers get a dose of mustard gas and hack their lungs out. Besides, the Sanders family has their fingers in other pies. Didn't they throw you out of your own cottage, so they could mine the slate away from under you? Now all that's left is a big hole in the ground, and the contracts are filled and the men are without work.'

Erin felt obliged to defend her employers. 'I couldn't have stayed in the cottage, anyway. I had no job to pay for food. And they gave me a room here, instead. I like it fine. It's warm here in the kitchen, and I get a good meal inside of me every day, cooked specially by the best cook in County Kilkenny.'

'Sure, but the pair of us had the devil's good luck to be kept on when they boarded up the house, when the rest of the staff was laid off and have no wages to rely on, else we'd be beggin' on the streets. 'Tis a lot of work for two pairs of hands, though.'

'Ah, but there's nobody here to make it dirty, and we can please ourselves, that we can. It's grand the pair of us living here all by ourselves. I feel as though I own the place.'

'Don't you go gettin' any fancy ideas, Erin Maguire. The

family will soon put an end to that when they come back. And they will, make no mistake.'

'It doesn't hurt to dream, Mrs Flynn. If I need to be reminded of my status here, the cleaning soon does that. But that's not to say I don't value my freedom from them, so I don't care if they never come back.'

Mrs Flynn nodded. 'Cliona Maguire wouldn't recognize you. You've got a healthy bloom to your skin now, and a woman's body coming upon you fast. The men have got eyes for nobody else when they see you coming.'

'Hah!' Erin said. 'I've got no plans for marriage and babies.'

'Just be careful, my darlin'. Loving feelings take a woman by surprise sometimes, and men are no respecter of that when it comes to their own needs.'

'They can keep their eyes and hands to themselves,' she said tartly. 'I'm saving up to go to London, to train to be a singer when I'm eighteen, and I'm never going to marry.' Indeed, Erin had saved most of her wages in a tin, and her second year's wages were overdue.

Not long after that conversation Mrs Flynn caught a cold that went to her chest. Her cough got so bad that Erin asked the doctor to call. He shook his head and called Father Brian. It was arranged for Mrs Flynn to go into the infirmary to be looked after by the nuns.

'She'll get better, won't she?' Erin asked the priest, and received an assurance that Mrs Flynn would get the best of attention.

Two weeks later, the priest came to collect the cook's belongings. As he opened Mrs Flynn's savings tin and began to count the coins, he told Erin, 'God has taken Mrs Flynn into His kingdom.' Pushing ten shillings towards her, he said, 'She didn't leave a will, but she told me on her deathbed that she wanted you to have her savings. You understand, Erin, I have to take the burial fees first, and she also mentioned a donation to the poor of the parish before she died, which she left to my discretion. I considered it my Christian duty to donate the money to the school which educated you.'

Erin felt like asking him if Mrs Flynn had been charged an entry fee into His kingdom, as well over thirty pounds disappeared into the priest's pocket. Father Brian then handed over a golden chain with a shamrock cross hanging on it. 'This is for you, too. It's gold, so look after it.'

Erin smiled at the sight of it. 'Mrs Flynn told me it was given to her by one of the little people after she followed him to the end of a rainbow.'

'You musn't believe in Celtic nonsense, Erin.'

'Who says I believe in it? We'd had a sip or two of the cooking sherry, and it was a bit of fun we were having. Mrs Flynn was like a mother to me, and I'll miss her something cruel.'

Erin added the ten shillings to her own rusty tin, then cried for an hour solid, before she got on with washing the kitchen floor. Mrs Flynn liked it to be spotless.

So Erin found herself living at Callacrea House by herself. It was a weird feeling to rattle around in a place this size alone. Over winter the house creaked and groaned, and sometimes the wind roared around it like a banshee looking for souls, and unexpected draughts stealthily opened and closed doors. When that happened, Erin snuggled in her narrow bed with a blanket pulled over her head, so she wouldn't be noticed.

She carried on with her duties, feeling as though she'd been forgotten. Starting at the top of the house, she cleaned it room by room, and then started all over again after she reached the bottom, keeping the main rooms dusted more regularly. But even if she'd wanted to leave she had nowhere else to go and the thought of going off alone to London Town when she didn't have to, was frightening. Mrs Flynn had once told her that, at Erin's age, the act of leaving the past behind was best born by thinking about it, rather than acting on it.

There were plenty of winter vegetables in the garden, and eggs from the hens. Then spring came and the urge to clean her large nest overwhelmed her. She opened the shutters to the sun, then polished the floors and shone the glass.

Anything Mrs Flynn had needed she had bought from the village shop, where a slate was kept for the Sanders. A bill was sent to their accountant once a month, and paid as regular as clockwork, Mrs Flynn had said, though she'd always kept a record of everything that was spent there to check against the bill, for madam was sure to want to see one, if she didn't.

Erin carried on the tradition, buying what was needed for the household cleaning, though she was frugal. She'd covered most of the furniture in dust sheets, so the rooms looked as though they were populated by statues.

Although Erin was lonely for most of the time, she was beginning to feel as though she was the mistress of the place, and that she'd grow old here, like Miss Haversham, who'd been disappointed in love, in a book called *Great Expectations*, which Erin had found in Catherine's room. She'd read it out loud to Mrs Flynn before she'd died, because the cook's eyes had not been what they once used to be.

Sometimes, she'd go into Mrs Sanders' dressing room and try on the clothes that had been left there. There was a big hat with ostrich feathers and some gowns that had gone out of fashion. Erin's favourite was a dark blue taffeta gown with a wraparound skirt. The bodice had a little stand-up collar and there was a matching coat with a nipped in waist.

Erin would dress up and go into the music room, where she'd stand by the grand piano and sing, as though she were entertaining guests. She'd learned to play the piano, too. Not as well as she played her harp, but like her singing, one day she intended to take lessons and learn how to play it properly. She hoped nobody would catch her at it, else they'd think she was moonstruck and put her in a lunatic asylum.

One day, when she was on her hands and knees, and her mind was a million miles away on some distant stage, an event took her unaware. She heard the sound of a car coming up the driveway.

It was Kell Sanders. Erin, ignoring Mrs Flynn's advice about guarding her heart, fell in love with him the moment he walked through the door.

'Now, there's a fine thing,' she said to herself in dismay, and sat back on her heels, polish rag in one hand and tin of beeswax in the other, just to take a proper look at him as he came in from the light, to the dark shadows of the hall.

She smiled as Kell threw his luggage on the floor, and his straw boater towards a hook on the hall stand.

'Damn,' he muttered, when he missed.

How tall and graceful a man he was. She felt like rising to her feet and dancing a sprightly reel to the rhythm of her fast beating heart.

He turned and called out, 'Don't be scared, Mrs Flynn. It's me, Kell Sanders.'

Erin said, 'Sure, but you'll have to shout louder than that to rouse Mrs Flynn. She was taken off by her Maker, last winter. The cough came on her something bad, so the priest carted her off to the infirmary.'

'Poor old Flynn.' His eyes narrowed in on her then. 'Is that you, Miss Erin Maguire? What are you doing on your knees in the shadows?'

She was surprised he'd remembered her name. 'Polishing the boards, since that's what I'm paid to do. Did you think I was praying like a pope, and myself with a polishing rag in one hand and a tin of beeswax in the other?'

He gave a bit of a laugh. 'Still as feisty as ever, I see. You're here alone, then?'

'Oh, the gardener drops in to pass the time of day. Or I go over to the stables and talk to the horses when the stable-hand's not there. Your Nero likes a bit of sugar. I'm trying to sweet-talk him into planting his hoof in the stablehand's backside when he bends over.'

'You don't get on with the stablehand?'

Erin scowled. 'He's got a way of looking at me that's uncomfortable, and hands that are sly. The man is old enough to be my grandfather, too. He should be ashamed, that he should.'

Kell couldn't quite hide his grin.

She pulled a reluctant smile to her face. 'Nobody else bothers with me. Most of the staff were laid off and they talked themselves into a ferment because Mrs Flynn and myself were kept on. And someone threw a stone through the pantry window, so the gardener had to board it up. When I go into the village now, it's noses in the air and a sniff or two or some mean remarks, like it was my fault they hold a grudge against me, the jealous cats.'

She stood. Suddenly aware of her position in the house and the untidy state she presented, she smoothed her apron over her skirt and began to roll down her sleeves. 'I daresay I sound just as bad. You'll be sorry you came, I think, for I haven't had one person to talk to over the last few months, excepting for my reflection in the mirror. I never get any sense out of her, so I'll probably talk your ears off.'

He chuckled. 'I've missed you, Erin. Nobody else can amuse me so.'

Amuse him? Was she a performing clown? She probably was to him, and she could already feel the heartache squeezing her at the thought. Her smile faded. 'Your room is clean, Mr Sanders. I'll put some sheets on the bed. Is the rest of the family coming?'

'Not for two weeks. Mrs Colby is no longer with us. She passed away over a year ago.' His eyes touched against hers as he told her, 'Mr Colby will be with us though. And there will be another guest. A young woman. Olivia Winslow is the daughter of a friend of my mother.' He shrugged. 'I daresay she'll be company for Catherine.'

So, Erin thought, she was to see her father again. She didn't know whether to be glad or sorry. She'd liked the little she'd seen of Charles Colby, and had considered him to be a kind man. The headstone he'd bought for her mammy's grave was made of white marble, with a little praying angel carved on it. And although the sun hardly ever shone on the damp little corner, the daffodils Kell had helped Erin to plant turned the ground into a cheerful gold in spring, as if the angels were standing there blowing their trumpets especially for her mother.

As for her father, he was a remote, shining star to Erin. The pride she felt in their kinship was out of proportion to his role in her life, but she was content with the image she carried of him, and didn't particularly want to be disillusioned.

She wondered if she'd be kept hidden from him again, in case the sight of her reminded him of his sin, and offended him. That would mean she'd be confined to the laundry again.

Erin gazed at Kell in dismay at a sudden thought. 'There are no other servants now, but me. I can't look after you all by myself.'

'Mother will bring her maid and the housekeeper. I'll ask

the village shop to put a notice in the window, to find us a couple of local women to help out next month. You can interview them. When did you last take time off for a holiday?'

Erin shrugged. Nobody had thought to ask her that before. 'I never have. I'm not the mistress of the house to please myself. And I can't afford a holiday, because I'm saving up to go to London when I'm eighteen.'

'Are you now?' He came up the hall, to stand in front of her. He scrutinized her face, his dark eyes engaging hers. Softly, he said, 'What do you intend to do in London?'

'Sing on the stage.'

'Ah yes . . . you had a lovely voice, as I recall. Perhaps you'd sing for me while I'm here.'

'I'd be too shy to.'

'Then how will you learn to sing on a stage with an audience? Best you learn among friends in the drawing room.'

'You're my employer, not my friend.'

He gave a soft sort of sigh. 'It's my father who hires you, Erin. Will you not sing for me? I'll be an audience of one to start off your career with.'

Head to one side, she asked, 'Will you play the piano, then?'

He nodded, his eyes on her mouth. Her lips felt dry. When she moistened them with her tongue his gaze moved up and engaged her eyes. 'You've grown into a beautiful young woman, Erin. Apart from the stablehand, do you have a sweetheart?'

That such a small compliment from him could make her cheeks glow so hotly, and her womanly parts flaunt a reminder of her own sinful nature, shamed Erin. She didn't know quite what to say.

But Kell Sanders was a man with great charm, and he wore a twinkle of mischief in his eyes when he lifted her hand and kissed it, saying, 'Let's pretend you're the lady of the house. Will you dine with me tonight, Miss Maguire?'

She giggled, reminded of her own pretensions. 'Hasn't that grand university you attend emptied your head of moonshine yet, Kell Sanders? I'm the maid of all work, but you're welcome to join me in the kitchen for a bowl of mutton stew.'

His eyes widened. 'Mutton?'

'And what's wrong with mutton, pray? Complain when you can't afford it for the stew, and there's plenty in Ireland who can't. I can make some dumplings to float on top.'

'Not much of a feast.' He gazed at his watch. 'I'll go to the shop in the village, and see what they have to fill the pantry. You can stop being the maid for one night. I don't want to eat alone, so we'll have your stew in the dining room, and we'll dress for the occasion.'

She eyed the dashing striped trousers he wore with their turned-up bottoms. With them he wore an immaculate navy blazer over a white shirt and knotted tie.

'In what, may I ask? I only have what I stand up in, and my church clothes. And one set is as bad as the other, now.'

'Oh, there must be clothing in the house. Mother and Catherine would have left something behind in their wardrobes that you can wear. Go and find something.' When she opened her mouth to protest he said, 'At once, Erin Maguire. When I get back I want to see you looking like a proper young lady.'

And here she was, all hot and sweaty from polishing. As soon as the car drove off, Erin put her cleaning rags away, poured some water into a bowl in the kitchen and washed herself all over, using pink carbolic soap.

With the house still quiet, she flew upstairs and pulled on the blue taffeta wraparound skirt and lace-trimmed bodice. Sweeping her hair up, she fixed it into position with some pins and a couple of fancy combs. Her curls took exception to the attempt to tame them into elegance, for wisps escaped the comb to spiral against her face and neck. There was something called eau de toilette evaporating in a bottle on the dressing table. Squeezing the bulb, she sprayed it on to her neck and arms.

Her nose wrinkled at the clash of soap aroma and fragrance. As she gazed at her reflection, she murmured, 'Now you smell like a lavender bag, Miss Maguire, and will probably attract all the stray cats in the district to dinner.'

How grand she felt, though. The car came back and she made her way downstairs taking small delicate steps as she'd seen Lady Sanders do. She reached the bottom just as Kell arrived. He was carrying a carton of groceries and whistling cheerfully. The noise ceased when he caught sight of her.

'Lordy me,' he breathed, his eyes widening. 'You're an engaging-looking puss, Erin Maguire.'

She dismissed his teasing. 'Sure, but I'm still the maid of all work under this fancy dress.'

'No, you're my dinner guest.' He picked up the cardboard carton and his smile became ironic. 'I'll carry this through to the kitchen and leave you to deal with it, shall I?'

She burst into laughter. She couldn't help it.

It was almost dark when they ate. Kell looked splendid in a dinner suit. The table was laid for two, the settings opposite each other. The silver cutlery Erin had kept lovingly polished over the past two years glinted in the light from the candles in silver candlesticks.

There were crystal glasses to hold the wine Kell had brought up from the cellar and decanted. A rich burgundy to go with the mutton broth, dumplings, and the dish of vegetables she'd roasted in the oven. There was sweet white wine to compliment the pudding of canned peaches and cream, cheese and biscuits.

Kell handed her a small glass of liqueur to drink with her coffee.

She giggled. 'I'm already as pickled as a caffler priest.'

Kell roared with laughter. 'It's only a small glass of cherry brandy to aid the digestion. Just sip it, Erin, it won't do you any harm.'

Erin wasn't sure her digestion needed aid, for she was as relaxed as she could be.

Kell was fun to be with. All through dinner he'd entertained her with stories about his fellow students at Cambridge. He dazzled her with his charm and flattery. Her blossoming body awakened, while the naïve child in her believed every word, because she needed to. Kell made her feel important. He made her forget her past – forget that the next week she'd be down on her knees scrubbing the scullery floor. She listened with rapt attention, becoming more and more enamoured with him. If anyone had granted her one wish, it would have been for this night with her handsome hero to last for ever.

'Look,' he said when they went into the music room carrying two glasses and the remaining wine. He rolled up the dust sheets so it was as if they had knees, seating the roughly fashioned dummies in the chairs. 'This is his Royal Highness, King George the Fifth. This is his lovely Queen, Mary of Teck.' He bowed to them. 'Welcome to my humble home, your Majesties.' He took Erin's hand. 'May I introduce Miss Erin Maguire, who is going to entertain you tonight. Curtsy,' he hissed from the corner of his mouth.

She entered into the spirit of the game and clumsily bobbed from the knees. 'Your Majesties, I'm humbled you've come all this way to listen to me sing.'

Kell led her to the piano, seated himself and played a trill. 'What will you sing?'

'"Kathleen"?' It was the first song to come into her head. His hands went to the piano keys, and she began to sing.

I will take you home Kathleen . . .

She finished singing and there was silence until Kell said softly, 'You deserved to win that festival medal. Catherine felt really bad about it.'

'I know. What made it worse was that Catherine sang my song. When she first told me she was singing "Kathleen", I had to change to something else, and that after I'd been rehearsing it for weeks. It doesn't matter now. It wasn't anybody's fault, and I got over it.' She grinned. 'They say disappointment is good for the soul.'

'Fetch your harp. Sing me the song you sang then.'

It didn't take long to run up to her attic room and down again for she felt as though she was floating on air. Placing it on her knee, she ran her fingers over the strings.

Black is the colour of my true love's hair,
His face is like some rosy fair . . .

A tender smile curved the length of Kell's mouth. She felt suddenly vulnerable, under his intense gaze.

I love the ground whereon he stands.
I love my love, as well he knows . . .

Her voice faltered and she stopped singing.

'That's too sad, let's sing something merrier,' she said.

He poured them a glass of wine apiece and handed her one. 'Let's not.'

Erin turned away from him to place the glass on the table, muttering, 'I'd better clean up. It's getting late.' When she turned back he'd moved closer.

'Have you ever been kissed?' he asked.

'Do you intend to kiss me, then?' Of course he did, why else would he have asked?

Head to one side he regarded her, a faint smile on his face. 'You have the softest lips, Erin. Will you allow me that liberty?'

Only a gentleman would ask so sweetly. Her heart was thundering in her chest. She shouldn't but, oh, how she wanted him to. One kiss wouldn't hurt, just so she'd know what it was like. And tonight, she wasn't the maid, but his dinner guest. A kiss would reward him for his kindness.

Shyness swept over her now she'd made up her mind and she shrugged, slightly embarrassed. 'Sure, but I don't know how to kiss.'

'You don't have to know.' He took her face between his palms, his dark eyes looking straight into hers. 'Right at this moment, I adore you, Erin.'

Happiness bubbled through her. Didn't she feel the same about him, like he was part of her heart for ever?

When his lips brushed against hers there was an instant melting inside her. How soft this kiss was, his mouth was a honey bee seeking nectar from a bud, and that bud gradually unfolded its petals to accept the plunder of its sweetness. But the flowering went further than her mouth. Sensing the danger in this kiss, Erin sighed, because she didn't know how she should proceed, or end it.

Her mouth cooled as Kell pulled away. He said, with laughter in his voice, 'There, now you do know how to kiss. It wasn't so bad, was it?'

Erin opened her eyes, aware of the love inside her, and knowing the nature of it. She wanted to rejoice with the sheer delight of it, and laughed with him. 'Sure, but wasn't that the grandest feeling. But now I've got to clear up the dishes, for it's getting late.'

He pursed her lips with his fingers and planted a smaller, more commanding kiss on her mouth. Then he let her go. 'We'll clean up together.'

He washed up the dishes. She wiped them dry and put them back in their proper places. Afterwards, she didn't know what to do, and fussed around, folding napkins and making sure the curtains were drawn across the windows.

Tension stretched between them now. She was aware of his eyes on her, of the smell of his skin and the aroma of brandy on his breath. They accidentally touched. It was like the stroke of ice against her heated skin, raising a shiver of little bumps that shot up her spine into her hair.

'I must remember to hang madam's gown back in the wardrobe.'

'Tomorrow I'll drive you to Dublin and buy you a gown of your own to wear.'

She gasped at the thought. ''Tis a long way to go.'

His shrug was careless. 'I've got some business there anyway. We'll stay in a hotel overnight and I'll take you to the theatre, for I doubt if you've ever seen the inside of one.'

Her eyes widened at the thought. 'What will madam say?'

'I dread to think. But how will my mother know unless you tell her? It will be our secret.'

Later, after she left him to his nightcap of brandy and went to her bed, her mind and body in turmoil, there came a hesitant knock at her door and the whisper of his voice against the panel. 'Erin, my love, you've forgotten to make my bed, and I don't know where the sheets are.'

She went to him in her bare feet and patched nightgown, her hair a cloud of darkness, to throw a white spread of virgin linen upon the mattress. The draught she created set the candle flame flickering. Kell's arms came round her body and his thumbs brushed against the innocent pink nubs of her breasts as he whispered words of love against her willing ear.

She made no resistance as he pulled her down amongst the sheets. His body slid naked from the silky depths of his robe like an oyster from its shell, and him all rampant in his maleness. She closed her eyes from the temptation of it. Her nightgown yielded to his conquering hands and joined his robe on the floor.

Her mother had said of Charles Colby, 'He was a man with hands so tender a woman's senses could drown in the sweet touch of him.' So it was with Kell.

'Erin, my own true love,' he murmured and his tongue sought the tips of her breasts, so they grew wanton into his mouth. After that, the night became one of endless delight.

Outside, the moon went behind the clouds and the April sky began to weep.

Seven

Callacrea was almost empty of people as they drove through, though a couple of constables stood talking on the corner. One gazed keenly at the occupants of the Morgan, as the three-wheeler drove through the main street. He touched a finger to his cap and nodded, obviously recognizing Kell.

'I wonder if something's up,' Kell shouted above the wind slapping at their faces.

Drawing her shawl tightly around her head, Erin held on tight as they bucked through the potholes, scared she'd be thrown out. But she was exhilarated by their reckless speed as they rounded the twists and bends in the road, honking the horn in case there was a donkey cart around the corner.

She couldn't believe she was going to Dublin with Kell Sanders, and was going to stay the night in a hotel. She couldn't believe they'd spent the night together either, and gazed at his profile, which was intent on the road ahead.

Kell had a nose like his father's, as straight as an arrow and with a little flare to his nostrils. His mouth was a soft, wide curve. She'd kissed that mouth. He'd insisted, smiling when she'd blushed afterwards. She grinned with the delight of knowing it.

He turned to her, and said softly, 'What are you thinking, sweet one?'

The walls and hedges had become a blur either side of them.

'I'm thinking that you're going to get us killed if you don't slow down, Kell Sanders.'

'Nonsense. She averages twenty-two miles an hour in trials.' He slowed down anyway, bringing the car to a stop. He stretched his arms above his head, and then pulled himself up out of the driver's seat. 'Move over, I'll show you how to drive her.'

Despite Erin's protests, driving wasn't as hard to master as she had thought it would be. Soon, she was steering them confidently along, if a little slowly. After a while, Kell took back control, saying, 'That was good, my love, but we'll never get there at this rate. You can have another go on the way back tomorrow.'

She was content to admire this hero of hers for the rest of the way to the city. She had never felt so happy.

Dublin didn't disappoint her. It was a grand place with a castle and a tower. 'The castle was built in the early twelve hundreds,' Kell told her. 'The tower is filled with records, and the Book of Kells is kept there.'

'Ah, I've heard of that. Father Brian told me it's a price-less manuscript from the eighth century. He said it's decorated with Celtic artwork and it once had a jacket of precious stones. Did your parents name you after it?'

'No. Kell is a Norse name. I was named after my great-grandfather.'

'Was he a Norse?'

Kell laughed. 'How could he be an 'orse when he only had two legs to stand on?'

When she gave him a black look he grinned and brought the car to a halt. 'What shall we do first? Perhaps buy you something to wear. We don't want you looking like a country bumpkin when we go to the hotel.'

She followed Kell into a ladies' establishment. When he turned to examine a lace-trimmed blouse, the shop assistant came over to look her up and down. The end of her thin nose pinched into the inevitable sniff and she said in a rather superior manner, 'Did you want something?'

Kell joined her. 'My cousin requires outfitting from top to bottom. Day wear, and something suitable for the theatre, as long as it's practical. That dark blue taffeta, with the lace collar looks perfect. And something along the lines of that pale grey two-piece with a pretty blouse.'

'Has your . . . *cousin* mislaid her own clothes?'

'As a matter of fact, she has. She was set upon by some thieves, who stole her luggage. They threw her in the mud and quite ruined what she was wearing. Luckily, a farm girl came to her aid.'

'I see,' said the assistant with a sceptical smile for the highly unlikely tale he'd trotted out.

'I do hope so,' Kell said pleasantly. 'I can't remember your face from when I last brought my mother here to shop. Are you new?'

Her nose elevated a little. 'I've been employed here for several years, and have recently been appointed manageress. It's possible I may remember your mother.'

'It's more than likely. She is Lady Sanders from Callacrea House.'

'Ah yes.' The girl lost her attitude and smiled at Erin. Her eyes though, contained the remnants of her earlier disdain. 'How unfortunate to have lost your luggage. I'll see what we have to fit. Come this way then, Miss . . .?'

'Miss Maguire,' Kell said. 'You may have heard of her. My cousin is a singer. They call her the Irish Nightingale in Callacrea.'

'Of course, sir. Perhaps I can show Miss Maguire other garments we have in her size.'

'She will need complete outfits. I'll leave the rest to her.' He gazed at his watch, a silver hunter. 'I need to go to the bank, Erin. I'll be back within half an hour. Is that long enough?'

Five minutes was too long to be away from him now, but Erin nodded, allowing him to make his escape.

The assistant began to show her some silk underwear, which she rather grandly called lingerie. The garments were pretty with lace.

'This camisole and the skirt knickers will be perfect under the blue dress, and the chemise and drawers will be comfortable under the suit. They're trimmed with Valenciennes lace.'

Erin didn't know what to say to such wicked finery, so said nothing. Then came stockings, fine and silky, with garters to wear above her knees to prevent the stockings from falling down. A small bell was rung and a girl came through from the back room. She was sent to the shop next door to bring a selection of shoes.

Erin chose button-up boots with low solid heels, and a pair of plain pumps with high heels. She felt a bit self-conscious about showing her ankles, and wobbled a bit when she walked, but most of the young women she saw on the street did the same.

She was wearing the suit when Kell returned.

His glance flicked over her and he smiled in approval. Handing over cash for the purchases, he took her packages from her.

'Your receipt, sir,' the assistant called out as they began to leave the shop.

'Send it to Mr Sanders, care of Callacrea House,' he said.

The hotel was a bit of a disappointment. Not one of the grander edifices, but more of a superior boarding house in a side street. But the room was clean, and the bed comfortable. Moreover, the woman in charge didn't even flicker an eyelid when Kell signed the register as Mr and Mrs Brown.

Erin said, as she removed the feather-decorated flowerpot hat that had come with the grey suit. 'That woman was so full of smarm afterwards, I thought she was going to kiss your—'

Placing a finger over her lips, Kell said gently, 'If you intend to go to London, you should aim to be less colourful in the way you express your thoughts, Erin.'

Mortified by the reprimand, her face flaming, Erin placed her hands against her cheeks, not knowing quite what to say.

She was pulled against his chest. 'I'm sorry, my love, I didn't mean to upset you. I'm telling you for your own good.'

'I don't know how to talk all lah-di-dah, like you.'

'You don't need to talk like me but, as an example, neither should you use such common phrases when describing the way I speak. It's not becoming. If you're to seek a career as a singer, and there's no reason why you shouldn't with a voice like yours, you'll be mixing with all sorts of people. You should learn to be less spontaneous in expression and a little more discreet.'

Now her heat had cooled a bit, she glanced up at him. 'Less Irish, you mean?'

He kissed the end of her nose. 'Not a bit of it, my darling. I love the Irish in you, and you'll never lose it however much you try because it's part of your heart and soul. Just think before you talk. Try to be pleasant, no matter what you feel about the person you're talking to.'

'But that shop woman treated me as if I was a beneath her.'

'She saw and heard a poor Irish girl, which is exactly what you presented her with. The mistake she made was to allow herself to let you know she thought she was your superior. We would have thought much better of her if her attitude been pleasant in the first place, would we not?'

'We would,' she said. 'I understand exactly what you are telling me, Mr Sanders.'

'Good girl. I've booked us tickets for the theatre, but not the Gaiety, since they're performing a Gilbert and Sullivan operetta, which I've seen twice before. There's a good variety show on at the Olympic, though, and they have a talent quest in the interval. I've entered you for it.'

She stared at him.

'Your eyes are as big as saucers,' he told her.

She scrambled for an excuse. 'I haven't got my harp with me.'

'They have an orchestra.'

'I'd be scared.' But it was an odd sort of scared, with a high proportion of excitement mixed in and butterflies in her stomach.

His eyes challenged hers. 'Pardon me for thinking you wanted to go on the stage, Erin Maguire. I'm disappointed. I offer you a chance, and you look as though you're going to run off like a scared rabbit.'

'Who said I was going to run? Can't you give a girl time to think on it?' she said, exasperated.

A grin edged across his mouth. 'The first prize is five guineas. Now, don't tell me you couldn't use it.'

She could put the money towards going to London. She drew in a deep breath, panicking a little. 'Sure, but I can't think of anything to sing.' But she could, for the next moment, the very first song she'd ever learned came into her head to prove her a liar. She beamed at him. 'What about "Spinning Wheel"?'

'Perfect.'

And it was perfect. Erin was last one of six, all singers. She stood there, feeling like a princess in her blue gown, a large matching bow catching the hair at the nape of her neck.

Beyond the glare of the footlights she couldn't see much, but she could hear people moving restlessly, the rustle of paper bags and the occasional cough. Her heart was thundering as she looked back at Kell, who stood off stage, smiling encouragement. He blew her a kiss.

When she began to sing she soon lost her nerves, and the orchestra picked up on the tune. The noise from the audience seemed to lessen, then it ceased altogether for her as she concentrated on her song.

> Mellow the moonlight to shine is beginning.
> Close by the window young Eileen is spinning . . .

Erin closed her eyes and thought of her mother. How proud she would have been to see her standing here. There was silence when the last note died away.

She opened her eyes and turned to look uncertainly at Kell. Applause broke out, then incredibly, people began to stamp their feet, whistle and shout, 'More . . . more . . .'

From the pit the orchestra leader looked up at her. 'Give them another. What will it be?'

'"Danny Boy".'

After she finished, a stout man in a tail suit came on stage, followed by the other contestants. He held up his hands for silence and the applause began to fade. 'There's no doubting who won the talent contest tonight.' Nevertheless, he consulted a piece of paper concealed in his palm in an attempt to prolong the tension. He took Erin's hand and held it high. 'Miss Erin Maguire from Callacrea.'

The competitors all bowed to the audience, then walked off to claps and whistles. Erin pushed her way through a forest of dancers in scarlet satin, boots and feathers. Their faces weary under their stage make-up, they smelled strongly of sweat. 'Well done, young un,' one of them said. 'You had everyone in tears.'

Shaking with nerves, Erin burst into tears herself when she reached Kell. He pulled her into his arms. 'You were wonderful.'

'Her first time on stage, is it?' the stout man said. 'You did well, young lady. The audience loved you. Bring her to the office and I'll give you her prize money.'

He handed Kell his card. 'I take it you're her manager. I'm Chauncy Green, and I'm only here for one more night, but if you ever come to London, look me up. I might be able to find a spot for her.'

They watched the rest of the show. Erin took special notice of the way the women singers moved around the stage, used their hands and interacted with the audience. She had a lot to learn, she realized.

As a finale, the dancers came on stage and went into a spirited number. The dance was a whirl of colour and noise. They kicked their legs high in the air to show a length of thigh above their black stockings, and gave a glimpse of their satin gussets as they cartwheeled across the stage, until, with loud squeals, they did the splits all along the line. The applause was deafening as people whistled, shouted and stamped their feet. Then they were being propelled through the theatre to the pavement outside, where a group of women stood waving banners. A placard was hoisted aloft.

'Support the war! Support conscription in Ireland!' one of the women shouted.

People began to jostle and shout good-natured insults.

'The English can go and fight their own battles. They're not getting my son.'

A cheer went up. 'You tell them, mother.'

The placard went under.

Kell shielded Erin with his body as he began to lead her through the crowd, but there was a moment when everyone was pushing and shoving, and a woman thrust something into Kell's pocket.

'Lord Sanders' son, isn't it?' she hissed. 'A fine example you are to your fellow men, enjoying a night at the theatre while they're dying in the trenches for the likes of you.'

Police whistles sounded, and Kell shouldered a way for them through the milling crowd. 'Let's get out of here before it turns ugly.'

They left the theatre behind them and strolled across a bridge spanning the dark flow of the Liffey. The demonstration had been unsettling, and there was a faint sense of uneasiness in the air, as if they'd suddenly been menaced.

Kell was quiet as they strolled back to the hotel, and Erin

could sense sadness in him. She gently squeezed his hand. 'What does conscription mean?'

'Enlisting young men into the army to send off to war, whether they want to fight, or not.'

'Will you have to enlist now you've finished your education?'

'It's my duty, though if my father has anything to do with it I'll probably find myself behind a desk, while the less fortunate are used as cannon fodder. They're sent off to die in the trenches by their thousands.'

'So, your Prime Minister wants Irish blood for his cause?'

'He already has it, but wants more. I doubt if he'll win enough support to introduce conscription here though. The Irish have their own cause to pursue. Let's not talk about war, Erin. Not tonight. London is full of it, and the women are sending their sons off to die in the name of patriotism.'

'What shall we talk about then?' Still buoyed by her success on the stage, and astonished by the way the women had flaunted themselves, Erin threw a remark into the silence. 'Those dancing girls were showing their underwear, the brazen hussies.'

Kell gave her a quizzical sideways look.

'I know, I should have thought it, but not said it. What's the use of thinking it, though, unless you can read my mind?'

Kell began to laugh. Taking her in his arms he whirled her around and off her feet. 'I do love you, Erin Maguire. I really do.'

Later, after they'd made love, she lay quiet in his arms long into the night, listening to him sleep, knowing she'd never be as happy as she felt at that moment. Kell had said he loved her.

She woke late, to find Kell fully dressed and sitting on the bed, watching her.

She pushed the hair from her eyes, and scrambled into a sitting position. 'Why are you dressed? Have you been out? What's the time?'

'It's late.' He opened his hand and a white feather floated down to the bedspread. 'One of those women put this in my pocket outside the theatre last night.'

'A feather. What of it?'

'It's a symbol of cowardice. They're right, you know. I was willing to sit out the war behind a desk while others died.'

Dread filled her. 'What have you done, Kell Sanders?'

'I've enlisted. I'm to be fitted up with my uniform in an hour's time. A truck will pick me up from Callacrea House tomorrow to take me to the Naas depot, then I'll have to report to my regiment.'

Tears sprang to her eyes. 'Oh, Kell, I'll miss you so.'

He traced the path of her tears down her face with his finger. Half smiling and half serious, he said, 'Nobody has ever cried for me before. Will you wait for me, Irish?'

'For ever. I'll never love another.'

'You're such an innocent, my darling. I can hardly bear to part with you.' He turned away. 'I've brought your breakfast up on a tray. You shall have it in bed while I go and transform myself into a proper soldier.'

Erin took Mrs Flynn's lucky shamrock from around her neck and placed it around his. 'Wear this always. It will keep you safe.'

'And be something to remind me of you.'

He rose, as tall and as elegant as a sapling. Erin couldn't imagine Kell killing anybody and closed her mind against such a terrible thought that somebody might kill him.

'I'll be back in a while and we'll go home.'

'Your parents will be expecting to see you when they arrive. What shall I tell them?'

'I'll leave them a letter.' He hesitated at the door, turned and said, 'It's best if they don't know about us until later, when you're a little older, perhaps. We'll keep it our secret.'

Our secret. She buried the thought deep in her heart.

The next day Kell departed. She could feel the uneasiness inside him, but he put a brave face on it. How proudly he wore his uniform, with the gold and green badge of the Royal Dublin Fusiliers. He was weighed down with a Lee Enfield rifle, trench coat, steel helmet and gas mask, and oddly, a certificate of employment. Erin tried not to think about what Mrs Flynn had said about the gas.

There would be a photo of him in his uniform sent to the house for her. 'A keepsake,' he told her. 'Keep a lookout for it.' Not that she needed anything to remind her of Kell.

'Where are they sending you?'

'I won't know until we get on the ship.' He placed a tender, lingering kiss on her mouth. 'Thank you for everything, Erin. I'll be back before you know it. I've left a token of my affection for you on the kitchen table.'

She watched from the upstairs window as the truck went off down the road. It had been raining, but as it rounded the bend and out of her sight, the sun came out from behind a cloud and turned the puddles into liquid gold. She took it as an omen.

God will keep you safe, my love, she thought.

In the kitchen, she found the money she'd won in the talent quest. Kell had added a pound to it, though she hadn't expected him too. She opened the small box he'd left on the table next to it. There was a ring inside, a small heart encrusted with tiny diamonds. Inside was inscribed, 'Kell & Erin, April 1916'. He'd included a golden chain to hang it on, to keep it hidden from curious eyes, when she had to.

Erin slipped the ring on to her finger. She had never owned anything quite so beautiful, and the sentiment behind it made her heart ache. Better still was the photograph that arrived later in the week. It was a portrait, and Kell looked so handsome in his cap, one eyebrow raised rather quizzically, as if he found the whole concept of going to war slightly amusing.

There was a similar envelope addressed to his parents.

Dorothea Sanders was incensed over her son's action, and said as much to her husband.

'You shouldn't have let Kell come here alone, Willie, you know how his head can be turned. Can't you do something?'

Thoroughly sick of the conversation, William sighed as he gazed at the photograph of his son in its cardboard frame. 'The boy has reached his majority, after all.'

'But he listens to you. He always has. The pair of you are as thick as thieves most of the time.'

William smiled at that, for he'd always enjoyed the company of his son and the confidences they'd exchanged. But not this time. Kell had acted on his conscience and, although William would have preferred his son in a nice safe post in London, he could only admire Kell's courage, while he feared for his safety. 'Have you managed to get some temporary staff?'

The change of subject didn't change Dorothea's need to complain. 'Not one person has bothered to come forward. Honestly, the people in the village are behaving in such a surly manner. Why didn't that wretched girl tell us that Mrs Flynn had died? I wouldn't have come if I'd known.'

'Probably because she didn't know how to contact us. She is only sixteen, after all.'

Dorothea stopped her tirade to stare at him. 'That's an odd thing to know.'

'What is?'

'The age of the maid of all work.'

'It's not as odd as you think, actually. I was guessing, since she looks so young.'

'Well, it's most inconvenient not having any staff. You shouldn't have laid them off in the first place. Mrs Baily can't cook very well, and the girl can only make mutton stew.'

'Which is quite delicious, if last night's dinner was anything to go by.'

'It made you repeat.'

He grinned. 'That's the sign of a good meal. Look, I've got a lot of work to get through, Dorothea. Why don't you take the girls out in the trap, enjoy the spring weather.'

Dorothea's head cocked to one side. 'Olivia is thinking of returning to London. She's quite gone on Kell, and is furious to be treated so shabbily. It really is too bad of him, since he led her to believe they were to be engaged. It will serve him right if he loses her.'

'I'm not particularly fond of the girl,' William said mildly. 'She displays a rather waspish manner, at times.'

'Olivia is the heir to a fortune, Willie. We mustn't forget that.'

'Mustn't we? Oh dear, I was rather hoping we could while we're in Ireland, and I'm in no hurry to see Kell wed. It's a big step for a man to take. The whole point of coming here is to relax.'

'And how can I relax when there's no staff? The people I've approached in the village were quite sullen. You'd think they'd be glad of the opportunity to earn some money. That dreadful girl forgot to make the beds this morning. When I reprimanded her, she burst into tears and said she was tired, and hadn't had time. Does she think she's the only one? I didn't have a wink of sleep last night. It's the damned silence.'

William felt a twinge of pity for the girl. 'She's rushed off her feet. Can't you make your own bed? I did, so did Charles and Catherine.'

'That's why we hire maids. It's really too bad. I'm thinking of returning home. I'm bored, and so is Olivia. At least I'll have my war work to fall back on.'

'Perhaps that would be for the best, my dear. Charles might be happy to accompany you.'

She lowered her voice. 'Charles is behaving quite peculiarly. He seems to have a fixation on the maid and can't take his eyes off her when he sees her. After I told her off he followed her into the hall, patted her on the shoulder and said, "Never mind, girl. Her bark's worse than her bite." I do hope there isn't going to be a *situation.* She's young enough to be his daughter and you know how untrustworthy Charles is with maids.'

William slit open an envelope with the paperknife. 'Charles is?'

'Don't play the innocent, Willie. I distinctly remember gossip about Charles and one of the house staff, several years ago.'

'One shouldn't listen to gossip, old girl. It does more harm than good.' Alarm thrust through him at the thought that Dorothea might discover who'd fathered the maid. William wanted a peaceful old age without a juicy scandal in it that would be endlessly discussed by his wife, especially when it was something in the past that couldn't be changed.

He was surprised to hear that Charles had shown the girl special attention; though Charles had never been predictable. He supposed he'd better have a word with him about it.

'It might be a good idea for you to return to London. I take it you've discussed this with the others over the last couple of weeks.' Of course she had, else she wouldn't have brought it up. Dorothea liked having numbers on her side.

Dorothea shrugged. 'Catherine wants to stay. You know how she loves it here.'

He nodded. 'You could take the Rolls and I can follow in Kell's car with Catherine, after I've supervised the packing and had the house boarded up. It's a waste of time coming back until the war is over. From what I've gathered, there are fears of continuing unrest.'

He opened the receipt he'd taken from the envelope. 'Hello, what's this?'

But Dorothea was leaving the room, her face wreathed in smiles now she'd got her own way. William wouldn't be sorry to be left in peace. He glanced at the receipt again. It was from a ladies' fashion shop in Dublin.

> Blue dress. Taffeta, lace collar.
> Grey suit.
> 2 pairs of ladies shoes.
> Silk camisole, Valenciennes lace trim.

William choked out a laugh as he realized the receipt belonged to his son. No wonder Kell had wanted to come early. Obviously, he'd brought a woman with him on the spur of the moment, and had wanted some privacy. He wondered if Kell had entertained her here, or in a hotel in Dublin.

He could ask the maid, he thought; then shook his head. If Kell had been serious about the Winslow girl he would have stayed, not run off to war.

Briefly, William wondered who the girl he'd brought here was. Some undergraduate Kell had met in Cambridge, perhaps? He'd heard that the intellectual types were a bit on the fast side. Still, a man needed to sow his oats before he settled down.

All the same, Dorothea would have a fit if she ever found out!

Eight

Erin was pleased when Lady Sanders departed, though the week before had been spent in a frenzy of packing, and Erin had spent it scuttling back and forth. Now, she was fair worn out.

She would be sorry to see the back of her father though, for Charles Colby had shown an interest in her, and had been kind.

Mrs Baily had left her final instructions. 'You're wearing yourself out, Maguire. Don't bother about keeping everything spick and span, just look after Lord Sanders and Miss Sanders while they're here. I'll make sure you get a good reference, and a letter of introduction to an employment agency in Dublin.'

Erin stared at her. 'Reference? Am I to be dismissed then?'

Mrs Baily avoided her eyes. 'If the house is to be boarded up for the duration of the war, you can't be boarded up inside it, can you? I'm sorry, Erin. You're a good worker.'

Erin's heart sank. What would she do without work and a roof over her head? 'Can't I go to London with you?'

'The London house is fully staffed. Perhaps you should talk to the master about your future. He's a good-hearted man, despite his stern manner.'

Erin dressed in her best suit for her appointment with Lord Sanders. He indicated a chair. 'What is it, Erin?'

She said it in a rush. 'Am I to be dismissed, sir?'

'Didn't Mrs Baily tell you that we won't be keeping any staff on once the house is boarded up? We've already sold the horses. I'm thinking of selling the estate, as well. We may never come back.'

'What will I do? Where will I go?'

'I'm sure you can find employment elsewhere.' He drew

93

an envelope from his drawer and slid it across his desk. 'Mr Colby has asked me to give you this. It should tide you over until you find work. And I owe you wages.'

His attention turned to her suit, frowning slightly he said, 'That's a pretty suit. It looks new?'

'Yes, sir. It is new.'

'You wouldn't have purchased something of that quality in the village.'

'No, sir. I bought it in Dublin.'

'You went to Dublin?'

She couldn't help but smile. 'It's a grand place with the castle, and all. I won a singing contest on the stage of the Olympic theatre. Five guineas, the prize was.'

Lord Sanders nodded. 'Is there anything else you'd like to tell me, Erin?'

She unconsciously fingered the chain hanging around her neck. 'No, sir.'

He brought out the receipt. 'This came from a shop in Dublin. It was addressed to my son. Do you know anything about it, my dear?'

Erin hung her head, hardly daring to breathe.

'Let me put it this way. Am I to understand that my son bought you that suit, and other, more intimate garments besides? I would rather you tell me than go and search your room.'

She lifted her head, her eyes defiant. 'Sure, but the pair of us love each other, and what's wrong with that.'

'He told you he loved you?'

She nodded.

'I won't ask you what went on between you, but I understand the attraction, for you're a pretty girl. However, you must realize that any sort of match between yourself and my son is impossible.'

'He asked me to wait for him.'

'You're sixteen years old, Erin. Too young to wait for any man, especially my son. My dear, put this foolish notion out of your mind. I'm sorry Kell trifled with your affections in this manner.'

'He didn't trifle with them. He said he loved me . . . twice.'

Lord Sanders' eyes took on an icy expression. 'Kell is engaged to marry Miss Olivia Winslow. Any relationship he pursued with you was for his own amusement. He would have left you a token, I imagine. Some money and a trinket, perhaps?'

His words were a dash of cold water in her face. Erin paled. 'I don't believe you!'

'Well, believe this, Miss Maguire. I took you in because I felt sorry for you, and this is how you repay me. Your relationship with my son is now at an end. I don't want to throw you out, since we need someone here. But when we depart, your employment is also at an end.'

'And if I choose not to stay?'

'You'll forfeit your wages for the entire year.'

She couldn't afford to lose her wages and protested, 'That's not fair.'

'I know it's not, but that's what will happen. So, are you staying or going?'

Grudgingly, she muttered, 'I'll starve without my wages, so I have no choice. Not that you care.'

'You're right, I don't, and I'd appreciate it if you didn't take that tone with me. Now, do stop being tiresome and go and get on with your work, there's a good girl. I won't confiscate the clothing, since you probably earned it.'

How sordid he'd made the love between herself and Kell sound. Surely Kell wasn't engaged to marry that awful girl, who laughed like a hen who'd just laid an egg, and whose nose was so sharp and beaky she could most likely stab a man to death with it.

Seething with shame and anger, Erin closed the door as hard as she dared, then went through to the kitchen to make herself a cup of tea.

She was tired from all the running around she'd been made to do, and doubt niggled at her. What if Lord Sanders was right, and Kell had been lying to her? Tears came into her eyes. Sitting in Mrs Flynn's rocking chair she moved back and forth for the comfort it gave her, then buried her head in her apron and began to sob.

After a while, she thought, she should be getting the tea tray ready for Miss Catherine and her father, not sit around and feel sorry for herself. Crying wouldn't help, and the scones she had in the oven should be cooked.

She dried her eyes, rose, and took the scones out, setting

them on the table. They hadn't risen as well as they should have. The firebox of the stove needed some more coal on it, else it wouldn't be hot enough to roast the chicken for dinner, or heat the water for the baths. Though it would serve Lord Sanders right if he had to use cold.

She set the tea tray and resentfully swiped a dish rag over the crumbs on the table. But it was no good grizzling about her lot. Once she'd been given her wage, she'd have nearly twenty-one pounds in her kitty, for Charles Colby's envelope had contained five pounds. There were her mother's sovereigns as well. That was more than most people had. She also had smart clothes, and a bag she'd found in Mrs Flynn's room to carry her worldly goods in when she was turned out of the house.

Erin drew in a deep breath. It was time to stop dreaming about London and go there. She would put her age up to eighteen, so if anyone asked, she'd be taken more seriously. And she'd cut her hair off; have one of those modern short styles. She might be able to sell the length of it to a wigmaker.

Erin began to smile as she picked up the brass coal scuttle, which was in need of a good polish. It could turn black now, for all she cared, for it would never get another spoonful of elbow grease out of her. Neither would anything else in this house.

The coal was in a bunker near the garden shed. It didn't take long to fill the scuttle. She carried her heavy load through the wet grass towards the kitchen door, two hands grasping the handle, leaning to one side and staggering a bit from the effort. Setting it down at the door, she carefully wiped her feet on the doormat.

As she placed the scuttle down by the stove and began to straighten up, Erin's eyes fell on the kitchen table. The scones were gone and so was the milk. And the larder door was wide open.

Across the kitchen floor was a trail of large muddy foot-prints going in, and another set going out. She went to report the theft to Lord Sanders.

Later, a constable came to the house. Erin was summoned to Lord Sanders' study, where Catherine gave her a re-assuring smile.

'They just want to ask you a few questions,' Catherine said gently.

'Where were you when the theft occurred, Miss Maguire?' the constable asked.

'Filling the coal scuttle.'

'And you didn't see anyone.'

'They slid in and out like they were skating on a streak of bacon grease. And my back was only turned for a few moments.'

The constable frowned at her. 'Are you certain you didn't see anyone? You're not lying, are you?'

'And why should I be lying? Do you think I've swallowed a dozen hot scones and a pint of milk in half a minute, especially with the scones as hard as pebbles because they forgot to rise.'

Catherine smothered a giggle. She received a stern look from her father which made her laugh. Lord Sanders smiled too, this time.

'Did you know that your brothers were released from prison two weeks ago?'

Erin stared at the constable, a yawning sensation in her stomach. 'No, I didn't,' she whispered before her voice strengthened. 'Patrick and Michael Maguire are no kin to me. I'd spit on them sooner than look at them.'

'Your father, Dermot Maguire, escaped from prison a few days ago, too. There are orders to shoot him on sight.'

'But why would any of them come here? Surely this is the first place they'd expect to be looked for.'

'Because Maguire swore he'd take his revenge on O'Connor and myself when I had him arrested,' Lord Sanders said.

Catherine's eyes widened. 'Daddy, we must leave here as soon a possible.'

Fear clogged Erin's throat and the colour drained from her face, leaving her feeling weak. Terrified by the thought that her stepfather might have walked into the house, she gazed at Lord Sanders. 'I didn't know any of this. I'd tell you if I saw him, I swear. He's a terrible hard man. I'm sore afraid of Dermot Maguire, of all the Maguires. They're a pack of mongrel dogs.'

Despite her own fright, Catherine crossed to her side to put a comforting arm around her shoulders. 'You look pale, Erin. Come and sit down. Father, do please stop bullying her. You can see she knows nothing and is frightened out of her wits.'

'You're right, my dear. I'm sorry, Erin, but we had to find out whether they'd made contact with you. From now on we must keep the windows shut and the doors locked, as a precaution, even during the day.'

'And we'll stay together all the time, Erin. I can help you with the cooking and everything, and we can sleep in the same room so we don't get frightened.' She added, as if struck by a sudden thought, 'How are we all to fit in Kell's car. Erin is coming with us, isn't she? You promised me she could be my maid when I was sixteen.'

Erin shrugged. 'I don't want to be a maid forever, Miss Catherine. I've decided to go to London anyway, to try and become a singer, like my mammy always wanted me to.' She flicked a glance towards Lord Sanders. 'Perhaps I can get a lift to Dublin on the shipping company truck, when they come to take the crates away, if it's not too much trouble. I don't want to be here by myself if the Maguires are on the loose.'

'I'll arrange it. It might not be them, you know. It was only a few scones and some milk. Perhaps it was local children who saw the opportunity for a feed, and succumbed to temptation. I'll ask the gardener to keep an eye out. O'Connor will be on his guard now, and will take a look around, too.'

The constable said, 'O'Connor and his family left Callacrea this morning to catch the boat to Liverpool. He said that as he's collected his pay he wasn't waiting around for Dermot to come calling, and was going to America. You should leave too, sir. As soon as possible.'

Lord Sanders nodded at the officer. 'Thank you for telling me. I'll keep my rifles loaded, just in case. And I'll keep a pistol within reach at all times. We'll only be here for another week or so, so should be able to manage.'

'I've got people keeping a lookout for them, so if they're in the district they're bound to be spotted. I'll drop by every now and then to check on you, sir. Don't hesitate to call us out again, if needed.'

After the constable had gone, Lord Sanders said, 'We must come up with an escape plan after dinner, just in case we need it.'

Later, when Catherine was taking her bath, Lord Sanders paid Erin her wages. 'Because of the danger, if you wish to leave earlier, you can. Good luck with your career, Erin.'

'Sure, but I wouldn't leave Miss Catherine to fend for herself. Though she tried to hide it, you can see what a stew she's in. And those footprints in the kitchen were too big for a child.'

He nodded. 'I saw them. You're a good-hearted girl, Erin. I wish things were different.'

Erin managed a small smile at the thought. 'Perhaps they will be, sir. Nobody can predict what the future has in mind for us. Not even you.'

But two days later, Erin wished she had been blessed with foresight.

Dermot Maguire had escaped prison during a riot in gaol, during which he and another inmate had fled, using a pre-planned route. The escape attempt hadn't been for him, but made on the behalf of his cell mate, a hard-faced man of few words – someone who Dermot had thought might be worth his while to befriend.

They'd lain low in a barge in the river, where they'd found a change of clothing waiting for them. After the hue and cry had died down, they'd made their way to the back entrance of a public house, situated in a dimly lit alley.

Men had greeted his companion – men with respect in their eyes who'd embraced his former cell mate. Dermot had been introduced.

'This is Maguire. He was born in Belfast. We can use him.'

Eyes turned his way; hard stares that made him feel slightly uncomfortable. He returned them. 'That's if I want to be used.'

Someone hit him and he went down, his face was pressed against the damp cobbled floor by a foot. A gun pressed against his temple. 'Either you're for us or you're against us.'

And if he was against them, a body would be found floating in the Liffey in the morning with a hole in its head. 'I'm for you.'

Hauled to his feet, he was then slammed into a chair.

'Fetch his boys down, so we know we've got the right man.'

So that's why he'd been encouraged to escape. Patrick and Michael were men now. Both of them were mean looking, but deferential, the least important in the pecking order of this group of men.

Father and sons made a show of clapping each other on the back. Dermot thought his sons fools to allow themselves to be used, but they had to make their own way in the world. As for himself, he was going to get out of the country as fast as he possibly could, and in any way he could. But first, he had some personal business to take care of.

'I'm going after Lord Sanders,' he told his sons, after they'd taken him to a filthy room they called home, which was in a building with a stink worse than the prison he'd just left.

His sons looked at each other. 'We have orders to shoot you if you try to leave.'

'Shoot your own pa? Neither of you have got the guts. But if you find some, shoot me after I've settled my debts in Callacrea, because those bastards who put me in prison are going to pay for it.' The boys seemed uncertain. 'Are you with me or against me?'

They'd all laughed at that. Now, the three of them crouched in the stables of Callacrea House, munching on the scones Michael had taken from the kitchen.

The horses had been saddled by the stablehand, another who held a grudge against the Sanders family. The man had promptly declared his intention to go straight to the pub and drink a jar or two of dark ale with his friends. He'd been assured that the horses wouldn't be harmed, but set free in some field, where they'd eventually be found and handed over to their new owner.

A can of gasoline had been brought there from the garage. Once the men had done their business, they intended to set fire to the house, to cause a diversion while they got away.

'I didn't expect to see our Erin working here,' Patrick whispered. 'I could have reached out and touched her titties when she came out for the coal, earlier.'

'She's got a nice pair, and a body on her. It's been a while since I had a woman.'

Dermot laughed softly. 'Erin looks like her mother did when I married her. Just keep your mind off your balls until after I've taken care of Sanders. There are two women here, and I fancy giving the Sanders girl the length of me. That'll teach her to look down her nose.'

'She's a cripple!' Patrick exclaimed.

'She's shite, but a man can still have his use of her, can't he? I reckon nobody's been allowed to investigate there, yet. It'd be a shame for her to die without experiencing the little treat I'm going to give her.' Dermot threw his younger son a frown as he began to cough on a crumb. 'Shut the feck up. You were a bloody idiot to steal the food in the first place. I thought we were going to be found out when the polis came nosing around, and Sanders is now on the alert. They've locked everything up.'

''Tis easy enough to open those windows. You just slide the blade of a knife along to release the inside catch,' Patrick said.

The men fell silent, the horses tossed, fretted and farted. The stable began to stink of moist dung.

Outside, the daylight faded. The gloaming was filled with soft purple shadows. Soon, the moon came up, creating little silvery patches.

They saw Erin and the Sanders girl in the kitchen, moving about. Dermot crept up the window and watched them. The pair were whispering and laughing together as they washed the dishes and put them away. How young they looked, their flesh unblemished and soft, their eyes wide and innocent, their mouths and bodies lushly curved to incite the lusts of men. They were ripe plums waiting to be picked.

Dermot felt no remorse for what was about to happen to them. There were hundreds of girls, just as young and pretty, waiting to trap some man into her honeypot in exchange for a wedding ring. The Sanders girl wasn't limping as badly as he remembered, though she still wore her ugly leg irons. He hoped she took them off to go to bed in.

101

He went back to his sons, who were eager for the hunt and the prize at the end of it. 'Not yet,' he said. 'We'll wait until after midnight. Sanders is usually in his study then, but the girls will have gone to bed. I'll take him. Michael, you can pour petrol around the house. Upstairs and on the staircase too, so it all goes up when we leave.'

'What about me?' Patrick said sullenly.

'You can fetch the girls down. Get our Erin first, she'll likely be in the servants' quarters in the attic. She can take you to the other girl.'

Inside the house, things were not as Dermot had imagined. The girls had remained fully dressed except for their shoes. They were to sleep in the music room on a mattress. If there was the need to escape, they would go out through the French windows on to the terrace and run around to the back, where Erin would take Kell's horse and ride into the village to alert the constables, while Catherine and Lord Sanders would escape in the car. The keys had been left in the car, and they'd been allowed a small bag apiece, which were already packed and in the car.

Both rifles had been loaded as a precaution, and extra ammunition set beside them. As Catherine had been taught to shoot, she was entrusted with her father's old pistol, which had been cleaned and loaded with its one shot.

Erin armed herself with a brass poker, just in case Catherine missed, and she wore her savings in a stocking tied around her waist under her skirt. She wasn't about to risk losing it.

Lord Sanders had stated his intention to sleep in the armchair in his study, which was right next to the music room.

It had been fun working out the escape plan; he'd made it sound like an adventure. Now, after ten minutes of whispers and giggles, the two girls fell asleep.

William smiled to himself. He had to admit, the pair of them had pluck. Erin Maguire had proved herself to be loyal. He was regretting his hasty decision to dismiss the girl, but now she was involved with his son, he had no choice.

He shrugged and poured himself a brandy. He warmed it

between his hands to inhale the bouquet released by the action.

Erin had stated her intention to go to London, too. And why not? he thought. Lots of Irish girls went over the water to work as servants. But he knew Erin Maguire had far grander dreams. He hoped she'd succeed where others had failed, as long as that didn't include marriage to his son. But Kell was no fool. Surely he knew the value of a good match and, like Charles Colby, wouldn't allow his head to be turned by a pair of Irish eyes, however beautiful.

He placed his glass on the side table, propped his feet on a stool and pulled a blanket over his legs. He doubted that Dermot Maguire would come all this way on the off-chance that the family was in residence, just to act out his threat. The house was as quiet as a grave, with not even a wind to disturb the trees.

Gradually, his chin sunk on to his chest and he nodded off to sleep.

Erin came awake suddenly, the hairs prickling at the back of her neck.

Her harp was singing to itself, the strangely haunting hum its strings sometimes made when a draft of air played over them. Her mammy had told her it was the voice of Ireland, and she should listen to it, not be frightened.

Erin suddenly sat up with a gasp as a thought hit her. If the harp was singing there must be a draught. Where was it coming from? At the same time, she heard a noise from upstairs, the click as a door gently closed.

'What is it?' Catherine said in alarm from beside her.

'Shush!' Erin got to her feet and, going to the door, placed her ear against it.

'The harp is playing by itself,' Catherine whispered.

'If there's a draught coming under the door it does that sometimes. There shouldn't be a draught. I'm going to wake your father.'

'I'm coming with you. I'll bring the pistol.'

'All right, but don't put your leg braces on, they're too noisy. And we'll open the French windows, just in case.'

Erin quietly opened the door and listened. There was a

soft scuffing noise coming from the dining room as a window was drawn upwards. The pair moved along the wall and slipped into the study. Catherine shook her father.

He was awake in an instant, grabbing for a rifle. 'Didn't I tell you to go out to the garage?'

But it was too late. The door slammed open against the wall and Dermot Maguire walked in. When William lifted his rifle to fire, Maguire calmly shot him through his head. There was no doubting that he was dead when he fell.

Catherine screamed and discharged her pistol at Dermot. The man dropped.

There was a strong smell of petrol, and shouts came from upstairs.

'Quick, out through the music room.'

'But my father.'

'He's dead, there's nothing we can do.'

Catherine's teeth were chattering in her head. 'Who's going to drive us?'

'I am. Now let's get going.'

Erin snatched up her harp and Catherine's leg irons as they went. They reached the garage without incident. There was crashing and shouting coming from the house. Suddenly, a red streak whooshed upwards and the house seemed to explode into a ball of flame.

The stable door was open and the horses milled about, making nervous whinnies.

The garage doors creaked noisily as they pulled them open.

'They're over there,' she heard Michael shout, then a scream. 'I'm on fire! Help me!'

Erin practically pushed Catherine into the passenger seat and piled the harp and leg irons on top of her. 'Here, hold on to those, and don't drop my harp.' The bags dug into her back as she tried to remember how to start the engine. Footsteps pounded towards them.

The engine started with a roar. Erin stuck her foot on the peddle and the car lurched forward. Patrick hurled himself on to the bonnet and was spreadeagled there. His fingers hooked over the front for grip.

As they passed him, Michael was on his knees, his arms

waving as he tried to beat the flames from his hair with fiery arms.

Beside her, Catherine screamed hysterically.

'Shut up and hit him with something,' Erin yelled at her, and was rewarded when her companion lashed out at Patrick's arm with her leg iron. When it fell from her grip, she threw the second one at him and caught him across the nose. Blood spurted.

Sliding to one side, Patrick cursed when he lost his grip, and just managed to fling himself clear.

The horses came out and began to follow the car. When she looked back it was to see Patrick trying to mount Nero. But the horse squealed and kicked out at him, breaking free.

Catherine shouted a warning, and Erin was just in time to turn the wheel of the car before they hit the gate pillar. Spooked now, the horses came galloping down the road after them, while Erin concentrated on trying to keep the car on the road. The back wheel bucked through the potholes, and something dug painfully into her spine. Thank goodness Kell had taught her how to drive the car.

Just as they reached the slope down into the village, the engine cut out and they coasted down the hill. In the sudden silence, the rush of air through the harp made it wail like a demented soul. The sky behind them turned redder, as though hell itself was on fire. Something exploded.

Next to her, Catherine began to sob.

As she steered the car to a stop outside the constable's house, Erin said, 'I think we've run out of petrol.'

Trembling all over, she squeezed the bulb of the horn, and kept squeezing it until the constable stopped her. Then she burst into tears.

Nine

The noise of the horn alerted the whole village. People poured from their houses and the bar.

The horses whinnied, squealed, nervously stamped their forelegs. Eyes wild, their hooves struck sparks from the road until their groom arrived to take charge of them, then they settled and crowded close to him, accepting the treats he had ready for them, used to his voice and handling.

He was respectful as he said to the constable, 'I'll take them to the smithy for now. He'll stable them until their owner can collect them.' His eyes shifted sideways a bit as if he thought he ought to explain. 'I was in the bar all evening, sir. Where's his Lordship?'

'The Maguire girl said her father shot him through the head.'

'A shame, since he was a lovely man.' There was shock in the man's voice. 'Dermot Maguire himself, was it?' There was a moment of silence, then a mumbled, 'Now there's a thing.' He ambled off, the horses following him like over-grown dogs.

The red glow in the sky took the villagers up towards Callacrea House, where they stood, arms folded over their chests, and silently watched the house burn. There was nothing else they could do, and although the fire cart finally came, the fire had gained too much of a hold. The heat reached out to them.

A gasp went up as the roof collapsed in a spectacular series of snaps and cracks, as if fireworks were going off. Then sparks whooshed upwards into the sky like a giant roman candle.

'Did everybody get out?' somebody thought to ask.

'Lord Sanders is still in there, I heard the Maguire girl say.'

''Twas Dermot Maguire's doing, she said. Her father shot his Lordship to death, hisself.'

'I heard they found the body of one the Maguire boys burned to a crisp.'

'Which one?'

'Only the devil knows, since it was too burnt up to tell. Perhaps those girls who were saved will be able to say.'

'I shouldn't be at all surprised if Erin Maguire had a hand in it. She's a dark horse. The Maguires were always a bad lot, 'tis in their blood.'

'May the good Lord cleave your wicked tongue to the roof of your mouth, Maureen Finnigan. The girl hasn't got a drop of Maguire blood in her. She's a bastard got on her mother by a relative of the Sanders. That's why she was kept on when the rest of you were sent packing. The Maguire men never failed to let Erin know it, either.'

'I saw her a while back, riding in Mr Sander's car, and them laughing together like the brazen pair they are. All night they were gone. She was all dressed up when she came back, like one of those fancy women.'

'Ah, shut your nasty chat, Maureen. It'll be interesting to find out what them girls said about this, tomorrow.'

Catherine was too distraught to say anything to anybody. Tears ran down her cheeks and she trembled with shock and clung to Erin, who hugged her tight.

'Poor dear girl,' the constable's wife said, prising them apart. 'I'll give Miss Sanders the spare room. It has a nice big bed so she can rest. I'll fetch her some warmed milk with brandy in it, to settle her down.'

Not so much fuss for Erin, who was handed a blanket and waved to a chair in the parlour, along with a cup of cold water. She shrugged, thinking, wait until you're famous, people will treat you better then.

Later, she was woken by the constable and subjected to rigourous questioning. She answered his questions, hoping she wouldn't have to lie.

'Dermot Maguire shot Lord Sanders. He was standing close and Lord Sanders only had time to raise his gun before the bullet got him in the head.'

'You're sure he was dead?'

'His brains were blown clear through the back of his skull and splattered all over the panelling.' She shuddered. 'It was a terrible sight, especially for Miss Catherine to see. The poor man. Dermot Maguire took a bullet and dropped like a stone, and it serve him right if you ask me.'

'Then what happened?'

Erin was relieved he hadn't asked who'd fired the shot that killed Dermot. 'The three of us had made a plan to escape if anything happened. I was supposed to use the horse because there isn't room for three in the car. But Miss Catherine didn't know how to drive, so I drove the car.'

She gave an account of the escape, of Michael catching fire and of Patrick hanging on to the car.

'So, Patrick Maguire is still alive and at large. There'll be a general alert out for him tomorrow and a watch kept on the ports. He'll be lucky if he gets away. And how did you learn how to drive a car, Miss?'

'Mr Sanders himself showed me, on the day he took me to Dublin with him. Sure, but you saw us go by, yourself.'

The constable nodded. 'I wondered what you were doing with Mr Sanders in the car.'

'And why should you wonder that? Mr Sanders was going to sign his name to becoming a soldier so he could go off and defend his country. Brave he is, or daft. One of the two.'

'Now don't you talk in a disrespectful manner about a man who knows his duty.' But the constable was smiling, all the same. He was an amiable man.

'Mr Sanders knew I was saving my money to go to London Town to be on the stage. Being the kind man he is, he took me to the theatre to enter a singing competition, just so I could see what it's like.'

'And what is it like?'

'It gave me the trembles at first. There was a proper orchestra, and a lot of talking from the audience. Then everyone began to listen. It was grand when they shouted for another song. My mammy would have been so proud to see me up there.'

'Cliona would have at that, for she had a rare talent for singing, herself,' he murmured.

'Afterwards, Mr Sanders found me a room in a boarding house and paid for it out of his own pocket, like I was the queen herself.' She managed a small smile despite the tragedy that had just taken place. 'I won the first prize of five guineas to put towards my fare.'

'That was at the Gaiety Theatre, was it?'

'It was not.' She pulled on a disapproving face for his benefit. 'The contest was held at the Olympia, where the dancing girls were a shameless lot of hussies with their feathers and painted faces. They kicked their legs up high in the air so their drawers were showing. When I said as much to Mr Sanders he just laughed and said I'd best get used to it if I'm going to be a singer on the stage.'

The constable smiled at that.

'Erin, where are you?' Catherine called out. 'I'm afraid to be on my own.'

The constable nodded. 'Go up and join her.'

'Your missus said I must sleep in the chair.'

'You go and keep the young lady company. The bed is big enough for two. I'll telephone the lawyer in Dublin, since he acts on the Sanders' behalf. He can contact the police in London, and they can go and inform Lady Sanders of what's happened. I'll want a written statement from the pair of you in the morning, too, for the records.'

Catherine was still crying when Erin joined her. 'How am I going to get home?'

'We'll sort it out tomorrow, Miss Catherine.' Erin undressed down to her chemise and slid into bed beside her. Both of them smelled of smoke. 'Listen, Miss Catherine,' she said. 'I know you've had a hard time of it, but tomorrow we have to make a written statement.'

'I'd better tell the constable I shot that man.'

'You'll tell him nothing of the sort, since a grudge might be held against you and his friends might come looking for you – that's if he's got any, which I doubt. Just tell him that Dermot died in an exchange of shots with your father. All right?'

'All right.' Catherine began to weep softly again.

Taking the girl in her arms, Erin held her tight. 'You've had a terrible shock, but you'll cope better after you've had a rest. Try to put everything from your mind.'

'Promise you'll look after me, Erin.'

'Of course I will. Go to sleep now, I'll sing you a song.' She softly sang 'Spinning Wheel', and by the time she reached, '*Slower . . . and lower . . . and lower the reel spins*', Catherine Sanders was fast asleep.

The best place for the poor girl, too, Erin thought. Easing Catherine out of her aching arms, she turned carefully on to her side and snuggled into the bed. She'd never slept on anything quite so soft, but couldn't help wondering what the morning would bring.

The morning brought Philip Flatterly from Dublin. He was a tall, brown-eyed man with a luxurious moustache under his nose that curled dashingly upwards at each end. The lawyer wore a sober, double-breasted suit and black tie.

Philip Flatterly had been to the gutted house, and had satisfied himself that there was nothing there left to salvage. He now supervised the written statements the two girls had made, making sure nothing compromising was present. He nodded with approval at the neat handwriting the pair presented, and was surprised by the maid's excellent grasp of words.

'That all seems perfectly clear, constable. I'll witness their signatures. I doubt if you'll need to keep Miss Sanders any longer. My instructions from her mother are to put her on the boat to London so she can be restored to the care of her family as soon as possible. Do you have any luggage, Miss Sanders?'

'One small bag in the car. What will we do with Kell's car?'

'My chauffeur will drive it to Dublin and I'll find room for it in my garage until other arrangements have been made.'

'There's no petrol left in it,' Erin said.

'I have a spare can in my car.'

Catherine choked, 'What about my father . . . his body? We can't just leave him there.'

Flatterly exchanged a glance with the constable. 'Perhaps you'd allow us a little privacy.'

When the constable had gone he patted Catherine on the shoulder. 'Lord Sanders' ashes will be sent to London as soon as it's humanly possible, my dear. You must understand, there will be very little of him left. The blaze was very fierce.'

To which Catherine began to cry again.

He handed her a handkerchief. 'Come along, my dear. I'm a very busy man and we need to get going else you'll miss the boat.'

'What about Erin?'

'Miss Maguire?' His eyes flickered over her. 'We're not responsible for the young lady. No doubt one of the local women will take her in, since she's one of their own.'

'Not likely,' Erin said with a snort.

Seating herself, Catherine folded her arms across her chest and said with unusual stubbornness, 'If Erin doesn't come, then I'm not going. She saved my life.'

'My dear girl. You can't expect your mother to give a home to a housemaid whose relatives killed your father.'

'Why not, since I killed her father?'

'No, shush, Miss Catherine . . .' Erin whispered into the silence.

The lawyer frowned and gazed at Catherine with some speculation. 'You didn't mention that in your statement, my dear.'

'Because Erin told me not to. She thought it better if I didn't.'

Erin became the subject of his uncomfortable scrutiny. 'Is this true, Miss Maguire?'

Obviously Catherine would have the deed on her conscience for ever if the truth were told. Dermot Maguire wasn't worth the burden of it, so Erin prepared to brazen it out.

'Is what true – that I told her not to say she shot a man? Yes, it is true, because of one simple fact.' She stared at him boldly. 'Miss Catherine didn't shoot anybody. She just thought she did. Her hands were shaking so much that the shot went into the ceiling. Lord Sanders shot Dermot Maguire at exactly the same time as Dermot killed him. I've made a statement to that fact, and I'll stand up in any court in the land and swear on a thousand Bibles that it's the truth.'

Catherine gave a small cry. 'But, I could almost swear it was me who shot him.'

111

'You were too shocked last night to think straight, that you were, Miss Catherine. I could see the way your thoughts were going, and that's why I told you what to say. I saw it happen with my own eyes. Don't you fret over it any more – your shot went into the ceiling. No doubt they'll find the hole it made if they look hard enough.'

Catherine's expression became one of relief. 'You don't know how happy I am to learn that.'

'I imagine the ceiling might have caved in,' Philip Flatterly said, with a wry smile.

'Fancy that.' Erin returned his smile. 'As I have said, Miss Catherine didn't shoot anyone, sir, so I thought it wiser that neither of us mentioned that she fired a shot into the ceiling, lest the constable tie himself in knots over it. It would only cause him extra work, if you see what I'm saying.'

He nodded. 'I see very well. Thank you, Miss Maguire. How can we reward you for showing such devotion to your employer's welfare?'

'Sure, it was nothing. But I'd like a ride into Dublin, if you would. I'm not staying in Callacrea, especially with Patrick Maguire on the loose. I'm going on the boat to London Town to seek my fortune on the stage, and it's a terrible long walk to Dublin carrying my harp.'

'I'm sure I can manage that.'

'We can be company together on the boat, and you can look after me,' Catherine said happily. 'That's settled then.'

Philip Flatterly reflected a moment. 'Lady Sanders expressed concern about you travelling alone, my dear. I'll telephone her and tell her you'll be accompanied. No doubt, she'll be relieved. I shall pay Miss Maguire's fare in return for the service she's done the family.'

'Good.' Catherine stood up. 'Now I must go and thank our host and his wife for their hospitality on behalf of Erin and myself.'

Something she wouldn't have thought to do. Miss Catherine had grand manners, and it wouldn't hurt if she learned a few herself seeing as she was going to London, Erin thought. And as Catherine walked away, she noticed with a slight frown that she hardly limped at all without her leg irons, though she stepped carefully.

After Catherine had gone the lawyer's glance came back to her. 'Lady Sanders will want to thank you personally, no doubt. Just remember she'll be grieving for her husband, so be grateful for her thanks and don't expect anything more. You have money of your own for the journey, I take it.'

Erin sighed as she pulled her shawl over the small bulge at her waist. She wasn't going to tell him how well off she was. That was her business, and it was money honestly earned and saved. But she doubted if any of them would believe she could have accumulated such an amount, and might think she'd stolen it. 'Lord Sanders had paid me my due wages before the fire—'

'But you lost it in the blaze, along with your other possessions, I imagine.'

She'd done no such thing. 'But—'

'Don't interrupt my train of thought, Miss Maguire,' he interjected smoothly, nodding to himself as he jotted down some figures in a notebook.

'Luckily, I had my best set of clothes in a bag, and I managed to rescue my harp, too,' she muttered. 'I wouldn't like to be without that, since it was my mammy's.'

'Quite,' he said. 'I'll make sure you're reimbursed for your other losses, of course. It will be taken into account when the insurance claim is settled. Ten pounds should cover it, I imagine.' There seemed to be a message in the eyes that engaged hers. 'I wouldn't like you to make claims against the family in the future?'

Make claims against the family, what the devil was he talking about? 'You mean the insurance will pay for everything of mine that was burned up.'

'Up to a certain limit.' He looked at his figures again and frowned. 'Perhaps fifteen might be a fairer figure. If you agree, I can settle the sum for you right now?'

If he thought a patched nightgown was worth that amount of money, who was she to argue with him? She'd be needing the money when she reached London Town. She'd heard it was an expensive place to live.

'Be quick, now. Yes or no.'

It would be so easy to agree and take the money, and the devil was sorely tempting her. How hard was it to say yes?

Harder than she expected, for the lie would not allow itself to be forced out of her mouth. The lawyer fellow must be as daft as a donkey, and she must be dafter to turn down the opportunity to double her money. She'd been brought up by her mother to be honest, and had told enough lies for one morning, but those couldn't be helped. She thought of Dermot Maguire and his sons. Erin didn't want to sink to their level.

'I don't think you understand, Mr Flatterly,' she said, resisting the urge to kick herself. 'I didn't lose anything of value in the fire except a ragged old nightgown, and I'm not about to claim that I did.' She patted her waist and lowered her voice, in case anyone was listening. 'I have my savings right here, in a stocking tied around my waist. When I reach London I'm going to put it in a bank for safe keeping.'

'I see.' He snapped his notebook shut and smiled expansively at her. 'It's a rare privilege to meet someone as honest as you are, my dear. I wish you good luck on the stage.' He plucked five pounds from his wallet, wrapped it around his card and pressed it into her hand. 'You may need some expenses for the trip, we can't have you spending your own money when you're doing the Sanders a service. No need to reimburse me. Call it a reward for your services, if you like. Do contact my office in London if you need any help. My signature is on the back of the card, just tell them that Mr Flatterly sent you.'

He looked up and smiled when Catherine came back. 'Ah, Miss Sanders, that was quick. Are we ready to go, then?'

Erin was more than ready. Her harp and their bags had been transferred to the larger car. As the two cars drove off they were watched by a small crowd of visitors.

'Good riddance to bad rubbish, Erin Maguire,' one of the women shouted out.

Erin was about to shout something rude back at her when she remembered she was riding in a posh car. How grand it felt, the leather seats all polished so she could slide her bum from side to side without a hitch. And what better a time to start improving her manners, when she felt like a princess. So she stuck her nose in the air and muttered, 'To hell with the harpy. I hope her milk goes sour.'

And later, when they were about to pass the churchyard,

she asked Philip Flatterly to stop the car, and she hurried down to the oblong bed of daffodils, where she said farewell to her mother.

'I'm leaving to sing on the stage, Mammy, and I don't know if I'll ever come back this way again. I'll work hard and make you proud of me, just see if I don't, though I'm as nervous as a turkey in December. As for Charles Colby, he's the grandest father a girl could ever have. No wonder you loved him all those years. Sure, but don't I feel the same way about Kell Sanders.' She wiped the tears from her eyes when the car horn was tooted. 'I've got to go now, Mammy darling. I'll see you in heaven one day.'

Erin ran back up to the car, tears pricking her eyes. Silently, Catherine handed her a handkerchief. When the car moved off, Catherine took her hand, a moment of empathy in the grief of mutual parental loss.

London! The Sanders' car was waiting for them, the chauffeur wearing a black armband. He touched a forefinger respectfully against his cap and held the door open for them.

As they wound through the crowded, narrow streets, excitement mounted inside Erin. There was a sense of bustle and purpose about the place. Men, tall and proud in their uniforms, strolled though the streets. Buskers played bugles, violins and mouth organs on every corner. Girls hurried about and smiled at the soldiers. The car overtook a Salvation Army band marching along.

They drew up at front of a large house, one in a curved terrace, with a flight of steps up to the front door. The door was opened by a maid.

'Lady Sanders is in the drawing room, Miss Sanders.'

Erin followed Catherine through. Lady Sanders was seated on a velvet chair by the window. She looked like a painting with the light slanting in on her angular face. Her elegant black dress and discreet pearls showed her off to advantage. Pale of face, her hair had been cut into the new style, which suited her.

She rose, tragic, but composed, a diamond ring glittering on one of the slim fingers of the hands she held out. 'Catherine, my dearest, such a tragedy to befall us. Thank

God you survived it. How shall we bear the loss of your father?'

They exchanged kisses, then Lady Sanders seemed to notice Erin. 'Maguire, isn't it? Mr Flatterly tells me you saved my daughter's life. I'm most grateful. And thank you for escorting her safely home.'

She rang a bell and a maid appeared. 'Tell the housekeeper to send some refreshment up, would you. And perhaps Maguire would like some tea before she leaves, so take her down to the kitchen with you, Prosser.'

'Yes, ma'am.'

When Erin was about to follow the maid, Catherine put a hand on her arm to detain her. 'You can't just throw Erin out. She's only just got here, and has nowhere else to go. Besides, she doesn't know anyone here, except us. Where will she go?'

Lady Sanders' lips tightened. 'Don't be difficult, Catherine. You know very well that we don't need any more staff. Besides which, it was the girl's family who committed the horrible crime against us.'

'But not Erin. At least you could offer her a room for the night. It's getting late, she can't just wander the streets alone, looking for somewhere to stay. Mother, you don't understand. I owe Erin my life.'

'I shall pay her something for the trouble. Oh, do stop being so dramatic, darling, and try not to contradict me in front of servants, it gives them the wrong idea. Very well, Maguire, you may stay tonight. Prosser, find Maguire a bed in the servants' quarters. Off you go now, the pair of you. I wish to talk to my daughter in private.'

As the door closed behind them, Erin heard Lady Sanders say, 'Catherine, you must not encourage this girl, else we'll never get rid of her . . .'

Erin's face began to burn with the anger of it. She wanted to march back in there and give her a piece of her mind. Instead, she thought, don't you worry, you'll soon be rid of me. I don't want to work for the likes of you, anyway.

Prosser turned to smile at her as soon as they were downstairs. 'She was lying when she said we didn't need any staff. Two of the maids have gone off to be nurses.'

'I don't want to work as a maid, anyway. I've been looking after that house in Ireland single-handed for the past two years.'

'Is it true that the house burned to the ground with the master's body still inside it?'

'It did.'

'And is it true that your family—'

'No, it is not. They're not my family. It was my step-father and his sons who were involved. Now, I'd be obliged if you'd kept further questions to yourself, Prosser. A fine man has died tragically, and the whys and wherefores of it don't concern you.'

'Aren't you the hoity-toity one? I was only trying to be friendly.'

'I know you were. You should understand though, that Miss Catherine and myself have had a bad time of it. Out of respect for a family who's mourning the loss of a loved one, I'm not of a mind to gossip about it.'

Mrs Baily appeared at the kitchen door. 'Well said, Miss Maguire.'

'The mistress wants her tea sent up,' Prosser told her, giving Erin a dark look.

'Cook's got the tray ready in the kitchen. Get about your work, Prosser, and leave Miss Maguire to me.'

When Prosser had gone, Mrs Baily said, 'Erin, you look tired. Perhaps you'd share refreshment with me in my sitting room, where we can be private. I can also have a mattress brought down for you to sleep on.'

Tears filled her eyes. 'Thank you, Mrs Baily. Why are you being so kind to me?'

'Because I know you're a hardworking and honest girl, and I think I might be able to help you find somewhere decent to live, and free of charge, if you don't mind doing a bit of minding.'

'I'm hoping to become a singer and go on the stage, Mrs Baily.'

'I know, but this shouldn't interfere with it, and at least you'll have a roof over your head. A relative needs someone to cook the evening meal and be a companion to his mother during the day, while he earns his living. My cousin is a nice

117

old lady, if a little difficult, at times. A woman comes in to do the housework twice a week. He'll provide room and board and five shillings a week, and you'll have your weekends and evenings free. It's my day off tomorrow. I could take you to see them, first thing. What do you think?'

Erin smiled.

Ten

They had left the Sanders house early, before Erin had time to say goodbye to Catherine, who was still in bed.

Erin had written her a farewell note and had given it to Mrs Baily.

> Dear Miss Catherine,
> I'm sorry for what happened to your father. He was a nice man despite being an English Lord.
>
> Mrs Baily has found me somewhere to live, so you won't have to worry about me not having a roof over my head any more. I will only have to do light work, so will have plenty of time to be a singer on the stage at the weekends.
>
> Although it's not my place to comment on my betters, you walk nice without your leg irons on, with hardly a limp, and you look grand, too, like a real graceful lady. Like your brother once told you, you should leave them off so your legs will get stronger.
>
> Thank you for being so kind to me.
> Yours faithfully,
> Erin Maguire (Miss)

There had been an envelope left for her in the kitchen by Lady Sanders. It contained ten shillings. She added it to her stocking.

Peter Gregory, blue eyes magnified by glasses, thin-faced and balding, worked for the government. He lived with his mother in a rather superior block of apartments, which were grandly named, Imperial Mansions. Inside the corridors, thick, dark blue carpet effectively smothered any noise coming from the outside. It created a rather claustrophobic effect.

The Gregorys' apartment was stuffy, but spacious and furnished comfortably with a chaise longue, and chairs covered in studded ginger velvet. There was a buffet with mirrored hutch covered in ornaments. White wallpaper was covered by swirling green leaves which reminded Erin of curly kale. The colour matched the green of the carpet. Thick lace curtains hung at the windows.

Peter Gregory stood up when Mrs Baily introduced Erin. She guessed he must be in his late thirties. He was of medium height and his thin brown hair receded from the temples. He gave her a brief smile, indicating that they both seat themselves.

'Miss Erin Maguire worked for Lord and Lady Sanders in Ireland, but recently lost her position because of the tragedy concerning Lord Sanders,' Jean Baily told him.

'Ah yes, a waste of a good man.'

'Yes, I agree. I thought Miss Maguire might suit the position you have on offer, Peter. I can personally recommend her. She's a hard worker, responsible and honest, and is able to work without supervision.'

His muddy hazel eyes gazed at her, then flickered away, his glance settling somewhere on her midriff. 'All those virtues in one so young. What is your age, Miss Maguire? Nineteen or twenty, I hope?'

Thank goodness for the poor light in the room. Erin thought quickly, and hoped his vision was just as poor. She could add three years to her age, if need be. She crossed her fingers behind her back, saying vaguely, 'My birthday is in October.'

'Good, good.' He went on to describe the position, something Mrs Baily had already done, then asked, 'Are there any questions you wish to ask me?'

'Yes, sir. Why did your last nurse leave?'

Mrs Baily put a hand on her arm. 'Erin, that's a question you shouldn't ask Mr Gregory.'

He smiled at that. 'Of course it is, Mrs Baily. For all Miss Maguire knows, I could be a bad sort.'

Erin said with a forced smile, for instinct told her she didn't quite trust the seemingly amiable Mr Gregory, 'If you're a bad sort, sir, I doubt if you'd tell me, now, would you?'

'You're right, I wouldn't.' His smile faded. 'My mother's last help left because my mother can be difficult. Because she can no longer do what she used to she gets frustrated, and she loses her temper sometimes.'

Erin looked around her. 'Where is your mother?'

'In her room. Would you like to meet her?'

'That depends, sir, whether you think I suit you for the position. Otherwise, what would be the point?'

'You suit me, but I'd rather like it if my mother approved of you too.'

'For God's sake, Peter, send the girl in and let me take a look at her,' someone shouted loudly.

'There's nothing wrong with her ears,' Erin said with a giggle.

A wry smile twisted his mouth. 'Indeed, there is not, though I'm afraid mother is not in a very good mood today.'

'We can't be happy all of the time, so I'll take that into account.'

Alicia Gregory was much smaller than her voice indicated. Aged about seventy, white-haired and frail-looking, she was seated in an armchair, her legs covered by a knitted rug.

The room was large, and as well as the daybed, had a spare armchair. In the corner, an upright piano stood, cluttered up with ornaments.

'This is Erin Maguire, Mother.'

Alicia frowned at her son. 'Is it now? Leave us, Peter.'

He shrugged with an apologetic look. 'Will you be all right, Miss Maguire?'

His mother sighed. 'Of course she will. I'm not going to eat her.'

Erin gave him a reassuring nod and, after he had gone, said pleasantly to the woman, 'To be sure you're not, Mrs Gregory.'

'Irish, are you?'

'That I am, and proud of it, too.'

'What are you doing in England, then?'

'My mammy died a couple of years ago, and my employer died recently. I needed a roof over my head and a wage with which to support myself. There was nothing in Callacrea where I lived. I only arrived yesterday, and Mrs Baily suggested I might suit you.'

'And if you don't?'

'I'll manage, no doubt.'

'No nonsense about needing a vocation where you can nurse the aged and infirm, like the last one? She was totally inept. I threw my breakfast at her, you know.'

'Then I'll make sure I stay out of range if I decide to work for you. Watch out though. More than likely I'll throw your breakfast right back at you.'

The woman cackled with laughter. 'I think I like you, Erin Maguire.'

'I haven't made up my mind about you, yet.' Erin wandered over to the piano and ran her fingers absently over the keys. 'This needs tuning.'

'I know. Can you play?'

'I was teaching myself. My mammy taught me to play the Irish harp. I have it with me and intend to become a singer on the stage.'

Interest came into the woman's eyes and she leaned forward. 'A singer, you say. What will you sing, pray?'

'Oh, I know lots of Irish songs. Listen.' She played a few notes then began to sing 'Danny Boy'.

Alicia Gregory began to nod her head in time to the music, then just before the end of the song she thumped her stick on the floor and said quietly, 'Enough of that caterwauling, girl. You know nothing about singing, and even less about playing the piano. Peter,' she called out, 'come here at once, and bring Jean Baily with you.'

'Did you know this girl intends to be a singer?' she said to her son.

'No, Mother.'

Her glance went to Mrs Baily. 'I take it that you did, Jean. Does she know about me?'

'Callacrea is a small village miles from anywhere. I doubt if Erin has ever been outside it, let alone to the theatre.'

'I have that. I went to the Olympia Theatre in Dublin

barely a month ago.' She couldn't help smiling at the thought of it. 'Kell . . . Mr Sanders took me. It was a rare treat. I won five guineas in a talent contest singing on the stage. The manager gave me a card to look him up if I got to London. He said he might have a job for me.'

'And you think that makes you a singer? It'll be selling tickets, or down on your knees and cleaning the stalls, no doubt.' Alicia nodded, as if she'd just assured herself that she hadn't been tricked. 'Have you ever heard of Alicia Sterne, Miss Maguire?'

'No, ma'am, but would I be right in thinking that Alicia Sterne was you once?'

'You would, though a name change doesn't mean I'm no longer me. I was famous in my day. I often gave a recital to the public at Covent Garden.'

'I've never heard of that place. I've never sung in a garden, but I used to sing in the public bar of the Shamrock Inn when I was a child. My stepfather kept all the pennies I earned, though.'

The old woman heaved an aggrieved sigh when Peter chuckled. 'You sound uneducated and naïve for someone who claims to be twenty years of age.'

Erin flicked a guilty glance at Mrs Baily, who gave a wry twist of the lips. She hadn't bothered to correct Peter's assumption the first time round, and didn't correct his mother's, now.

Jean Baily was doing her a favour. Obviously she'd recommended her for the job because Mrs Gregory and herself had singing in common. She wouldn't know whether to be pleased or dismayed by this, until the point of it was revealed.

Alicia Gregory spoke again. 'I admit, I'm intrigued by Miss Erin Maguire. Although she has too pert a way with her, she has no pretensions, just illusions. I'll soon dispel those and make her mind her manners, just see if I don't. You may hire her, Peter. I shall teach the baggage to sing, and knock the rough edges off her. It will give me something better to do than stare at these four damned walls and wait to die. That is what you wanted, isn't it, Jean?'

'In addition to finding someone to look after you, yes.'

Erin's eyes widened. 'I'm not a baggage, and I haven't said I'm willing to be hired yet.'

'If I say you're a baggage, you're a baggage.' Alicia dismissively waved her hand towards the door. 'Your room is through there. Fetch your suitcase and get yourself settled in while I talk to my son. If you would rather not be hired, or feel unable to take advantage of my kind offer as a singing coach, you know where the door is. Which is it to be, miss?'

Erin didn't bother making a pretence of thinking about it, the woman was too sharp-witted to be fooled, and she'd be an idiot to turn down free tuition. Make the right impression, Kell had told her. 'I'm sorry if I appeared churlish. I'm happy to accept. Thank you.'

Mrs Gregory gave her an approving smile. 'Good. You may bring your harp in here.' Her eyes slid to Mrs Baily. 'Jean, you have displayed an extraordinary talent for slyness in this affair.'

'Thank you, Alicia.'

Erin's move into Imperial Mansions was immediate, and so began her occupation as carer and pupil to the formidable Alicia Gregory.

She just hoped Kell Sanders would be able to find her when he returned from the war.

At that moment, Kell Sanders wished himself anywhere, but in the trenches of the Somme. This was no longer the pleasant continent he'd once idled through, spending many hours exploring its delights, but a strange, wrecked landscape of mud, pockmarked with water-filled holes and littered with bloated bodies in different stages of decomposition.

He hadn't been prepared for this – the constant explosions, the whistle of bullets, as thick as bees in an English country garden in summer, but their sting more lethal. Nor had he expected the all-pervading stench of rotting flesh. When compared to the smell of his unwashed body, now infested by lice and worms, he knew he smelled all the sweeter for the life still in it.

And with that life came hope, though his initial idealism and patriotism had given way to the realities of war, and there was certainly nothing heroic about the way he felt. If

he could find a sheltered place in this hellhole of a landscape, Kell thought, he might be tempted to crawl in there
and hide.

Was his former life only a few weeks in the past? He'd
give anything for a warm bath and a cup of strong tea. He
missed London and Ireland. His fingers touched against the
lucky shamrock hanging over his heart. He gave a faint smile
as he wondered what Miss Erin Maguire was getting up to,
alone in that big house in Callacrea. Was she still singing to
an imaginary audience and saving up to go on the stage?

Erin's wide blue eyes came into his mind, and the way
her mouth curved into a smile. She'd been a delightful
companion, though Kell now felt guilty at the way he'd taken
advantage of her youthful innocence. His feelings towards
her were very tender. He shrugged ruefully. Erin Maguire
was completely unsuitable, of course. Men like him simply
didn't marry girls like her.

The whistle blew for the next advance. The men in the
trench scrambled out and began to run, slipping and sliding
in the mud and shooting their rifles. God only knew what
they were shooting at. Around him, his companions began
to fall and the wounded began to cry out in agony.

There came the whistle of shells flying overhead, the
crump, crump as they landed.

The ground seemed to open in front of Kell. Clods of mud
flew at him and a hand bounced off his shoulder, splattering
him with blood. Lifted off his feet by the blast he flew backwards, landing on his back in the same trench he'd started
out from.

A small shard of hot shrapnel sliced across his upper arm,
leaving the material of his coat smoking. 'Shit!'

This was not a good place to be, he thought, rising to his
feet. His arm still worked so he picked up his rifle. Dazed,
he scrambled out of the trench again and, taking advantage
of the low lying smoke, he ran pell-mell towards the next
trench.

He fell into it just as the smoke cleared, reloaded his rifle
and joined a fellow soldier. 'Where are the rest of the men?'
he asked.

The soldier didn't answer. When Kell touched him he

toppled sideways. There was a neat hole through his head.

Someone touched his shoulder, his sergeant. 'Sanders, you're the best shot, follow me.'

Bent double, the pair ran through a network of trenches to where the remainder of his unit was crouched. Filthy with mud, cold and weary, the five survivors gazed at one another.

'There's a sniper in that trench over there, just to the left of the wire,' the sergeant told him. 'See that dead soldier between him and us? We're going to provide cover fire until you get to him. You should be able to pick him off from there. Get down the trench a bit and line up that bit of a tree stump for cover if you can.'

Kell experienced a sinking feeling as the sergeant pulled out a grenade and threw it. It came up short but provided enough diversion for Kell to wriggle over the top. There was a whole barrage of shots from his companions. He rose to his feet, bent double and ran like hell, eventually flopping down behind the shattered remains of a very slim trunk, panting for breath.

So far, so good, he thought. His next spurt was made on his stomach as he dragged himself rapidly across the stinking mud with his elbows.

The soldier's body was still warm, his stomach covered in fat blowflies. Head turned slightly towards Kell, his eyes were a half-open glint of shining blue. While the next barrage of shots claimed the sniper's attention, Kell lined his rifle up across the stomach of the corpse.

'Move it a little to your left,' the soldier whispered.

Kell jumped. 'Christ! You frightened the hell out of me. We thought you were dead.'

'I will be soon. Shrapnel has sliced up my guts, and a bullet has lodged in my neck. I can't move a soddin' finger or feel a fuckin' thing. Do me a favour, will you? There's a letter in my breast pocket. After you've killed that bastard, take it with you and post it to my mother.'

'Will do. What's your name, soldier?'

'Danny Robinson,' he said tiredly.

The young man had a London accent. 'I'm honoured to meet you, Danny. I'm Kell Sanders. I'll deliver the letter personally and tell your mother how brave her son is.'

He managed a faint smile. 'She'll like that,' he said. 'Are you a good shot?'

'The best in the regiment.'

'Good, because you'll be lucky to see him. There's a small forked twig standing up there. Get it between your sights and you'll see the whites of the bastard's eyes when he blinks.'

Kell's eyes narrowed in as he concentrated, then he whispered, 'Got him.'

'Give him one for me, then,' Danny whispered, but Kell was already squeezing the trigger. When the sniper's head exploded, his regiment gave a cheer and came scrambling over the top.

'Don't leave me here like this,' Danny said, as Kell took the letter from his pocket and stood up. He gave a faint, apologetic grimace. 'I'd do it myself if I could move.'

He had blue eyes, like Erin Maguire. Kell remembered her singing 'Danny Boy' in the drawing room. It seemed like years ago now. Tears coming to his eyes, he placed his pistol against the young man's heart and smiled at him.

'Thanks,' Danny said.

The memorial service for Lord Sanders had been held, the ashes interred; the soberly dressed mourners were gathered in Lady Sanders' drawing room, talking in muted voices.

Charles Colby was one of them. He was not an outgoing man, but he edged closer when one of the men said to another, 'It was bad luck, William copping it like that. The daughter was lucky. She escaped just before the uprising in Dublin.'

'A bad business that. They're getting themselves organized over there, and I can't help feeling there's going to be trouble ahead in Ireland.'

'Isn't there always? Young Catherine brought her Irish maid over with her. Dorothea was not amused, since the girl's family was responsible for the fire. The pair have been at loggerheads about it ever since.'

'I hear that the son has joined the Dublin Fusiliers and is in the thick of things, in the Somme.'

'Let's hope he survives it then. They're dropping like flies.'

The pair moved off.

Charles edged over to where Catherine stood by the open French windows. 'Hello, my dear,' he said. 'How are you coping?'

There were tears in the sad eyes she turned his way. 'It's hard to hear people talking about my father when he's not here. I expect him to walk through the front door any minute.'

When he placed a comforting arm around her, she rested her head against his shoulder. 'I miss him, Uncle Charles. I'm trying to be brave, but I wish Kell was here. I could always talk to him. Mother won't listen to anything I want to discuss about Daddy's death. She says that talking about him won't bring him back, and it's not done to show your grief in public. She wasn't there, but you'd think she'd want to know how it happened. And she keeps blaming Erin Maguire, who was only related to the criminals by her mother's marriage.'

'People cope in the best way they can with grief. I believe your mother has written to someone to try and get Kell home on compassionate leave.'

'They told her he couldn't be spared. Kell will be all right, won't he, Uncle Charles?'

Charles could only offer her platitudes. 'Of course he will. That brother of yours has always lived a charmed life.' He tucked her arm into his. 'Come on, let's go for a walk in the garden. We can sit in the alcove and you can talk to me, if you want.'

It was mid afternoon. After the smoky atmosphere of the drawing room, the air seemed fresh and clean outside. Flowers lined the paths. The apple and pear trees, espaliered against the wine-coloured brickwork of the surrounding walls, wore an abundance of pale-pink blossoms. They drifted in the wind, scattering on the paths and the manicured lawn like bridal confetti.

Charles followed Catherine down the pathway and past the elegant birdbath to an alcove covered in ivy. As they seated themselves on a wood and wrought-iron garden seat, he said, with some surprise, 'You're not wearing your leg irons now.'

'D'you know, you're the first person to notice. Erin told

me I could walk perfectly well without them.' She gave a faint smile. 'I can, too, though my legs ache sometimes. You know, nobody ever told me to take them off, except, Kell did once. But the doctor said it was too soon. No one even suggested I could walk without them until I threw them at that horrible stepbrother of Erin's. They caught him such a crack across the nose and he fell off the car.' Catherine sighed. 'I was hoping Mother would give Erin a home, but she wouldn't, even though Erin saved my life. Mother said I mustn't mention her again.'

'Did Dorothea say why?'

'No, but there seems to be some mystery about Erin. Do you know what it is?'

'A mystery?' he spluttered, taken aback. 'Good Lord, Catherine, old thing. What an odd notion.'

The girl looked disappointed. 'I thought Erin might have been my half-sister, or something equally scandalous. Why else would Mother forbid me to see her again?'

'Your half-sister?' He managed a nervous laugh. 'Of course she isn't. It's a silly idea that you must drive from your head, because it's simply not true. Your father wasn't like that.'

She shrugged. 'You're right, Uncle Charles. You know, Daddy had made plans for us to escape from Callacrea House, and they didn't include Erin, at first. What I'm saying is, if Erin had been related, he'd have cared more for her. He wouldn't have intended to leave her behind to starve, would he?'

Guilt attacked Charles. Her words had made him realize what scant regard he'd had for his only child's welfare, even though he was interested in her now. 'No, I don't suppose he would have.'

'Erin had nowhere to go. No family to care for her. She would have starved on the street, or worse. It's not fair, is it? People like us, who have everything we need, just can't understand how hard it is for people like her.'

'No darling, we can't.'

'Mummy only gave Erin ten shillings, after she risked her life to save me. To be quite honest, I was in a bit of a funk and I didn't know what to do. Erin took charge. She was wonderful. Frightfully bossy, though I daresay I needed it.

Thank goodness Mrs Baily found her a job to take up in London, where she has a roof over her head.'

Charles kept his voice casual. 'D'you know who with?'

'I don't know. I wanted to go and see her, but Mother found the letter Erin left for me with Mrs Baily and confiscated it. She threatened Mrs Baily with dismissal if she disclosed Erin's whereabouts to me.'

'Bad luck,' Charles said sympathetically and squeezed her hand.

Catherine's eyes were brown and pleading, and she looked for all the world like a little dog he'd once had. 'If you run into Erin, you'll make sure she's all right, and tell me, won't you Uncle Charles? And if she's down and out, give her some money to help her out.'

'Of course I will.'

She threw her arms around him. 'Thank you, you're a darling.'

Catherine's breast pressed softly against his arm, her thigh against his. She was wearing a black dress of some silky material and her hair was worn in a long braid. How old was she? Seventeen? Too womanly to treat an uncle like this, now. Awkwardly, he patted her on the shoulder. 'Better let me go now, Catherine, dear.'

'What on earth is going on here?' Dorothea said coldly. 'Catherine, you should be inside with our guests, not indulging in such unseemly behaviour with my brother-in-law, especially on the day of your father's memorial.'

Colouring at the rebuke, Catherine rose to her feet and hurried towards the house.

'It wasn't anything, Dorothea, old girl. A bit of coltish behaviour on Catherine's part.'

She said tartly, 'Then I'd be obliged if you'd discourage it. Catherine is not one of the maids at Callacrea House.'

He wondered if she was referring to Cliona Maguire and decided to brazen it out.

'I don't know what you're talking about, Dorothea.'

'Oh, don't play the innocent. I'm referring to Erin Maguire, of course. I saw the way you looked at her when we were last in Ireland. It was undignified and disgusting, and I don't want Catherine to be subjected to such advances.'

Blood rose to his face. 'Don't be so bloody silly, Dorothea.'

'Silly, is it? I remember some whispers about you and one of the maids some years ago.'

Charles had always thought Dorothea to be a beautiful woman, in a classic way. Now he saw that her face was disagreeable in temper, and her eyes were as mean as wasps.

Her lips pursed into a web of lines and she tossed her head. 'I won't have you pawing over Catherine the way you did Erin Maguire. D'you understand? She is hardly out of childhood.'

'Neither of them are.'

'Exactly. Erin Maguire is not the innocent she seems, though. The silly girl gazed at you with adoration in her eyes when you paid her some attention.'

'The bee in your bonnet is without foundation. I'll go as far as to say that you have a filthy mind, Dorothea.'

She gave an outraged gasp.

Charles rose to his feet, saying quietly, 'Let me reassure you about something. I always have, and always will treat Catherine with the utmost respect.' He gave a faint smile because the relief of what he was about to say was already giving him a sense of freedom. 'As for Erin Maguire, the girl is my daughter. Her mother was Cliona Maguire, a woman I loved with all my heart from the moment I set eyes on her, and who I have loved for every day of my life since. I would have married her if I'd been free.'

Dorothea's mouth fell open.

Inserting a finger under her chin, Charles closed it with a snap. 'There, now you know.'

Dorothea found her voice again, and it was annoyed. 'Did Willie know?'

'Of course. He arranged for Cliona's marriage to Dermot Maguire and gave them the cottage on the slate field to live in. I paid the rent. Even Kell knows the true story. Willie told him when he was old enough to understand.'

'And it was kept it from me all these years. I'd never have allowed that girl in my house if I'd known.'

'That's why we didn't tell you. But you needn't sound so affronted. You're a hypocrite, Dorothea. I know about that affair you had with Bobby Dengate. Oh, don't bother,' he said when she opened her mouth to deny it. 'Your son saw you with Dengate when he was small, and told his father.'

'Willie knew about it? He never said.'

Charles shrugged. 'Willie was a true gentleman, and more than you deserved, for all your airs and graces. I'll say goodbye now.'

She placed a hand on his arm. 'It was nothing, just madness. Willie was so boring sometimes, especially about Ireland. You know, I'm glad the house has burned down. It means I'll never have to see it again.'

'Or your husband?'

'People like us don't marry for love, do we? I'd be most grateful if you didn't mention this conversation to anyone. After all, you wouldn't want anyone to know that your bastard daughter is a maidservant.'

When he said nothing, her eyes narrowed and the tip of her tongue moistened her bottom lip. 'When I said, *most grateful*, I meant it. You're a handsome man, Charles, and I've always had a soft spot for you. We're both widowed now. What harm would there be in companionship?'

He stared at her with contempt, then walked away.

Eleven

Erin had been stung when Alicia Gregory had described her singing as caterwauling, but under the woman's tuition she began to improve.

She was kept busy. First thing in the morning she helped Mrs Gregory ready herself for the day. After that, she cleaned up the breakfast dishes and made the beds. If there was shopping, she was given a list to take to the local grocery store, and the goods were added to the account and delivered by a young boy on a bicycle. Washing was taken to the laundry in the basement, where it was dealt with by the Imperial Mansions' laundry staff, and charged in the form of a service fee. Erin also cooked the evening meal from a menu handed to her, along with a recipe book.

Peter Gregory interfered very little with the running of the house, and went out a lot in the evenings, sometimes staying out all night, always politely inquiring beforehand whether she'd be staying in.

She wondered why he wasn't married, and mentioned as much to Mrs Gregory.

'Oh, Peter's not the marrying kind,' she'd said vaguely. 'He's much too shy to meet women. It's his lack of height, I think. He's too conscious of it.'

Once Mrs Gregory was ready for bed, Erin had her evenings to herself, but it was usually too late to go out. Sometimes she'd sit in her room and read to herself, mend her clothes or darn her stockings. And although her weekends were supposed to be free, Alicia spent four hours on Saturday morning at her tuition, and she was expected to go to church on Sunday with the family.

Alicia was often impatient, but Erin soon came to read

her moods and knew they arose from the frustration she felt. Except for her visit to the church, tucked up in a basket chair and wheeled by her son, Alicia had made herself a prisoner. That made Erin feel closed in too.

Alicia's leg muscles were wasted, and her skin was a mass of scars.

'How did they get to be that way?' Erin asked her.

'Some scenery fell on me. I was trapped from the waist down and the nerves in my spine were damaged. The doctor stitched my cuts, but he couldn't fix the rest.'

'I'm sorry.'

'Don't be. I don't like pity.'

'Being sorry for somebody who has had an accident isn't the same as feeling pity for them. Is that why you never go out, except to church?'

'Who said I never go out?'

'Your son. Besides, I can see, can't I?'

'He should mind his own business and so should you.'

'I know I should, but my mammy told me that if I don't ask questions I'll never learn the answers to anything.'

'She should have taught you that curiosity killed the cat.'

'I'm not a cat though, I'm her daughter. She probably thought her advice of more use to me.'

Alicia gave a cackle of laughter. 'You've got an answer for everything, haven't you?'

'No, Mrs Gregory, but if I keep on asking questions I might have someday.'

'Then God help us. Tell me about your mammy. What did she die of?'

'One babby too many,' Erin said. 'She said the infants that Dermot Maguire planted inside her wouldn't stick to her womb. The last of them killed her, and just when she thought she was free of my stepfather, too.'

'Do you know who your real father is, Erin?'

Erin had the feeling Mrs Gregory had learned that from Mrs Baily. She heard the wistfulness in her own voice when she told her, 'I do, but I'll keep that to myself, if you don't mind. He's a fine gentleman, that he is. Someone to be proud of. My mammy loved him all her life. She had a song to remember him by, and it's my song too, now.' Though Erin didn't tell Mrs Gregory that it brought a memory of Kell Sanders to her own mind.

'What's the song called?'

'"Black is the Colour".'

'Ah, yes,' Alicia said, 'I know it. Fetch your harp and sing it to me, my dear.'

For once, Alicia Gregory didn't interrupt, but leaned back in her chair, her eyes closed. As Erin sang the slow, poignant song, tears gathered in her eyes and tracked slowly down her cheeks, for it brought to mind her mother, her father, her lover, and Ireland.

When the last note died there was silence. After a while Alicia's eyes opened. They were also moist as she whispered, 'Yes . . . yes, that was exquisitely sung, Erin.'

Erin was too choked up to answer. *I love my love*, she thought and yearned to see Kell's smile, full of teasing, and his eyes so alight with laughter. And as she thought that, she began to perspire and her head became light. The harp gave a discordant trill as her hands fell from it to support her swimming head.

Her employer looked anxiously at her. 'How pale you've become. What ails you?'

Erin drew in a deep breath, steadying herself as she tried to control the slight feeling of sickness in her stomach. 'Nothing. I felt faint, that's all. It's stuffy in here.'

'Put your head between your knees.'

Erin did as she was told and began to recover. She lifted her head to smile at the old lady. 'Sure, but I don't know what came over me.'

'I think you need some fresh air to get the roses back in your cheeks. Open the window and take some nice deep breaths.'

'No. I'm fine now, Mrs Gregory. Honestly.'

'Nevertheless, you must open the window. It's a lovely day.'

Outside, the road was busy with traffic. There was a bus stop a few steps further up the road. The buses were open fronted and the top floor had no roof to shelter passengers when it rained.

There was a soldier waiting at the bus stop. An officer.

He looked very smart and upright. It could have been Kell waiting to board. He could have been taken to the army headquarters office, wherever that was, and there, he could be helping to plan the war, just like his father had wanted him too.

But Kell had wanted to fight, to stand beside his fellow men where the real war was. He was a hero, who hadn't wanted to hide behind a desk like a coward. She sorely missed him, and worried about his safety.

The bus arrived, gaudy and gay in a coat of scarlet paint. Its engine thrummed, just like the Zeppelins that flew over now and again to drop bombs on the English. Not that she'd seen or heard one yet, but the hall porter had told her about them. The bus had Schweppes Tonic Water advertised along the side, and Iron Jelloids on the step. There was a coat of arms too, with 'The King' written under it. Very patriotic, she thought. Erin hadn't seen His Majesty yet, either, even though she'd heard that Buckingham Palace was only a short trot away.

A uniformed lady conductor in a hat turned up at one side, stood on the platform at the back of the bus, where a staircase curved towards the upper deck. She handed out tickets in exchange for the thruppenny fare.

The soldier didn't get on when the bus stopped. Smiling, he held out his hand to help a woman alight from the platform, waiting until the bus moved off before he kissed her.

Erin heard her laugh as they linked arms and walked off up the road together.

Imagining Kell greeting her in the very same way, she turned and asked Mrs Gregory, 'Do you think the war will be over soon?'

'Who can tell. Do you have a sweetheart in the forces, then?'

Erin nodded, but shyly. 'I can't tell you his name though, since I promised to keep it a secret.'

'Why is that?'

'Because he's a gentleman.'

'Ah, I see. Men can be fickle creatures, Erin. How can you trust a man who won't acknowledge you?'

Pulling the neck chain from under her bodice, Erin showed

the ring to her employer. 'He gave me this before he went away. He said he loved me.'

Alicia gently squeezed her hand. 'A pretty token of his affection, my dear. Just be careful, a heart can so easily be broken by a personable young man. You must remain a good girl until you marry.'

'Yes, ma'am,' Erin murmured, reckoning it was too late for that.

'Now, wheel me across to the piano. You will do your voice and breathing exercises, then you'll learn a new song. You'll need to expand your repertoire if you are to sing on the stage.'

Pulling in a deep breath, Erin placed her hands on her stomach. 'Which bit's my repertoire?'

She saw Alicia Gregory hide a smile. 'That's your diaphragm, and I've already explained its function with regards to your singing. Your repertoire is the number of songs you've learned, and can perform when the need arises.'

'I know six songs by heart, already.'

'Then we must add to those, and they will need to be varied. Most of your songs are emotional, which is all well and good since you have a feeling for them and they appeal to the heart. But you need some variety, some lighter ones to amuse and, because we are at war, a patriotic song or two. And you need to learn how to read music.'

And so, the real work started for Erin. As the weeks passed, she noted the improvement in her voice. But something more disturbing had occurred, her monthly bleed had ceased, and her waistband had tightened considerably. Having watched her mother go through countless pregnancies, Erin knew exactly what that meant.

One day halfway through August, she stood in her petticoat in front of the mirror and placed her hands over the gentle curve of her stomach. Although worried, because she was bound to lose her position and, with it, her voice coach, she delighted in the thought that inside her she carried Kell's infant. But she'd be sorry to leave Alicia Gregory. Erin had grown fond of the woman, despite her unpredictable ways.

To save being dismissed in disgrace, Erin handed in a

month's notice, hoping she could hide her situation until she found somewhere else to live.

Alicia Gregory was furious with her. 'You ungrateful wretch. After I've spent all these weeks coaching you, you decide to leave me. Why, Erin?'

'I can't tell you that, Mrs Gregory.'

'Can't tell me? Of course you can tell me. Have you got another job? Do you need more money? I'll ask Peter to pay you more.'

'It's not money. I have my savings in the bank.'

'Then what is it?' Alicia took a surprisingly strong grip on her wrist and growled, 'You look me in the eyes, girl. I'm not going to let you go until you tell me.'

She couldn't lie to Alicia Gregory: she'd know. Reluctantly, Erin lifted her head. 'I'm expecting a child.'

There was a harsh intake of breath from her employer, then she said, 'When?'

'Halfway through January.'

'You knew this when you came here to work?'

'No, ma'am. I didn't.'

Colour flooded the woman's cheeks and she lashed out with her stick, striking Erin several times across her shoulders and arms, and shouting, 'Liar! Liar!'

Erin managed to free herself from Alicia's grip but, as she tried to escape, one blow caught her across the stomach. 'Don't hurt my baby,' she cried out. Falling to her knees she curled her body around her infant.

Alicia Gregory had run out of strength. The woman was breathing harshly as Erin scuttled across the floor to her room. Pulling herself up, she went inside, closing the door behind her. Her shoulders ached from the beating but, worse, her heart was sore from the unfairness of it.

Going to her bed, she curled up on her side and began to sob quietly to herself.

'Dirty Irish tramp,' Alicia said from the other side of the door. 'Oh, I know your type. You're after all you can get. I suppose you thought I'd take pity on you. Well, I won't, d'you hear?' She rapped on the door with her stick. 'Feeling sorry for yourself won't sway me, missy, so cry all you like. When you come out I'm going to give you a taste of this again.'

Erin sucked in a deep breath and rose from the bed, her dander rising. That's what she thought!

Alicia looked taken aback when Erin suddenly opened the door.

Taking the stick from her hand, Erin marched to the window, opened it and tossed it into the garden below. She turned to the woman, saying quietly, 'Lay one finger on me again and I'll throw you out after it. You're a stubborn, bad-tempered curmudgeon.'

'Curmudgeon and bad-tempered means the same thing, you ignorant creature.'

'Ignorant, is it? Then it must be obvious to you from what I've just said that you've got a double dose.'

'I will not be spoken to like this. Get out!'

'I most certainly will not . . . at least, not until your son comes home to look after you. Then I'll decide what's to be done about you.'

'About me? What nonsense is this? It's you who's in trouble.'

'There must be some law against beating people with a stick. Assault they call it, I believe.'

'Assault?' Alicia gave an incredulous laugh. 'I hardly touched you. It would be my word against yours and it doesn't take much intelligence to guess whose word they'd accept.'

'It's me who has the bruises and welts, Mrs Gregory.' And she did, her body was aching and sore from the assault. A sudden thought occurred to her. 'What if you've caused me to lose my infant?'

Alicia gazed at her, unsure. 'For someone in your position, I imagine that would be a blessing.'

'You're wrong. I want this child. I love its father, and once this damned war is over he'll find me and we'll get married. Call me names if you must, but you have no right to hit me when you're having one of your childish tantrums. No right, at all.'

'Childish tantrums!'

'That's what she said, Mother.' Peter threw her stick on the table. 'This nearly brained me as I was coming in, and I could hear you shrieking at Erin from outside.'

'The girl—'

'I heard everything,' he said sternly, 'including the names you called her. You sounded like a fishwife. It's not up to you to judge her morals. I want you to apologize for your treatment of her.'

'I mean it, Mother,' he said when Alicia opened her mouth in outrage.

'It doesn't matter,' Erin said. 'I'm sorry this has happened and I don't want to be the cause of trouble between you. I'll go and pack my bag.'

Alicia smiled triumphantly.

'I'd prefer it if you'd stay and work your notice out, Miss Maguire, otherwise I shall have to put my mother in a nursing home.'

'You will not,' Alicia said sharply.

'Since you can't look after yourself, I might have to.'

'She must leave.'

Peter ignored his mother. 'Are you willing to stay for a while, Miss Maguire? It will give me time to find someone to replace you.'

Erin nodded. 'I have nowhere else to go, anyway. I need time to find somewhere else to live.'

'I refuse to allow her to touch me again.'

'So be it.' Drawing Erin from the room, Peter led her though to the drawing room. He avoided her eyes. 'I can't pretend I'm not disappointed with you, Miss Maguire, but I apologize for my mother's behaviour.'

Erin looked ruefully at the bruises on her arm. 'It's not your place to apologize, Mr Gregory. Your mother would have come to her senses, you know.'

'I know. But this time she went too far. She had no right to set about you. I'm going to teach her a lesson. Perhaps you'd like to get on with dinner now.'

The lesson was a harsh reminder of Alicia's helplessness. Come bedtime, Alicia Gregory was left in her bath chair.

'Erin,' she shouted. 'Come here at once!'

'Go to bed,' Peter ordered.

Erin thought what he was doing was cruel. 'We can't leave her. She'll need to use the commode.'

But Peter did leave her.

Erin pulled the blanket over her head while Alicia Gregory

shouted and raged, then the woman fell quiet. Erin heard her quietly weeping. She couldn't stay in bed and listen to that while the poor woman suffered. Pulling on her robe she went through to her and placed her arms around her thin shoulders.

Alicia's head came against Erin's shoulder. Her voice was contrite. 'I'm so sorry for beating you, my dear. Can you ever forgive me?'

'Of course. I'll ready you for bed. Do you need the commode?'

'It's too late for that. I'm so ashamed of myself. You will stay until we get someone else, won't you? I couldn't bear being put in a nursing home.'

'Hush . . . there's nothing to be ashamed of and, yes, I'll stay until you can find a replacement.'

Erin put her employer to bed, then went to warm her some milk. Peter came into the kitchen in his robe. It was loosely tied, showing an expanse of hairy chest. Erin didn't know where to look.

He moved close to her, and she could smell alcohol on his breath. 'I'm sorry. I didn't mean to wake you,' he apologized.

She wished he'd move away. 'You didn't.'

He glanced at her stomach, saying quietly, 'I didn't think you were that type of girl, Erin.'

She coloured. 'What type?'

His words came out clipped and angry. 'The type with loose morals. Is that milk for you, or for mother?'

She could hardly look at him. 'Your mother. I can't leave her sitting in her chair in her own urine, weeping all night. It's cruel.'

Taking a bottle of medicine from the cupboard, Peter added a spoonful of liquid to the milk.

'What's that?'

'A sedative the doctor prescribed. It'll give her a good night's sleep. I'll see you in the morning.' When he turned abruptly, walking away without another word, she felt relieved.

By the time Erin had finished cleaning the basket chair and the wet patch on the floor, Alicia was sound asleep. She looked peaceful, like a child. As Erin straightened, there was a tickle of movement inside her.

Her infant! she thought, grinning with delight in the wonder of it as she put the bucket and cleaning rag away, then made herself a cup of cocoa and went through to her room. Opening her diary she recorded the event in it, addressing her thoughts to Kell, as she always did.

> Kell, my dear love, there was a terrible argument today about my condition, and I am to leave. But then came a miracle. Our baby moved inside me, and the shame Alicia made me feel was replaced with joy. It was such a tiny flutter, like a butterfly stretching its wings towards the sun.

Erin only lasted another two weeks in her position. During that time Peter Gregory watched her, his expression often speculative. And sometimes he stood too close and his hands would accidentally brush against her body, so she now felt uneasy in his presence.

Although a petulant Alicia Gregory had stated she would not be satisfied with the third applicant who applied for the job, on the Saturday, Peter Gregory employed a robust-looking, older woman who had trained as a nurse at St Thomas's hospital. She was to start the following week.

Alicia Gregory complained bitterly, and threw a tantrum, throwing things around her room. Sedated by her son, she was put to bed early.

Peter went into the drawing room and poured himself a whisky. Erin noticed that his hands were shaking and the decanter had gone down considerably. His voice slurred, he said, 'Have a drink with me, Erin.'

'I don't think so, Mr Gregory,' she said politely, though disturbed by his slightly agitated manner. 'I'm too young to drink strong liquor.'

'But not too young to be used by a man, eh? How old are you, girl. Not twenty, as you claimed.'

She didn't see any harm in telling him the truth, now. 'I'm nearly seventeen.'

His hand loosely circled her wrist. 'You're a pretty girl, Erin.'

'I'd prefer it if you didn't speak to me in such a familiar manner, sir. It makes me feel uncomfortable. I'm going to my room. I'll fetch myself some cocoa later.' She walked away from him and, after checking on Mrs Gregory, went through to her own room and began to sew a panel in her best skirt, so it would be more comfortable for her expanding waist.

Tomorrow was Saturday, and she intended to take some time off. The hall porter had given her the name and address of a boarding house. His nephew was going off to war, and would be vacating his room there soon.

'It won't be much, lass, because Cheapside is not much of a district,' he said. 'But beggars can't be choosers, and the rent'll be affordable. It's about a half a mile from St Paul's.'

She was debating whether or not to go to bed when a knock came at the door.

'I've brought your cocoa. I'll leave it outside on the table,' Peter whispered. 'I'm sorry I upset you. Goodnight.' He shuffled off, and she heard his bedroom door close behind him.

At least he'd apologized, she thought, and it was nice of him to bring her the cocoa. Fetching the cup from the table, she took a sip and grimaced. Lord, but he'd put a lot of sugar in it. She sipped it as she wrote a list of what she thought she might need for her room.

After a while her eyelids began to droop. Jerking awake she placed her pencil to one side and yawned. She felt as weary as a dog lying in the sunshine. Undressing, she slid under the covers, drifting into sleep almost immediately.

The clock in the hallway chimed midnight. A door opened and closed. Erin half woke. She felt heavy limbed and too lethargic to move. Her mouth was dry and thick, as if her tongue had swollen to fill it.

Moonlight drew changing lacy patterns on the wall as the curtain moved with a faint breeze that came through the window, open just a crack.

As the satin eiderdown slid from her body, the breeze stroked her body, raising goosebumps against her skin. Her eyes closed, then opened again when her nightdress was pulled upward to cover her face.

143

Now she felt hands exploring her body, rolling the tender nubs of her breasts. Then they moved between her thighs, pinching the flesh, touching and squeezing the softness of her, making her sore.

Her attempt to protest came out a cracked sort of grunt. When she tried lift her arm to push the intruder away, she found it was too heavy to lift from the bed.

It was a dream, a horrible dream, she thought, as a shadow moved over her. But it was frightening one. Tears streamed down her face.

Then the intruder tried to push himself inside her, and his mouth was panting harshly against her ear. His breath smelt of stale whisky. 'Love me, Erin. Make me feel like a real man.'

She found her voice, a small whisper. 'Don't . . . don't . . . you coward.'

His mouth slid to her breast and he bit her. She groaned with the agony of it. 'Be quiet, else I'll kill you,' he said roughly.

He dragged her head back by her hair as he began to shove himself against her, gripping her painfully as he did. But he was small in his maleness and his assault could not be maintained. He collapsed against her, cursing as he did. 'It's your fault, you Irish slut. You women are all the same.' A slap across her face, and her attacker was gone, sobbing under his breath.

Erin lay there in the moonlight, her body throbbing from the assault. After a while the shocked clamour inside her eased off.

Some movement returned, as if the paralysis she'd been suffering from was fading. She managed to pull her nightgown down over her body. Still lethargic, she refused to believe what her mind was telling her. It must have been a nightmare. She rolled painfully on to her side, pulled the sheet over herself and escaped into sleep, though tears still squeezed from under her lids.

As soon as daylight crept into the room Erin woke. The day was a dull grey and rain splattered the window. Alicia Gregory was calling her, her voice thin and dissatisfied.

It's supposed to be my day off, Erin thought, wondering

why her body ached so much as she swung her legs over the side of the bed. But she couldn't leave the old lady to her own devices and went through to help her on to the commode, going through to the kitchen afterwards to make them some tea, while giving her some privacy.'

She'd just got Alicia dressed and settled in her chair when the woman touched her chest. 'What's that? It looks like teeth marks. Do we have rats?'

Going to the mirror, Erin undid the top buttons on her nightdress. There were bruises on her breasts, and an indentation from a bite. She gazed at them in horror. So, she hadn't dreamed it! Her cocoa cup was on the table. Holding it to her nose, she inhaled. It smelled odd. Peter Gregory had drugged her, and then . . . *he'd tried to rape her*!

She couldn't stay here now. Rushing through to her room, Erin quickly dressed herself, and packed her bag. She took it through to Alicia's room, where her harp was.

Alicia looked up. 'You're leaving me?'

'I have to – ' and she opened her bodice – 'Your son did this to me. He was drunk last night. He drugged me with that medicine of yours, put it in my cocoa. Last night . . . I thought it was a bad dream.'

Alicia's face paled. 'But he can't have. He's incapable, he was born . . . different to other men, you see.'

'That may be so, but it didn't stop him thinking that way, and trying. I can't stay here any longer. I'll wake him up as I go out.'

Alicia nodded. 'You won't say anything, will you, Erin? He is so embarrassed by it. He'll never be able to marry or father children. If it gets out, people will think he's one of those men who are . . . *different*. He'd lose his job. Peter doesn't know I'm aware of his condition. I'll pay you to keep quiet.'

Sadness filled her. 'Goodbye Mrs Gregory. Thank you for the singing lessons.' Picking up her harp, Erin walked away from her.

She stopped to collect a jug of water, then rapped on Peter Gregory's door.

'What is it?' he said, his voice thick with sleep.

She marched in. 'Get up, you coward,' she hissed. 'Your

mother needs seeing to, and I'm leaving.' Emptying the water jug over his head, she left him spluttering as she slammed the door behind her.

Outside, a bus was coming along the road. She stuck out her hand and it waited for her at the stop for her to board. She paid her thruppenny fare and the bus went bumping off through the potholes on its solid rubber tyres.

'Where are you going, luv?' the clippie said.

Erin didn't know, and she didn't care.

Twelve

The room the doorman had told her about was already tenanted.

'If you'd come last week, I could've let you have it,' the boarding-house owner told her.

Disappointed, Erin turned away, her heart heavy. At least the rain had stopped, but the roads were wet and the potholes full of puddles, so the passing traffic sprayed water on to the narrow pavements and the bottom of her skirt was covered in mud.

She was hungry too, and wished she'd stayed for breakfast instead of rushing off without even a cup of warm tea in her stomach. She should have taken Mrs Gregory's conscience money, too. Pride was a fine thing, until your stomach was rattling from the need of something to fill it.

Still, she had a few shillings in her pocket, and twenty-six pounds in the bank. But she was keeping her savings for a rainy day, since she didn't know how long it would be before she found work, or somewhere to live. There was a smell of food in the air. All she had to do was follow her nose.

So she did, and found herself in a queue outside a hall.

'Is the food here cheap?' she asked the person in front of her.

'You'll get a free bowl of soup and some bread if you've got a good story and let them preach to you. They like to save souls.'

'My stomach needs saving more.'

The queue inched forward, and eventually Erin found herself facing a gimlet-eyed woman in a black bonnet.

'Name?'

'Erin Maguire, ma'am.'

'Do you work, Erin Maguire?'

147

'I lost my job, ma'am. I've been wandering round looking for somewhere to stay, and I'm terrible weary.'

'Why did you lose your job? Are you a lazy girl?'

'No, ma'am.' Erin lowered her voice. 'My mistress found out I was in the way and dismissed me.'

The woman sighed. 'Are you married?'

Erin thought quickly. 'Sure, but my man's gone off to fight in the war.'

'I see.' There was a sceptical look on the woman's face. 'I can't see a ring on your finger.'

'I sold it for a florin. Now I can afford a bed for the night if I can find one, so I can. Only I can't afford food as well.'

The woman handed her a ticket. 'All right, Maguire. Go through. You'll be expected to attend the service afterwards.'

The soup was pea, flavoured with ham. It was thick and filling. She placed the chunk of bread in her bag for later. After listening to the sermon and joining in the hymns, she asked the Lord to forgive her for lying, since there were so many people who seemed worse off than she. Then she thanked her hosts and left, walking aimlessly, her harp becoming heavier by the minute.

The sound of a violin attracted her. Around the corner, in a busy street lined with prosperous-looking shops, a lonely figure stood in the alleyway. People hurried by. Well-dressed woman and men, and soldiers by the score. Now and again, one would stop to throw a penny into the youth's violin case.

The musician was oblivious to all of them, his eyes were closed and he wore a dreamy expression on his pale face as he listened to the music he was making.

Erin walked up to him, as the melody finished. 'If it isn't Nevin O'Connor. I thought you'd gone to America.'

The bow stopped its movement and his eyes focused in on her. He gave a shy smile. 'Erin? What are you doing here?'

'The Maguire men burned Callacrea House down and Lord Sanders with it. Patrick Maguire is the only one left alive, and he's on the run. So I came to London to make my fortune on the stage.' She gave a wry smile. 'At the moment I haven't got a job, or a roof over my head.'

'Neither will I have unless I can earn my rent. I was going to put my age up and go into the army, like Liam.'

'Your mammy didn't mind?'

'She did that. She nagged me about it for ages, until my pa told her to shut her mouth. He said that nobody made their fortune from playing the fiddle. Being a soldier would make a man out of me, he said, and it would save him paying my fare to America. So they left me with Liam.'

'So why didn't you go into the army?'

'I'm getting to that. The doctor said I was too small, my chest was weak and my feet were flat. But the family had taken the boat by then. I'm going off to America to join them as soon as I can afford it, but I can't find a job.'

Erin noticed his hat only contained a few coins. 'You're not collecting much, either.'

'It's been raining.'

'Tell you what, Nevin. If I sing, perhaps it will bring in more. In return you can let me stay at your place until I can sort myself out.'

''Tis a hovel mind, Erin, but you're welcome to move in and share the rent.'

'Better than sleeping in a shop doorway. We'll give them a taste of some real Irish. How about "Danny Boy"? It always brings a tear to the eye.'

They followed that with a faster song. Soon, a small crowd of people gathered and money began to clink into Nevin's violin case. The impromptu concert was abruptly terminated when it began to rain again. People scattered.

Nevin put his violin away and grabbed up her bag. 'Come on, that's enough for one day. We have to be careful of the polis. They don't like beggars.'

She laughed as they headed off down the alley, partly because she had somewhere to stay, and because she no longer felt so alone. 'Beggars, is it? As far as I'm concerned I'm a singer and you're my accompanist. Did we earn enough to pay the rent?'

'We did that.' The smile that lit his thin, pale face held relief. 'There was silver amongst the copper, too, so we'll be eating well for the rest of the week.'

Nevin had not been exaggerating when he'd said he lived in a hovel. The attic room was situated in a tall, gloomy house halfway down an alley. There was an unhealthy stench inside, a mixture of mice pee, boiled greens, cockroaches and damp. The room was bigger than Erin had expected though, and was lit by a skylight, through which water dripped into a bucket.

Erin placed her harp in a corner. 'You're not much of a housekeeper, are you, Nevin O'Connor?'

Shame came into his face when she brushed mouldy food into a sheet of newspaper with her hand and wrapped it. 'I haven't had time to clean up today.'

'Or any day by the look of it.' She sighed. 'I suppose it can't be helped. Like most men, I expect your mammy did for you from the moment the knot was tied in your belly button.' Her glance swept round the room, taking in two rusty iron bedsteads, a torn screen, a sagging sofa, a rickety table and two chairs.

She reminded herself she mustn't complain, even though it made her previous room at the Gregory's seem like a palace. It could have been worse. At least there was a small gas stove to cook on, and a solitary gas bracket on the wall, though it needed a new mantle. She gazed at the stump of a candle in a saucer.

'You know, we can make this place more comfortable.'

'How?'

'Repair that window to start with. It won't take long to put some new putty in where it leaks, and I'll buy a new mantle for the light.'

'I'd better put some money in the meter then,' Nevin ventured. 'And we could whitewash the walls so we can see the cockroaches.'

'A good idea. We can trap them with some molasses in a jar. Once the place is clean, it'll look much better. Where d'you get your water from?'

'There's a pump downstairs, and the privy is out the back.' He blushed as his eyes went to the chamber pot under the bed. 'I forgot to empty it.'

'Well, empty it when I'm out. I'm going shopping. I saw an ironmonger around the corner, and should be able to get a bit of putty there. I'll be after the landlord to reimburse me for it though, so don't you go paying the rent until I come back. Put the money we earned in a pot, and we'll work out what we need for the week. I'll fetch us something back to cook for dinner. You look as though you need a good feed. Where do you buy your groceries?'

'There's a market around the corner.'

'Good. I'll use it. Pass over that basket, then.'

It occurred to Erin she was taking charge, but Nevin didn't seem to mind, so she said, 'You can find a broom and start sweeping the floor while I'm out. You do have a broom, don't you?'

A grin crossed his face. 'And a scrubbing brush, bucket and soap. And behind that screen, a tin bath. There are some spare sheets for the bed too, though they'll need some darning.'

'Then I'd best buy a needle and thread, as well. Well, go on, Nevin O'Connor. Start sweeping then, and no slacking mind.'

It was late when she got to market, so she was able to haggle the stall-holders down. Soon, her basket was filled with vegetables and fruit, and she bought some mutton hocks for the stew, and a pot to cook it in, made of cast iron.

She found the room reasonably clean when she got back. There was no sign of Nevin. He came back just after she'd put the stew on to cook, carrying a tin of whitewash and a wide brush. He smiled, handing her a flaming red chrysanthemum in a pot.

She smiled at him, saying quietly, 'We musn't waste money on things we don't need. And don't you start getting any ideas about me, will you, Nevin. My heart belongs to another.'

''Tis only a flower.' A blush tinted his face. 'And it's not only your heart involved, it seems. I've got eyes in my head. Who's the father?'

'None of your business.' She slipped the chain out from under her bodice and showed him the ring. 'My man's away at war now, but we're engaged to be married.'

'It's not our Liam, is it? He said that you and he—'

'Liam O'Connor is a dirty liar, and if you mention his name to me again, I'll slap you from here to Sunday and back. *Hah!* I'd rather throw myself under a bus than allow him near me. Thank you for the flower, lonely little soul that it is. We'll put it under the skylight, so it can see the sky.'

Soon, Erin was settled into her new abode, and it began to look like home. They managed to earn enough money to make ends meet, but as it neared Christmas the weather grew cold and people hurried past, eager to get home to their firesides.

Although reluctant, Erin was forced to withdraw some of her savings. She needed clothes for the baby and a cradle. Then it was money for gas, rent and food. Soon there was nothing left, except the gold sovereigns she'd found in her mother's tin. There were other options, she thought.

She took out her mother's purse and gazed at the half-penny, folding it in her palm. It was a coin she would always keep. Her mother had died hungry, and she had no intention of doing the same. If necessary she'd find out where her father lived, and ask him for a helping hand.

That night she wrote in her diary.

> Kell, my dearest,
> Our infant will be born in four weeks and I'm suffering from the cold and hunger. I know you would help me if you could. It's too cold now to sing in the streets for my supper. Because it's Christmas, and a time of goodwill, I've made up my mind to ask your sister Catherine to help me.
>
> I will give her this diary to post on to you, so you'll know how we are faring.
>
> Stay safe, my love.
> Your own, Erin.

The day was icy with wind blowing sleet. Erin stopped for a moment. In Lady Sanders' window stood a Christmas fir tree, covered in festive ornaments and garlands. There was a holly wreath on the door, dark glossy leaves, sharp with prickles, and stalks laden with flaming berries.

Erin went to the basement entrance and knocked.

Mrs Baily opened the door and stood silent for a moment, then she stood to one side, saying, 'Alicia told me what happened. I'm so sorry.'

'Sure, but it wasn't your fault. How is Mrs Gregory?'

'Unhappy now she has nothing to interest her. They're keeping her sedated.'

It was obvious that Lady Sanders was entertaining guests. Plates of food covered the table and maids came and went, giving her curious looks. From upstairs came the faint sounds of laughter and talk.

'Come into my sitting room,' Mrs Baily said. 'We'll be more private there. I'll bring us some refreshment.'

Food came. A plate of bread and butter, some pieces of chicken, and a slice of cake.

Erin placed her newspaper-wrapped parcel on the table. 'Sorry,' she said after she'd wolfed down the food. 'I haven't eaten today. I'd like to leave this with Miss Catherine, if I may.'

'I'll have to ask, but I know what the answer will be. Eat your food while you can, dear, and tell me what you've been up to.' Neither of them mentioned the baby.

Lady Sanders was still dressed in black, and was not pleased to see her former maid.

'What is it, Maguire?'

She indicated the parcel. 'I came to leave this with Miss Catherine.'

'My daughter is staying with her grandmother.' The woman shot the housekeeper a look. 'Mrs Baily should have told you that.'

Mrs Baily's lips tightened. 'I'm sorry, ma'am. I thought you'd rather tell her yourself.'

Erin pulled the ragged blanket around her, hiding her stomach and burying her pride. She kept her voice humble. 'Then perhaps you would help me, Lady Sanders. I need some money to buy food with.'

'And what is that to do with me?'

Erin hated asking her for money, but she only had the sovereigns left, and she didn't want to part with them, since she might need them for her baby. 'Because it's Christmas, I thought you might find it in your soul to be charitable.'

'Did you . . . did you, indeed? You're being a nuisance. I'm not in the habit of feeding every beggar who knocks at my door, Christmas or not.'

Erin's face flamed, but she couldn't afford pride if she was to raise the rent. 'Then perhaps you'd allow me to sing to your guests. You could pay me a fee.'

'Good Lord, what an awful suggestion.' She turned away. 'Get rid of her, Mrs Baily. Don't let her in here again. We owe her nothing.'

Lady Sanders was halfway across the room when Erin stated flatly, 'I'm carrying Kell's child.'

Mrs Baily gasped.

Dorothea Sanders stopped in her tracks. Then she turned, her glance falling on Erin's stomach. Her expression became glacial. 'What trickery is this?'

'No trickery. It's the truth.' Erin picked up her parcel and held it out. 'If you can't find it in your heart to help me, perhaps you would send this to Kell.'

Mrs Baily placed a hand on her arm, murmuring, 'Oh, my dear.'

'My son is missing, presumed dead.' For the first time, Lady Sanders' voice faltered, reflecting her feelings on the matter.

The blood all but drained from Erin's face. Kell was dead? Her lover, the keeper of her heart, was gone from her. How could a man so good, so handsome and so alive, be dead?

'He can't be dead, it's too cruel,' she whispered, her hands going protectively to her stomach.

Air hissed angrily through Lady Sanders' teeth. 'Anybody could have fathered the child you're carrying, Erin Maguire. Given your history, I doubt if you know who did, since you appear to be as promiscuous as your mother was.'

Feeling sick and dizzy, Erin replied sadly, 'My mother was a fine woman. She wouldn't have entertained her friends while her beloved child was thought to be dead. She would have grieved that loss, as if a piece of her heart had been torn from her. I'm carrying Kell's child. Whatever you choose to think, there's no mistake about that. Are you completely lacking in compassion to turn your back on your own grandchild?'

White lipped, Dorothea Sanders turned, her hand slashing across Erin's face. The diamond ring the woman wore cut into her lip.

Already shaking from the shock of learning such distressing news, Erin slid to the floor.

She came round to feel a cloth, cool against her forehead. There was no sign of Lady Sanders. Mrs Baily helped her to her feet. 'As soon as you feel able to walk, I'm to take you home.'

They walked in silence for a while, then Mrs Baily said, 'You were a fool, Erin. If you wanted money for food from Lady Sanders you should have been more humble.'

'I'd rather eat a sewer rat for breakfast.' There was a black empty space inside her, and it had nothing to do with hunger.

The housekeeper gave a dark laugh. 'You'll probably end up doing just that. However, Lady Sanders has given me a generous amount of money to help you out. In return you're to sign a paper stating that Kell Sanders is not the father of your child.'

Erin's eyes glinted. 'I certainly will not, for it would be a lie.'

'In that case, I'm to inform you that you'll get nothing. Think about it, Erin. Lady Sanders has been generous.'

Her chin lifted, even though she knew she was being stupid. If Kell was dead, he would never know she'd denied his child his name. 'I've no need to. Kell Sanders wouldn't have abandoned his baby, and I want it to grow up knowing who its father is.'

'When is the baby due?'

'Next month.'

'How will you manage with another mouth to feed?'

They drew to a halt in front of the building she lived in. 'I'll manage. I might have to approach Mr Colby. Do you know where he lives?'

'I'm afraid not.'

Tears came to her eyes. 'I can't believe Kell is dead. How did it happen?'

'I don't know, my dear. I imagine he was shot. Such a waste of a life, but thousands are dead and dying now. You were unfair to Lady Sanders over it, you know. She wouldn't leave her room for a week after she was told, and Catherine was so upset, they sent her to the country to stay with her grandmother.'

'Then you would have thought she'd be happy about Kell's baby, not deny its existence. Kell and I loved each other, you know, even though he was engaged to that other woman, Olivia Winslow. He promised to come back to me.'

'If he said so I'm sure he would have, because he was a fine young man. As for Olivia Winslow, you're mistaken, my dear. Kell was never engaged to her. His parents were hopeful, of course, because she's heir to a fortune. Mr Sanders told his parents that he'd only marry when he fell in love – and fortune wouldn't be a consideration.' Mrs Baily gazed up at the house. 'Is this where you live?'

'At the top. I share the room with Nevin O'Connor, from Callacrea. He wanted to be a soldier, but they wouldn't take him because he's too small, and is not very strong. But he plays the fiddle like an angel, and we perform in the streets for pennies. Pickings are bad in the winter. We haven't got much, but you're welcome to come up?'

'No, I'd best get back. Some other time, perhaps. I'll call on you in a month or so, just to see if you're all right.' Taking Erin's hand, Jean slipped some money into it, then kissed her on the cheek. 'You can repay me when you've become a singer.'

Impulsively, Erin hugged her. 'You've been a real friend to me, Mrs Baily. I'm sorry I've let you down.'

'You haven't.' She gave a small, tentative smile. 'I had a daughter myself once. She had blue eyes and dark hair like yours. Scarlet fever took her off when she was barely a year old, and my husband a year later. If she'd lived, she would be your age now.'

'What was her name?'

'Lillian. Lily for short, after the flower.'

'That's pretty.' Because Jean Baily had been so kind to her, Erin resolved to call her own baby Lily if it turned out to be a girl.

The next three weeks turned out to be hard, even though Erin carefully eked out the money she'd been given. The weather was freezing, ice glazed the puddles. To distract her from constantly thinking of Kell lying dead in the mud some-where, Erin kept herself busy, though she wept silently at night and hoped her sorrow wasn't communicated to the child, now pushing heavily against the pit of her stomach, but giving an occasional painful stretch to ease its cramped position. She had sewn some baby garments of warm flannel, and made some squares to wrap around its little behind.

156

She bought Nevin a warm scarf for Christmas, and a jacket from a second-hand stall, taking up the sleeves and patching the holes in the elbows. It was too big, but Nevin was grateful for the warmth.

He shyly handed her over a parcel, watching her unwrap the baby shawl, which was made of crocheted squares of coloured wool. 'Thank you, Nevin,' she said. 'It's just what I needed.'

His face lit up. 'I bought it in the market. It didn't cost much.'

The following week, Erin sold one of her mother's sovereigns so they could eat, pay the rent and warm themselves. Thank goodness she'd paid for the professional midwife's services with thruppence, a week in advance, she thought, when, finally, her water broke and the first cramping pain dug its claws into her.

Before darkness fell, she sent Nevin to fetch the midwife. When Nurse Rowe arrived, she was dressed smartly in her uniform and hat, and carrying a black bag. Donning her apron, the midwife set about examining her, then sent Nevin away. 'Go for a walk. It shouldn't take more than an hour.'

'I'll sit on the stairs in case you need me.'

They then got down to the business of birthing her infant.

Up till then, Erin had been holding back from expressing her pain so as not to scare Nevin. Now she grunted and groaned as the labour pains came thick and fast, sweating with the effort, despite the cold. After a while she felt herself beginning to stretch as her body strained to push the child from inside her.

'Good. Stop pushing a moment.'

The effort of not pushing was worse than the alternative. 'Go.'

As Erin heaved, her infant slithered from her in a gush of warm liquid. The relief was enormous.

'You have a son.'

When her son gave an aggrieved, warbling cry, Erin craned her neck to see him, but only caught a glimpse of a dark capped head.

Soon, Nurse Rowe finished her tasks and Erin's son was placed in her arms. She'd never seen a baby quite so beautiful. He looked like Kell, with his liquid dark eyes – and his hair was already curling.

Tears came to her eyes as she kissed his forehead and whispered, 'So like your daddy, you are, my love.'

The midwife took out a pencil and notebook. 'I'll fill out the details for the birth certificate. Do you have a name for him?'

Erin had already decided she'd call a son after his grandfather and father, so he had a tenuous family connection. 'Colby Kell Sanders.'

'A nice name. What's his father's name?'

'Kell Sanders.'

The nurse's eyes met hers. 'The lad living here isn't your husband, then?'

'He's a friend from home. We're looking after each other. Colby's father is a soldier in the war.' Erin omitted telling the woman that Kell was probably dead. She didn't want to think about it, and certainly didn't want the woman's sympathy. If there's a heaven, Kell would be there. He'd know of Colby's existence and would guide him through life, with no nonsense about class or birth status.

'It's a bad business. My husband is in the war, too. He's a doctor, and is working in a field hospital. I'll be glad when it's over and we can get back to normal. We'd only been married a month before he left. I was hoping I was carrying myself, but nothing came of it.' Her eyes went to the baby. 'He's a good size and there were no complications with the birth. You should put him to the breast before he goes to sleep. He'll need to learn how to suckle. I'll make you some tea while you do that.'

'I don't think we've got any tea.'

'I carry my own, just in case.' She took a small glass jar of tea leaves from her bag and headed over to the gas cooker and put the kettle on.

Colby took to the breast easily. Erin liked the feeling of his mouth tugging at her and his little fists kneading. He fell asleep after a few moments, his long dark lashes resting against his pale skin.

Love for him overwhelmed her and she feathered kisses over his head.

'Tell Nevin he can come in, would you?' she asked the midwife, who was preparing to leave. 'It's cold on the stairs.

He's not very strong. Sometimes he suffers from croup and finds it difficult to breathe.'

'Next time, make him put his head over a bowl of steaming water. It will help ease it.'

When Nevin came in, his face was pinched with worry. 'I heard you cry out.'

'Of course I cried out, for didn't it hurt like bejesus? You look like Murphy's cow when she's got the gripe. Stop glowering and give us a smile, for heaven's sake. What do you think of my handsome son? I've called him Colby.'

Relief inched across Nevin's face at the sight of the boy. 'I don't have to ask who the father is now, for he's the very image of Kell Sanders himself. But I'm thinking it will be nice for you to have another man to boss around, besides me.'

'Men, is it? When the both of you are boys. Go and fetch yourself a cup of tea, now. Nurse Rowe brought some with her. We can brew it up again in the morning, so don't you throw the leaves away.'

She couldn't help thinking of Kell as she gazed at Colby. How sad that his grandmother had denied herself the sight of him. Erin wondered if it was worth trying to change Lady Sanders' mind. She shook her head. The woman didn't have a motherly bone in her body, that she didn't.

In February, Catherine Sanders turned eighteen. She infuriated her mother by refusing the ball Dorothea had wanted to hold for her.

'How can I enjoy a ball when our men are dying just a few miles away, and when people are dropping dead in the streets from cold and lack of food?'

'We can't be held responsible for that, my dear. Besides, I'm sure the soup kitchens can cater for them. I passed one the other day, and the soup looked very thick and satisfying.'

'I know that, Mother. I work in one. It's just that the war is so awful, and I keep thinking of Kell, wondering if there's some chance he might still be alive.'

'If he was, he'd have been in touch,' her mother said briskly. 'No, we must put Kell behind and get on with our lives. We can't grieve for ever. At the moment I'm trying to arrange your birthday celebration. What about a dinner party then? There are some young people I want to introduce you too.'

'Eligible men, you mean.'

'And why not? There will be a shortage after the war, and those who come back might be maimed in some way.' She shuddered. 'It will be in both of our interests to find you a husband before it ends.'

Catherine sighed. 'I don't think I want to get married yet.'

'Don't be silly, dear. I need to get you off my hands.' She shrugged delicately. 'I might be getting married myself, soon, you see, and having a grown-up daughter living at home is definitely a disadvantage.'

Catherine wasn't surprised. 'Oh, which one of your suitors do you have in mind?'

'Harold Templeton.'

Now she *was* surprised. 'But he must be over a hundred years old. I was rather expecting that it might be Jonathan Granger. He's such a pleasant person, and nearer to you in age.'

'Jonathan has that awful daughter with the funny name. Darling, you know I can't tolerate other people's children. They never seem to have any manners. I could hardly stand my own, and was probably the worst of mothers. Luckily, we could afford nursemaids.'

Catherine gave the expected reply. 'Of course you weren't, Mother. I was perfectly happy being brought up by the nursemaid.' She surprised herself by being unable to resist a jab. 'Besides, Father was always sweet and attentive, so any motherly effort by you would have gone unnoticed.'

Dorothea raised an eyebrow, then gave a brittle laugh. 'What a caustic remark to make, Catherine. Something of me seems to have rubbed off on you, after all.'

'I shouldn't think so. I like children, and consider Sabrina to be a sweet girl. She's at that teenage stage where she's aware of herself.'

'Self-centred and spoilt, you mean. Thank goodness you were never like that. As for Jonathan, he's handsome and self-assured, but rather vain. Woman are attracted to him though.'

160

Feeling compelled to defend him, Catherine said, 'He can't help it if women like him. He's a good listener, and he makes me laugh. I like him.'

Dorothea's eyes sharpened. 'You sound as though you're sweet on him yourself.'

Her mother stared hard at her and blood rose to Catherine's cheeks. 'Don't be silly. He's much too old for me.'

'If you say so, dear. Jonathan's not interested in me, though. He has his eye on the main chance and is after the management of the company when Eric Glover retires at the end of the year. Or perhaps it's you he's interested in. You'll be quite well off when your father's estate is settled. Older men like a young woman in their beds, especially those with no experience. I take it you're still a virgin.'

Dismayed, Catherine stared at her. 'Mother! How could you?'

'Oh, don't sound so prissy. Older men make good husbands, they're more experienced.'

'What about love?'

'There are more sensible reasons to wed. For instance, Harold Templeton has a title, and a fortune. He has no heirs to pass it on to, so I might as well have use of it. I want to travel after the war is over and done with. Your father was such a damned stick-in-the-mud.'

'Mother!' Catherine exclaimed again, shocked to the core.

'Oh, do shut up, dear. I take it then, it's to be a dinner party? I shall invite Jonathan Granger and flirt with him a little. See what he's made of. I wonder if he's noticed your limp yet? That's what most men notice first. Poor Catherine, you're so old-fashioned. You really should do something about yourself if you want to catch a man.'

Pressing her hands to her burning face, Catherine wanted to kill her mother, even though it was the truth. Hardly anybody noticed her and she felt lonely. She wished she had a close friend to talk things over with, wished she knew where Erin was. Though Erin was so capable that she was content with her own company, and hadn't seemed to need friends.

Catherine thought Mrs Baily knew where Erin lived, but she'd said that she didn't. Her mother would have ordered

Mrs Baily to keep quiet and threatened her with dismissal, though. Still, Catherine couldn't help wondering how Erin was managing, and she knew they would have been friends if only Erin would forget she was once their maid.

Had Erin had her hair cut into the modern style like they'd talked about on the boat? Should she . . . and would Jonathan like it if she did? Oh, why was she thinking about Jonathan Granger? Surely he wasn't interested in her. Damn Mother for putting the idea in her head. If only Kell was here to advise her. Olivia Winslow suddenly came into her mind.

Thirteen

Erin and Nevin scraped through the winter, which was the coldest either of them had ever known. The skylight was patterned each morning with lacy ice crystals from their breath. Erin was down to her last sovereign when the equally cold spring arrived.

Nevin's cough had been continual over the cold months, following severe attacks of croup in the mornings. The steam eased it a little.

'You should see a doctor and get some medicine,' she'd told him, but Nevin had dismissed the suggestion.

'I've had this since I can remember. 'Tis caused by the foggy smoke in the air from the chimneys. The cough will go as soon as the weather warms up.'

And it was beginning to ease off. But still, Erin was worried about him.

Her son had thrived. She'd been lucky. Pleasant natured when he was awake, Colby rarely complained unless she kept him waiting for his dinner, and he slept like an angel when he was supposed to. Motherhood had come easily to Erin despite her youth. But her son was breaking her heart, for each day he reminded her more of Kell – his smile in particular. How she wished that his father could see him.

April arrived, and still the cold persisted. But eventually the trees in the parks and gardens began to wear tender green leaves, and daffodils triumphantly nodded at each other. With the sun came a new optimism: hope that the war would soon be over. Soldiers on the streets were quiet and weary-looking, their sad eyes reflecting too many horrors.

The pair had spent the winter rehearsing different songs. When he played the violin, the anxious, pale-faced Nevin

163

was transformed, his expression reflecting the emotion of it, whether it be a jig or a reel.

'We must go out and earn some money,' Nevin said, one day.

'Do you feel up to it?'

'Sure I do. I've been living off you for long enough. Besides, you have Colby to look after.'

Erin noticed the clear blue sky above the skylight. 'We'll go after I've fed him. I daresay he'll enjoy a little outing. There should be a matinee on at the Empire.'

'That's a burlesque theatre. It's got a bad reputation.'

'So what? It's popular with officers. We can work the queue.'

'We'll probably get moved on,' Nevin said morosely. 'I hear it has a new owner.' He turned away when Erin began to undo her bodice, took out his violin and began to tune it.

The queue outside the theatre was long. With Colby tied in a shawl against her chest, Erin began to sing the old favourites. Thank goodness she had such a good accompanist, for she wouldn't be able to handle both her harp and young Colby.

Her sleeping infant brought smiles to the faces of the theatre's patrons, and money tinkled into the violin case as the queue shuffled forward. The queue ground to a halt when she began to sing 'Danny Boy'.'

She'd just finished her song when a man she recognized came from the foyer and grasped Nevin by the collar. He gave him a shake. 'Move on or I'll break your fingers off for you.'

Erin's hands went to her hips. 'Will you, now, Chauncy Green? You've heard of Roaring Rory O'Roarke, the Irish wrestling champion, haven't you? He's our uncle.'

The man grinned as he let go of Nevin and stared at her. 'I've never heard of him, and neither have you. Where do you know me from?'

'I won a contest in the Olympia Theatre in Dublin a year ago.' She bent the truth a little. 'You promised me a job if I came to London.'

'Ah yes, I remember. Where's your manager?'

'Gone to the war. He's missing in action,' she said,

swooping in a breath to take away the ache she felt at the thought of such a finality. 'Are you going to give us a job, or not? I have a child to feed.'

Chauncy gazed at Colby, who had woken up and was staring around him with interest. 'We do have a spot open. Can you dance?'

'I'm not taking my clothes off if that's what you're after. I sing and Nevin accompanies me. That's it.'

'We have an orchestra for that, and besides, you haven't got enough on top to make a burlesque dancer. But you need to do more than sing. You need to move about the stage. Can you manage that?'

She'd watched the singers go through their routines in the theatre in Dublin. 'Sure, I can.'

Dubiously, Chauncy nodded towards Nevin. 'How old are you, lad?'

Her heart beating fast, Erin lied, 'He's eighteen, a year younger than me. He can play the fiddle until his finger-ends catch fire, like the very devil himself.'

Chauncy chuckled. 'He doesn't look very strong.'

'He's strong enough. He's small for his age, that's all.'

An undecided expression settled on Chauncy's face. 'I don't really need a fiddler.'

'It's both or nothing,' she said quietly. 'As it is, we make good money singing on the streets.'

'Can the lad not speak for himself?'

'Course he can.' When Nevin opened his mouth, Erin kicked him on the ankle. 'You heard him play, didn't you? What more d'you need to know about him?'

Chauncy flicked a glance at the open violin case and his eyes widened a fraction. 'I'll give you a try-out.'

A job! Erin couldn't help but smile but she tried not to sound too eager. 'When?'

'Tonight. You'll be on first. One of the dancers will look after the kid when you're on stage. Make sure he's full, so he doesn't squawk. What are you called?'

'I'm Erin Maguire and he's Nevin O'Connor.'

'The name of your act?'

Erin and Nevin stared at each other. 'We haven't got one.'

'Then we'll call you The Shamrocks. The stage door is

up the lane around the corner. Be there at seven. I'll tell the doorman to let you in.'

'Wait a minute,' Erin said as Chauncy turned away. 'We haven't discussed payment.'

'You'll be singing for what the audience throws at you for the first week, to see how you go. After that, we'll see.'

'No we won't. We want two pound guaranteed, up front,' Nevin said, surprising all of them.

'See, I told you he could speak.' Erin grinned widely at him. 'I bet you wish he hadn't now.'

Laughing, Chauncy held out his hand to Nevin, and the pair shook on it.

Later, the pair of them were nervous. Being the first act on, the audience was still settling into their seats, rustling bags and talking when the curtain rose. Erin forgot to use the stage until after her first song, when Nevin reminded her. Beyond the footlights she could see very little, but she began to enjoy herself during the second song.

The applause was startling and coins began to rain down around them. While Erin scrambled to pick them up, Nevin played an Irish jig. The audience whistled and stamped their feet in unison. When Chauncy beckoned, they bowed to the audience and ran off stage.

Chauncy looked happy. 'Nothing wrong with the music, but you need to work on that act. I'll ask Dolly to work up a routine for you. Come in tomorrow morning, and she'll take you in hand.'

Dolly was Chauncy's wife, and a former dancer. She was a hard taskmaster, but soon they had a couple of acts they could call on, and within a month, as they gained in experience, their appearances were increased to two.

In one, Erin was a poor Irish girl and Nevin a leprechaun who she followed to the end of the rainbow, where she found a pot of gold. In the other she was dressed in rags with a baby in her arms, waiting for her husband to come home from the war. But only his ghost returned, to accompany her on the violin as she was forced to sing in the streets. In it, she sang tear-jerkers, such as 'Danny Boy' and 'Black is the Colour', and her performance brought muffled sobs from the audience.

Erin cried too, for she always though of Kell and her mother when she sang. Nevin said it made him homesick for his family, though he had not once received a letter from any of them. Liam O'Connor's name had been on the casualty list in the paper the month before. Nevin had said nothing, though he'd cried himself to sleep that night.

The German army had retreated to the Hindenburg line in February. News from headquarters said there had been a revolution in Russia towards the end of February and early March. Tsar Nicholas had been forced to abdicate.

It was now halfway through April, and there was a rumour that the Americans had declared war on Germany too. Kell hoped it was true, for the troops on the Western Front were exhausted.

Kell had received letters that week. One was from his Uncle Charles, posted over a year earlier, informing him of the death of his father, and of the burning of Callacrea House. Of course, he'd been officially told his father was dead many months ago, but although he'd absorbed it, he hadn't had the time to grieve. Now he was used to death – to seeing men drop to the ground around him, their voices cut off in mid-sentence, leaving only a momentary impression of what they'd been about to say in their eyes.

His uncle wrote:

> My dear Kell,
> It's my sad duty to inform you that your father is no longer alive, and Callacrea House is no more. William was shot, but he was already dead when the house was torched by the Maguire men in a revenge attack, so he did not suffer. Erin got Catherine out. They escaped in your Morgan, and were put aboard a ship to England by Philip Flatterly. The girls were very brave. Of the Maguires, Dermot and Michael were killed – one by your father. The other was burnt alive. Patrick Maguire is still on the run . . .

Kell stared into an imagined landscape of a past tragedy and wondered when his turn to die would arrive. He hoped it would be quick and painless when it did. He read the letter for the umpteenth time, then folded it and placed it back in his pocket. There was a letter from Catherine too, also telling him about the tragedy, and describing their miraculous escape. Rather proudly, she informed him she no longer needed her leg irons, and had thumped Patrick Maguire with them. Nothing from his mother. Still, letters took ages these days. He imagined that sometimes they never caught up with the thousands of soldiers struggling to stay alive.

Nothing seemed real to him any more. One day dragged into the other, equal in misery, even in the periods when they were being relieved at the front, when it seemed that they only had time to take a deep breath before they were back in the thick if it again.

There had been a lull in the shooting lately. He took out his shaving kit. Propping a small mirror on the side of the trench and using a tin mug of muddy water, he proceeded to scrape the stubble from his chin, trying not to cut himself in case it became a festering sore.

His hands trembled slightly and he felt hot. He thought he might be burning up with trench fever again, a condition brought about by the invasion of lice, amongst other things. He'd had several bouts already, usually ending up in the field hospital until it had run its miserable course.

The last time he'd had a lucky escape. The hospital truck, a converted London bus, had taken a direct hit. Blown clear, he'd landed in a shell crater. The only survivor, his hair had been singed and smoking, his clothing blown from his back. Except for a few burns and a collection of shrapnel – which a fellow soldier had later picked from his skin – he'd been unharmed.

Stripping the uniform and boots from a dead soldier occupying the same crater, and with a rifle and ammunition taken from the same source, Kell had simply joined up with the nearest regiment and had carried on fighting until he could rejoin his own men, despite his fever.

During his time in France he'd rapidly risen through the ranks and now had his captain's pips up – filling dead men's shoes every step of the way. The landscape was a shambles, and he hoped his luck didn't run out.

Pulling the lucky shamrock from under his collar he rubbed it, smiling at the thought of Erin. His sister would probably have crumbled to pieces when faced with danger – but not Erin. She'd have put up a fight.

He wondered what she was doing, whether her dream of performing had materialized. He remembered her in Dublin, her blue eyes bright with the wonder of being on the stage, her body quivering with excitement, singing her little Irish heart out.

Suddenly, guilt stabbed at him. He shouldn't have taken advantage of her. But she'd been so lovely, her adoration for him written plainly on her face. He hadn't been with a woman since, and had lost any desire to, thank goodness.

Did he love Erin? He'd thought he had then, but it seemed a world away now. He found love hard to define in the face of this carnage around him – any emotion come to that. Erin had been ethereal in her innocence, he remembered. He'd *known* he loved her then, for he'd loved her from the moment they'd met. But the war had changed his perspective. Would she wait as he'd asked her . . . perhaps for ever? And if he survived this hell he was in, would he be able to recapture what he'd felt then – or would he disappoint her?

His smile faded and fear ran through him. He squashed it, afraid it would take over and turn him into a coward. Which didn't mean he was reckless. He ducked as a shell whistled over him, and dropped the shamrock back inside his shirt. They were in a forest of splintered tree trunks with a bare sky shining above where the canopy of leaves had once provided shade for lovers. There was a dull crump as the shell landed.

He suddenly remembered a postcard he'd received from his mother as a child: *France in Spring is a delight. Wish you were here.*

Kell wished he was anywhere but *here*. Pulling on his tin hat, he hunched into his collar as splinters of wood and clods of earth rained down on him.

The man next to him jerked out of sleep to complain bitterly, 'You'd think the bastards would let a man have a lie-in on Sunday morning, wouldn't you, sir?'

Kell managed a thin smile. 'You would indeed.'

His luck ran out a few days later. Almost delirious with a bad bout of trench fever, he was on the way to the hospital for treatment when they ran into an ambush. Shots were exchanged, the cart lurched sideways; Kell rolled out and the cart rolled on top of him.

When he regained consciousness both his legs and one arm were encased in plaster, and he was lying in a hospital bed.

There was a man talking with another not far away – in German!

Catherine, feeling sophisticated in her new persona, was enjoying her birthday dinner until her mother decided to notice her.

As usual, Dorothea held court, elegant in a finely-pleated grey silk gown, with a wide belt embroidered with rose buds, one designed to show off her tiny waist. The colour of the rose buds matched the ruby necklace and earrings she wore, a gift from Lord Templeton.

Dorothea, animated after a couple of glasses of champagne, caused a stir when she daringly smoked a cigar. Then she flirted with Jonathan; Catherine nearly gritted her teeth with the embarrassment of it.

Her mother made her feel dowdy, despite the efforts of Olivia Winslow. Although Catherine's blue gown was of the latest fashion, the ankle-length hobble skirt with gathered overskirt drew attention to her limp. She'd never worn Louis heels before.

Olivia had said rather impatiently, 'Don't worry about the limp. It's hardly noticeable now, and you'll soon get used to the heels.'

Olivia had just become engaged to a dashing pilot in the Royal Army Corps. 'Anthony is a banker in real life. He's going to teach me to fly as soon as the war is over. He knows Jonathan well. The pair of you should make up a theatre party with us the next time Anthony is on leave.' She'd sighed. 'I'm not really over your brother yet.'

Catherine had been surprised. 'I didn't know you were involved with Kell. He never said.'

'We weren't involved, at least, not in anything but a casual way. Kell would never have married me, you know. I was one of the crowd to him. I believe he cared for that Irish maid of yours more than he did me – the one who saved your life. He was always talking about her.'

Catherine's eyes widened at the thought. Her parents wouldn't have allowed that if they'd known. She remembered how it had struck her then that there seemed to be some mystery about Erin Maguire.

Her mother's strident voice dragged her into the present. 'You should wear flat shoes if you can't manage heels, darling,' she said to her in front of everyone, so their attention was drawn immediately to her feet. 'And whatever have you done to your hair?'

'I had it cut into the latest style,' she said, feeling slightly desperate when all eyes then came up to scrutinize her shorn head. Her glance went to Olivia for support, with no result. She was in a corner with Jonathan, the pair smiling as if they'd just shared a private joke.

Dorothea shrugged. 'Oh well, you know best, I suppose, though if I may make comment, I always considered your hair was your best feature. Didn't you, Charles?'

Charles Colby took her hand in his, gently squeezing it, as if he knew exactly how she was feeling, and saying gruffly, 'I like Catherine's new hairstyle, it shows her pretty face off to perfection.' He kissed her on the cheek. 'Damn it, my dear, your father would have been proud to see you looking so grown-up.'

When her faint blush brought a smile from Jonathan, Dorothea's eyes glinted. 'Of course he would. Willie was always so proud of his children.'

Charles turned to Dorothea. 'It doesn't seem long since you were eighteen, and newly engaged to Willie, Dorothea. How young we all were then.'

'Oh, do stop talking about the past, Charles. We're supposed to be celebrating Catherine's birthday.' Dorothea sounded quite cross.

'Quite,' Charles said.

Ignoring him, Dorothea gazed from Harold to Jonathan. 'Now, which of you fine gentlemen will I allow to escort me in to dinner, I wonder?'

Harold said firmly, 'Don't put Jonathan on the spot, Dorothea. You know very well he had every intention of escorting Catherine.'

'Damn,' said Charles, jokingly. 'As her godfather, I was going to claim the honour for myself, but I'll defer to Jonathan.'

'The birthday girl has two arms, so we shall claim one each,' Jonathan said.

Lord Templeton stood up and leant on a silver-topped cane. He was small and neat, with twinkling blue eyes, his kind face topped by silvery hair. Catherine was sorry she'd been mean about his age, for really, he was not much older than sixty. And she'd heard that he still rode with hounds.

'Which reminds me, Catherine, I've brought you a gift.' He handed her a jewellery box. Inside rested a gold bar brooch, the centre set with a pearl surrounded by half a dozen each of diamonds and sapphires.

Catherine gasped with delight. 'It's so pretty. Thank you, Lord Templeton. You really shouldn't have.'

He was gruff. 'Nonsense, my dear.'

'I shall treasure it, always.' She kissed his cheek.

Dinner was called.

After they'd eaten, Jonathan asked to speak to her in private. She took him into her father's study, which was exactly the same as when he'd left it, except tidier. This was her favourite room. Everything smelled of wood, tobacco, leather and books. There were hundreds of them lining the walls, of different colours, most tooled with gold lettering. There was a portrait of her parents over the fireplace: her mother confident in her beauty, her father with a twinkle in his eyes as they sat together on a sofa.

Portrait photographs of herself and Kell were on her father's desk. She picked up a pipe to inhale the aroma of the bowl. Her grief came, short, sharp and urgent.

First her father, then Kell. How quickly death had claimed them. But she did not like to recall the time of her father's demise because panic always welled up in her. She picked up Kell's portrait. 'I miss them both so much. Kell was such a nice brother to have. He always had time to listen to me.' She looked at Jonathan. 'Do you have any brothers or sisters?'

172

'No. I'm quite on my own.'

'Except for Sabrina.'

'Except for Sabrina.' He cleared his throat. 'I was wondering, Catherine . . . I rather thought it would be nice if we were engaged to be married. I mean, we always get on so well together, despite the age difference. I need a wife and Sabrina needs a mother.'

There was something charming and easy-going about Jonathan, as if he didn't take life seriously. 'I was thinking about doing some war work,' she said.

'I wouldn't stop you doing it, since it helps the war effort. Come to that, we needn't get married until after the war. It's bound to end sometime.'

Catherine wondered if Jonathan loved her. He hadn't mentioned it. Indeed, she wondered if she loved him. Marriage, and the responsibilities that came with it, wasn't something she really wanted to rush into.

But Jonathan had a little ring box in his hand, and was showing her a pretty ring with a cluster of glittering diamonds on it. 'I hope you like it. We can change it if you don't.' It was slid on to her finger with no fuss, and she was suddenly engaged, without even being given time to answer.

Jonathan had a rather endearing smile on his face now. 'Shall we go and tell everyone?'

'Do you love me, Jonathan?' she asked.

His eyes flickered away. 'Of course, my dear. Didn't I say so?'

So why did she feel so disappointed by his answer. It was being here in this room, so filled with ghosts, she thought. She placed her hand in his and allowed herself to be led away.

The news of the engagement was received with a smile from her mother, and a kiss on the cheek for Jonathan. The rest of the guests seemed surprised. Olivia looked shocked.

Amidst the congratulations, Charles Colby took her aside to ask, 'Are you sure you're doing the right thing?'

'I don't know. It just seemed to happen. And it will be convenient for the company, and . . . everyone, I suppose.'

'Convenient for Catherine Sanders, as well?'

She shrugged. 'I do like Jonathan and his daughter, and we're not getting married until after the war is over.'

'Well, just make sure he's the right man, and that you love each other. Personally, I think he's too old for you. If you ever need anyone to talk to, you know where I am. I'm sure your father wouldn't mind me acting on his behalf.'

She was grateful to him. 'Dear Uncle Charles. I do wish things had been different for you.'

The sigh he gave had a lonely sound to it. 'So do I. But there, things can't be changed now. You haven't heard from Erin, I suppose?'

Catherine shook her head. 'If I do, I'll let you know. She may have gone back to Ireland.'

Charles hoped not as he accepted a glass of champagne from the housekeeper. Soon it would be time for the entertainment. 'Are you going to do a turn?' he asked his niece.

'Mother insists I must sing.'

'Make it something Irish especially for me, Catherine, love. I always used to enjoy those evenings we had at Callacrea House.'

Mrs Baily, hovering nearby with the tray, said quietly, 'If I may say so, sir, you should attend the show at the Empire. It has an Irish act called The Shamrocks, and I've heard they're very good indeed.'

Charles nodded. 'Perhaps I will. Thank you, Mrs Baily. Kind of you. I hear you're leaving the employment of Lady Sanders.'

'Yes, sir. My second cousin has been called up to drive ambulances, and I'm needed to look after his mother. She's an invalid.'

'I see. Well, if you're ever in need of a reference, don't hesitate to call on me.'

'Thank you, sir. I will. Don't forget to go and see that act, sir. I can guarantee you'll be glad you did.'

Charles remembered Mrs Baily's words a couple of months later.

News of the allied push at the start of spring had been heartening. Now it was July. At his club he learned that the Germans were using mustard gas to try and break the British lines. Casualties were severe, and the allied forces were paying a high price for the small gains in territory.

Charles seemed to be at a loose end now William Sanders had died. He missed his brother-in-law. Dorothea had become engaged to Harold Templeton, and they were to be married in August.

He felt a certain disdain for her now. He'd not realized how terribly self-centred Dorothea was, and she spent money without thought for the future, entertaining constantly.

His ears pricked when he heard Gerald Compton mention The Shamrocks, recalling that Mrs Baily had told him about them before.

'The singer's voice is quite beautiful, and the young man is a wonderful violinist. It's worth putting up with the rest of the show, just to see them.'

Charles decided he might take a look at them. He turned, saying, 'Forgive me for butting in, Gerald, but I couldn't help overhearing. What theatre are The Shamrocks playing at?'

'The Empire. You'd best get there early, though, if you intend to catch their act. It was standing room only, the last time I went.'

Charles duly presented himself early, and joined the front of the queue. Within ten minutes it stretched back down the road behind him. He managed a scat in one of the boxes overlooking the stage and looked around him.

The seats were old and frayed, the carpets soiled, and the stage curtains, dark red velvet fading to pink with tarnished gold fringes, displayed several rips and darns. The theatre was shabby, the scrolls and other decorations losing their gilt and glitter, and covered in dust.

A great deal of money would need to be spent to bring it back to its former glory, he thought, as the lights dimmed.

There was a loud whirring noise and the curtains drew jerkily back to reveal a backdrop of a park. There was a bench under a gaslight. A woman sat there, her head bowed in her hands. She was dressed in rags. The audience began to clap and cheer, and stamp their feet.

When the sound of a violin came from offstage, there was an instant hush. Charles could hear his own heartbeat. The violin was playing a slow romantic tune. A young man walked on to the stage and went to stand under the lamp, playing to her.

When the girl gradually lifted her head, the youth handed her a red rose. She was young. Her eyes were of the purest blue, her hair as dark as night as she cupped the flower in her hands and held it to her nose to breathe in its perfume. Then she began to sing, her voice soaring as clear as a bell, so he was entranced by it. He could almost smell the mists of Ireland in her voice.

Red is the rose that in yonder garden grows . . .

'Erin,' he breathed. So enamoured was he by the beauty of this daughter of his, he ignored the tears that filled his eyes and trickled down his cheeks.

The next day, Charles hired a private box for himself for the season. Every evening for the next week he sent Erin a bouquet of flowers.

'There's a note with these,' Chauncy told her as he handed over a bouquet of pure white roses.

Opening the envelope, Erin grinned. 'He wants me to take refreshment in his box with him, during the interval. What's he like?'

'A gentleman, and well-heeled by the look of him. But too old for you, my girl,' Chauncy cautioned.

'I can't come to any harm with him in such a public place.' Erin twisted her mother's wedding ring, which she'd taken to wearing. It saved awkward questions when she had Colby with her. 'I'll thank him for the flowers, and I'll tell him I'm married if he looks as though he's going to get out of hand.' She gazed at Colby, who was sprawled on his back in a basket in their dressing room. He could sleep soundly anywhere. 'Will you keep your eye on his lordship, Nevin?'

Erin hurried up to the box, still in her stage make-up and her costume rags.

When she entered, a man rose to his feet. There was a bottle and two glasses of champagne on a table. When he turned to smile at her, her eyes widened.

'Pa . . . Mr Colby. I wasn't expecting to see you.'

'I wanted to congratulate you, Erin. I've been wondering what happened to you, and I found you quite by accident.'

A smile came and went on her face, her heart was warmed by the thought he'd been thinking of her. 'I can't stay long, I have to get ready for my next performance.'

'I'm quite amazed by your talent for singing. I'm so proud of you.'

She shrugged. 'I was lucky that I was able to take some singing lessons.'

He took her hands in his and drew her down on to the seat next to him. 'I'm sorry I wasn't a better father to you, Erin. I'd like us to meet now and again, if you'd allow it.'

'Of course, Mr Colby. I'd like that too.'

'Could you bring yourself to call me Father, d'you think?'

She nodded shyly, then kissed him on the cheek. 'Sure, but I'd be proud too . . . *Father*.'

They exchanged a smile and Charles handed her a glass of champagne. 'Welcome home, Erin,' he said.

Fourteen

Erin thought it wiser not to tell her father about Colby. Not that she'd set out to deceive him, but she treasured the growing relationship with him, something she'd missed out on while she was growing up. It was precious to her and she was frightened of losing it.

Young Colby had other ideas, though. By August he'd found he could get around quite easily if he put his mind to it. And he found the theatre an exciting place to explore. As a result, the props man built him a pen. Colby stood up on the mattress and rattled his prison bars ferociously back and forth.

The carpenter, sitting on a box right next to him, said, 'You'll never get out of that however hard you try, young man.'

But Colby did. As soon as the man left, he placed one foot through the bar on to the box and hauled himself up over the top, to tumble down the other side.

As he sat up, wondering whether to cry or not, he heard his mother begin to sing. He saw her in the distance, surrounded by light. Chuckling with delight, he headed for the stage at a fast crawl.

Erin was singing 'Danny Boy' when somebody in the audience laughed. Others joined in. She was puzzled by it, usually they were dabbing at their eyes, by now. Her song trailed to a halt when Nevin stopped playing and began messing about with two notes on his violin.

The audience dissolved into laughter.

When she turned, Erin saw Colby crawling across the stage in time to the music. She began to laugh. Waiting until he reached her, she scooped him up. 'It seems that my son wants to be introduced instead of sleeping,' she said to the audience.

Colby beamed a pleased smile all round, then stuck his thumb in his mouth. He was tired, Erin saw it in his eyes as he snuggled his head against her shoulder. Erin abandoned 'Danny Boy' and instead, began to sing 'Irish Lullaby'.

The audience settled down, and when she reached the chorus they sang along with her. 'Too-ra-loo-ra-loo-ral . . .' quieter and quieter until her son was fast asleep. Blowing them a kiss, Erin walked off stage, followed by Nevin.

'Wonderful!' Chauncy declared, taking Colby from her. 'We'll work him into the act. He'll bring the house down.' Indeed, the audience were clapping in unison and demanding more.

'Give them an encore,' Chauncy said.

When she and Nevin went back on stage, the audience erupted into cheers. But her heart sank when she looked up at her father's box, for it had been abandoned. She sang 'Kathleen', which was another audience favourite, then went to claim Colby.

She found him cradled in his grandfather's arms. Charles looked up at her. 'Why didn't you tell me, Erin?'

She shuffled her feet. 'I don't know. I thought you'd be ashamed of me if I did.'

Nevin looked from one to the other, then disappeared towards the dressing room, saying, 'This sounds to me like a private conversation.'

'The baby looks like Kell. Would I be mistaken in thinking he fathered him?'

'He did.'

'Does Dorothea know?'

'I went to her for help, but it came at too high a price. She wanted me to sign a paper denying Kell was Colby's father.'

'You called him after me. I'm honoured. You should have come to me, you know. I wouldn't have turned you away.'

'I thought about it, but I didn't know your address, and Jean Baily didn't dare go against Lady Sanders and tell me, though I think she wanted to. How is Mrs Baily? Have you seen her?'

'Mrs Baily has left the Sanders family. She's looking after her cousin. Somebody had to when the son was called up. She seemed well when last I ran into her.'

'That's good. The sovereigns you gave to my mother saw us over that hard winter, you know. Nevin and I can manage now we have regular work.'

Looking amazed, he said, 'Cliona kept that money all those years?'

'As a legacy for me. A good job she did, else I'd have starved to death by now. Promise you won't tell Catherine about me, or the baby. Her mother dislikes me, and it will only cause trouble if Catherine insists on seeing me. Best if it's kept quiet.'

'If that's what you want, my dear. Catherine is engaged to be married, now. Her mother wants her to wed in the spring, but Catherine wants to wait until the war is over.' He hesitated for a moment, then said, 'About Kell . . . did you love him?'

'Of course I did.' Erin showed him the ring Kell had given her. 'He asked me to wait for him.'

Smiling a little, her father kissed her gently on the cheek. 'I'm so glad to know his intentions were honourable. He knew how much you meant to me. You know, I think you and I need to talk, Erin. May I escort you home?'

She nodded. 'We'll fetch Nevin on the way.'

'Nevin's gone off to a party with a couple of the dancers,' the doorman told her when she asked if he'd seen him. 'He said not to bother waiting up for him.'

Her father might as well see where they lived. She and Nevin had made their attic room more comfortable with a rug for the floor, some patchwork quilts for their beds, and some bright cushions for the armchairs. It was far from luxurious, but it was homely and clean.

Even so, her father frowned when he saw it. 'I think you should come and live with me, Erin. This isn't a good place for my grandson to grow up in.'

She shook her head. 'I can't leave Nevin. He needs somebody to look after him. Besides, having a bastard daughter is bad enough, but having a bastard grandson, as well, would make you an outcast. We grew up in very different worlds. After a while you'd feel ashamed of me.'

'Never,' he said, though he winced at her forthright language.

'What about my career? I've only just got my foot in the door.'

He said nothing, but his eyes were sad. 'The boy needs a better chance in life than you can give him. I can pay for his education, at least, enrol him into a good school, the one his father attended. Will you allow me to do that? And we should find a better place for you both to live. An address like this will disadvantage him.'

'By the time Colby is aware of his surroundings, I'll be earning enough to afford something better. Our contract is due to end soon, and we're going to ask Chauncy Green for a raise.'

'Allow me to act in that matter for you, then, if you will. I imagine I'll be better at negotiating the financial side than you will.'

Erin and Nevin were pleasantly surprised by the large increase Charles negotiated. 'You're to get a small percentage of the box-office takings, as well,' he told them, a pleased smile on his face.

The act continued to draw crowds over the summer. Erin didn't have time to celebrate her eighteenth birthday. To her surprise, her father remembered it though. He bought her a necklace of pearls.

In November, Chauncy announced that the theatre was to be refurbished over the winter months. The dancers grumbled at being thrown out of work, though Chauncy did his best to help. Erin had no trouble. She was to be the princess in the pantomime, Cinderella.

'But I don't know how to act.'

'Neither does anyone else in the cast. Don't worry, the kids will love you.'

'What about Nevin?'

'Sorry, love. I did my best, but they wouldn't take the pair of you. It's only for a few weeks. You'll have top billing afterwards. Try and work on a couple of new acts in the meantime. Nevin, if you find money tight, I daresay I can manage a loan.'

'No need, I have a bit put by. I'll look after Colby,' Nevin offered. 'He's getting a bit of a handful now he's begun to walk. It will save you paying someone to look after him.'

Nevin was looking a little tired, and the onset of winter had started him wheezing again.

On Christmas day, Nevin went off to Mass. He returned, his face streaked with tears.

'What is it, Nevin?' Erin asked.

'I saw our Annie. She looks terrible.'

Hearing the anger and despair in his voice, she said, 'You should have asked her back for dinner.'

'She wouldn't come. I told her I'd be back at the theatre in March, just in case if she ever needed help. Begging on the street, she was. A little girl hanging off her skirt. I gave her the couple of shillings I had in my pocket, but I was glad she didn't want to come back home with me. Now I hate myself for thinking that way.'

'And so you should, Nevin O'Connor. Didn't we once sing for our supper ourselves?'

'Annie isn't singing for hers. She's . . .' He shrugged. 'Well, you know.'

Erin sighed as she handed him a package. 'Here's your Christmas present, darlin'. 'Tis a bowler hat like Charlie Chaplin wears, so you'll look like a proper gent instead of a raggy-arsed Irish lad with legs like chicken bones. And here's a letter from America.'

Placing the hat on his head and beaming a smile, Nevin went into a dance routine, using it as a prop. Nevin was nifty on his feet, and graceful, even though he ran out of breath quickly.

'Sure, you are as sprightly as a spring lamb,' she said when he'd finished, and she swept her son up to plant a kiss on his cheek.

Colby smiled at her through Kell's eyes. The sudden surge of love she experienced for her son made her feel happy that she'd loved his father. She was becoming more adult in her thinking, though, and had begun to doubt that Kell would have returned to wed her.

She was also aware that Nevin didn't need her so much, though she thought he might have grown fonder of her than he should be. He was more manly, and a favourite with the dancers. He'd learned to flirt, too, and was self-assured, despite his tears over Annie.

182

Hands on hips, Nevin was bent double, trying to catch his breath.

'You know, Nevin,' she said. 'Once we get back to work, I think it's about time I started looking for my own place. Don't think I haven't noticed the dancers making flirty eyes at you. You have a life of your own to lead, and so do I.'

He straightened up to smile easily at her. 'You've been reading my mind, I reckon. I don't know what I would have done without you, though.'

A lump stuck her throat. 'Nor me without you. I was at my wits' end when we ran into each other. I had nowhere to go—'

'And walked into my flat without a by-your-leave and took over with your bossy ways, Erin Maguire.'

'You needed bossing and I needed someone to boss, and that's the truth of it.' She laughed. 'Come over here and give me a big hug before you go off to read your letter.'

1918 ticked over. It was reported in spring that the troops were suffering from a bronchial disorder that infected them by the thousands. It turned into influenza, and by summer the infection reached England. Men in masks sprayed the streets, but the disinfecting didn't seem to make any difference and people began to die by their hundreds.

Jean Baily and Alicia Gregory invited Erin to tea. The old lady seemed glad to see her, but she'd lost some of her spark.

Alicia Gregory told her, 'That new nurse went off, taking half the silver with her. She said she hadn't been paid for months.' Tears came to her eyes. 'And Peter was killed in action.'

'I'm so sorry.' Erin kissed the old woman's cheek. 'I do hope he didn't suffer.'

'It's nice of you to say that, considering you and he didn't see eye to eye.' It was said rather aggressively, as if what had happened had been Erin's fault. 'I hear you have a son.'

'Yes, he's in the drawing room with Jean.'

'Then you'll know how I feel about Peter – why I couldn't take your side. He died a hero, you know. They'll be sending his medal when the war is over,' she said rather abruptly, then added, 'Are we going to let bygones be bygones?'

'If that's what you want.'

'You wouldn't be here if I didn't. Bring the lad through so I can see him. There's a present for him under the tree.'

Colby smiled winningly at Alicia when she stroked his curls. 'A handsome lad,' she said. 'Let's hope he doesn't have to go off to war and get himself killed one day.'

Erin's blood ran cold at the thought.

After tea, Alicia insisted that Erin sing, smiling in approval afterwards. 'You're a little ragged in the high notes, but I taught you well. I hear you're at the Empire, my dear.'

'Yes, but it's closed for refurbishment, and I haven't been keeping my voice exercises up. Nevin and I will be topping the bill when it reopens.'

'I must come and watch you perform, if Jean can make arrangements to get me there.'

As they were about to leave, Jean Baily took her aside and whispered, 'Peter was shot for desertion, you know, but don't tell her that.'

Erin's eyes widened. 'How dreadful. But she told me the War Office was sending a medal after the war.'

'I'll find one to send her. Wounded soldiers are selling them on the street for the price of a meal. It's wicked that they have to resort to that, but she won't know the difference.' Jean took a deep breath. 'Alicia and I were wondering if you'd like to move in with us?'

Erin remembered Alicia's temper. 'It's tempting, but I can't risk it. What if she sets about Colby?'

'It was Alicia's idea. Despite everything, she's always liked you and she feels guilty for throwing you out. She's changed since Peter died. The doctor has put her on some new sedatives, which keep her calm. To be honest, he doesn't think she's going to last out the winter. Her heart is terribly weak.'

'I can't look after her like I used to, Jean. I have my work to consider. There are routines to rehearse and songs to learn.'

'We could work out a routine between us. Having you here would give me some respite, and Colby will have me to look after him when you're on stage in the evenings. Alicia would help you learn your songs. It will give her an interest, stop her feeling sorry for herself.'

Erin discussed it with her father.

'Do it, my dear. A good address is hard to come by. I'll be more at ease knowing you're in a nicer area. My chauffeur will drive you home from work at night. Jean Baily, I know, of course, but I'd like to meet Alicia Gregory. Will you introduce me?'

'If you'd like. Mrs Gregory wants to come to the theatre and see me perform.'

'I have a box. Shall I arrange an outing for opening night? I can collect Mrs Gregory in my car and escort her.'

Erin moved into Imperial Mansions the following week. On opening night, Colby was left with a nanny her father had hired, after carefully checking her credentials.

Dressed in a lilac gown and a fur coat, a frail Alicia was conveyed to the theatre and settled in her father's box with a rug over her lap. Jean Baily was in attendance, pretty in pale blue. The theatre looked its best. There was a corsage of flowers for both women, champagne and chocolates. Alicia was pale, but spots of colour in her cheeks gave her excitement away.

It was a good evening, the new acts were interesting. For once, Erin and Nevin got to dress up. Erin had bought herself a gown of dark blue lace over satin, with a wide buckled belt.

Nevin was bursting with pride at being top of the bill. Erin scrutinized him carefully, to make sure he'd been looking after himself.

'Are you eating properly?' she asked as she smartened the knot on his tie.

He grinned. 'Don't I look as though I am? The woman who lives downstairs cooks my meals now.'

'Make sure she gives you plenty of meat and vegetables, then.' She tutted. 'That shirt needs a button sewn on it. Give it to me after, and I'll repair it.'

'I have hands. I can sew on my own buttons.'

They both laughed.

She said, 'I never thought I'd say this to an O'Connor, but I do miss you, Nevin . . . though you've become a cheeky little wretch in your old age. And are those whiskers I see growing on your chin?'

'Can't a man have some privacy round here?' Nevin smacked a kiss on her cheek and strutted on to the stage, his violin and bow held over his head while he played a jig and danced a few steps to it. He wore his bowler slanted at a dashing angle, his blue checked trousers were held up by braces, and a darker blue waistcoat was worn over his shirt.

When the audience began to whistle and clap, he turned his head towards where she stood. He was laughing, enjoying every minute of the performance.

As usual, there was standing room only, and the applause was deafening.

Erin could feel the warmth of the response flowing towards her, even though she couldn't see past the first few rows.

If she'd been able to see past the footlights, she would have seen the Sanders' party. A sour expression had settled on Dorothea's face when she'd recognized her former maid.

Catherine was gazing at the stage in delight, her face wreathed in smiles. Her escort, Jonathan, was enjoying her reaction to the surprise he'd cooked up with Charles Colby. 'We're invited to the backstage party afterwards,' Jonathan whispered in her ear.

Curious about the child Erin had supposedly been carrying, Dorothea swallowed her ire and decided to be gracious. It wasn't as if the girl could marry her son now, so neither she nor her offspring posed a threat to her own well being.

When they met face to face, she looking at Erin, a faintly patronizing expression on her face. She conceded that Erin was striking with her Irish colouring and fine features. It was possible that Kell, with his passion for all things Irish, had fallen for her. Would it have been so awful to have this girl in the family? she thought. After all, Charles Colby was quite well bred, and he seemed to have acknowledged her as his daughter.

'Lady Sanders,' Erin said, a faintly ironic smile on her face. 'I do hope you're well.'

Spoken rather gracefully, considering the circumstances. The girl was surer of herself now, and she'd learned some manners.

'I'd forgotten what a lovely voice you have,' Dorothea said.

'Thank you, Lady Sanders.'

'An entertaining act altogether, Miss Maguire.' She noticed the wedding ring on Erin's finger. 'Do you have any children?'

Not at all taken in and, refusing to satisfy her former employer's curiosity, Erin smiled. 'Yes, I do have a child. Have you met my singing teacher, Alicia Gregory, yet? She used to sing at Covent Garden.'

When Catherine headed towards her, Erin excused herself. Their reunion was less restrained. Catherine threw her arms around her and hugged her tight. 'You were quite wonderful, Erin. And so is your partner. Isn't he Nevin O'Connor, from Callacrea, who won a medal for violin when we were children?'

'Indeed, he is. You have a good memory.'

'Then I'd better go over and say hello, to remind him of it. After that I'm going to seek out Uncle Charles and tell him off. He promised to let me know when he found you.' As she went off, Erin was glad to see that Catherine was hardly limping.

The man with Catherine smiled indulgently. 'It seems that I've been left to introduce myself. I'm Jonathan Granger, Catherine's intended. I've heard a lot about you, Miss Maguire.'

She gave a light laugh. 'I hope I don't disappoint, then.'

His glance lingered on her body longer than was polite, then flicked up to her eyes. 'On the contrary, you're everything Catherine said, and more.'

Wolf! Erin thought. Then wondered if Patrick Maguire was still at large.

With several days' growth on his chin, Patrick Maguire was hunched in an army coat he'd stolen from a soldier earlier in the day. The man had been huddled in a laneway, nearly unconscious.

'Help me,' he'd begged, his voice slurred. 'I'm ill; I need to go to hospital.'

Patrick knew a habitual drunk when he saw one. Face flushed and hands shaking, the man had been half delirious. Patrick had found some money in the pocket of the coat, enough to buy a pie to temporarily fill a hole in his stomach.

He'd been in London for over a month, finding food and shelter where he could, begging, or preying on others down on their luck when he needed to. He'd been looking for an opportunity to earn himself some money with the least effort, enough to disappear for good. Now he seemed to have found it.

Opposite, and a little to his left, was the stage door of the Empire. There was a poster at the front of the theatre. He'd recognized the picture of Erin straight away, and was waiting for her to come out.

He cursed as a clock on the church struck eleven. He hadn't expected them to be so late. The door suddenly opened and several girls exploded through it, chattering, laughing, and bidding each other good night.

Patrick's eyes narrowed as a car came to a halt alongside the stage door. He silently whistled as Erin came from the theatre with a young man. She was wearing a smart suit and her looks made him suck in a breath. All he wanted from her was a boat fare and a little left over to live off, so he could get away to America. He didn't have time for anything else. Erin looked as if she could afford that.

'Are you sure you don't want a ride home, Nevin?' she said.

Patrick recognized the youth as one of the O'Connor brood. The small, ratty one. He waved her into the car with an exaggerated bow. 'Since when have I needed a lift? I only live around the corner?'

'You were coughing more than usual tonight. You should look after yourself with all this Spanish influenza going around. They say that eating lots of porridge will keep the germs at bay.'

'Stop worrying yourself over me, Erin.'

Taking his face between her hands she kissed his forehead, as if she was his mother. She grinned when he frowned at her. 'Worrying about you has become a habit, and nothing you can say will stop it.'

She entered the car and it drove away. Nevin O'Connor gazed after it for a moment, then turned and walked off up the lane, one hand in his pocket, the other carrying his violin case. He whistled happily to himself, giving a skip now and again.

Patrick followed after him, glowering. The O'Connor rat was dressed decently. He could hear money jangling in his pockets. It would be easy to knock him over the head, empty his pockets, then take his violin off him and sell it.

He was just about to quicken his pace, when a woman stepped out of the shadows and accosted Nevin. She had the look of a whore.

Patrick drew into the shadows, recognizing her as Nevin's sister, Annie O'Connor. There was a short conversation, one which ended when Nevin opened his wallet and handed over some notes.

'No more,' Nevin said. 'I've got to eat too, and I have my rent to pay.'

'You're earning plenty now, our Nevin. I bet you've got a whole heap of money tucked away in the bank. Pickings are light tonight. Everyone's frightened of this damned flu.'

'Get off home with you, Annie. Nobody asked you to go on the streets.'

'Had no choice did I? Not with a child to feed. Come on, our Nevin; you don't want her to go hungry, do you?'

Giving a sigh, Nevin withdrew another note from his wallet and handed it over. 'That's it. Don't bother me again. I've got my own life to lead.'

'That Erin Maguire has put grand ideas in your head, that she has. She's no better than me, and neither was her mother.'

'You shut your mouth about Erin. She's been good to me, when she had no reason to be, better than my own kin ever was, 'cepting my mother. Now, get about your business, and don't come back.'

'Got eyes for her, have you?' Annie sneered. 'She won't give you the time of day, you should know that. She always thought herself a cut above the rest of us, and has her sights set on something better than a Callacrea lad.' Stuffing the notes inside her pocket, she turned away. 'All right, I know where I'm not wanted. I'm going.'

As she came along the street towards Patrick, Nevin disappeared into a doorway. Patrick took note of it.

Waiting until Annie was level with him, he stepped out in front of her. She didn't recognize him straight up, but her hands went to her hips and her pelvis thrust forward in the time-honoured advertisement of her trade as she whined, 'After a woman are you, sir? I'm clean.'

Like hell she was! Her eyes widened when Patrick grabbed the front of her throat. She looked like hell, did Annie, and smelled worse. 'Hand over your money.'

Quick as a flash her fingers clawed at his hand and her knee came up to connect with his crotch. But he was ready for it. Catching under her knee with the other hand, he pushed against her neck, sending her sprawling backwards on to the cobbles.

Quickly he knelt on her stomach and slid the money from her sleeve. That done, he spat in her face, then stood up and walked away, leaving her spitting out obscenities at him.

From the darkened doorway, Nevin watched Annie pick herself up and straighten herself up. She was crying, taking big gulping sobs, so he thought his heart might break. She looked unwell, too, her face flushed and her voice husky, as though she was suffering a sore throat. She was his sister, after all. But Annie's path was set, and Nevin knew nothing would change her now.

The existence of the child bothered him a little. The poor little mite would probably be put to work in the same trade as her mother, and at an early age. He intended to talk to Erin about her, perhaps pay for the girl's schooling, so she could find useful employment when she grew up.

A man came down the lane, weaving drunkenly from side to side. Annie blew her nose on the hem of her skirt when she saw him, then went wearily into her stance. Soon, she was attached to his arm and leading him towards a dark doorway.

Nevin took off up the road. He had nothing left in his wallet to give her, and he didn't want Annie to know where he lived – or Patrick Maguire, someone he'd recognized straight away. He must warn Erin about him tomorrow. She might want to inform the authorities.

Annie went home in the early hours and gazed sourly at her daughter. The brat was a nuisance. She wished she was a bit older so she could make some money from her.

Annie's head was throbbing, her temperature soaring. The

man she'd been with had been rough, and had only paid her half of what she'd demanded.

The room Annie lived in was a hovel. Rats ran along the corridors and cockroaches up the walls.

For two days, while Annie shivered and shook, her daughter played quietly. She didn't cry. She'd been trained not to make a noise while her mother slept.

On the evening of the third day, Annie's laboured breathing ceased.

By that time the child was sick herself. She lay next to her mother's body, thirsty and weak, grizzling quietly to herself now and again and waiting for her mother to wake up.

They weren't missed for a few days. The authorities were called. A neighbour identified Nevin as Annie and her daughter's next of kin.

Fifteen

In June, Alicia Gregory died peacefully in her sleep. Jean Baily inherited her cousin's estate, except for the piano, which had been bequeathed to Erin. The estate consisted of the Imperial Mansions accommodation and an investment portfolio which provided an income.

'Blue chip,' Charles Colby told Jean when she asked for his advice. 'Hang on to it, and to the property if you can. After the war, accommodation such as yours will command high prices.'

'You must allow me to pay rent now,' Erin told her.

Jean laughed. 'Certainly not. I valued your help with Alicia, and you already contribute towards the services and food bill.'

Since Alicia's death Jean had begun to look a little younger, as if the release from the responsibility for her cousin's welfare had peeled ten years off her. Despite their age difference, she and Erin got on well together.

With Charles as a constant visitor, young Colby received plenty of attention, too.

Summer brought warmer weather, but no respite from the illness sweeping England. As the influenza epidemic worsened, people began to die in their thousands and the city was gripped by fear. Masks were being worn and chemicals were being sprayed in public places.

The audiences started to stay away from the theatres, and if they had to queue anywhere, they wore scarves over their noses and mouths, and no longer stopped to chat.

Some of the entertainers were afflicted by illness, the line of dancers shortened and the acts disappeared as rapidly from the stage as the audience from the queue.

'We'll be out of work soon,' one of the dancers grumbled

to the other, and there was a general atmosphere of gloom about the theatre.

Looking harassed, Chauncy called the cast together and confirmed the dancer's prediction. 'I'm sorry folks. I can't afford to operate on an empty house. I'm closing the theatre until this epidemic is over. I can afford to pay you up to the end of the week. Check back with me from time to time.'

Nevin and Erin gazed at each other, and shrugged. 'I can manage on my savings for a while. How about you, Nevin?' she asked.

Her partner mumbled an affirmative, lying, because he'd just had to pay for his sister's burial. Nevin had also been sending money to his family in America on a regular basis, since his mammy had written to say that his dad had injured his back and was now out of work.

He'd written to her, bragging a little, telling her of his success on the stage and, as he always had, he sent her money to help out. But she kept asking for more, even though he'd told her he was trying to save enough money to join them. He'd not told her about his partnership with Erin Maguire, though, or that Erin had kept him going through the lean times and had, in fact, been more of a mother to him than his own mother had ever been.

Yet Nevin was torn between the need to see his family and his loyalty to Erin, even though he knew she didn't need him. He wondered if he could manage without Erin's input. He could always play on the street again, but he wouldn't tell Erin, for she'd disapprove. They'd taken a step on the ladder to success. For her, the only way was up, not backwards.

'You watch out for Patrick Maguire,' he warned her. 'That money he took from Annie will have run out by now.'

She shuddered. 'I imagine he's long gone by now.'

Erin discussed the situation with her father, who was sympathetic. 'I have a cottage in the country we can use. Let's get out of London and go down there until the theatre opens again. I need a holiday, and Colby will love having a garden to play in. It will get us away from the influenza. We can stay there indefinitely if need be.'

'I'll let Nevin know where I am, in case he needs to talk to me.'

'You must give him the telephone number of the cottage.'
He scribbled it on the back of his card and handed it to her
before looking across at Jean. 'Perhaps you'd like to join us,
Mrs Baily. Unless you have something better to do?'

Jean went pink with pleasure of being an invited guest.

It was arranged that they'd leave on the following Saturday.
The day before, Erin went to the attic flat she'd once shared
with Nevin.

'He didn't come down for dinner last night, so I don't
think he's in,' Molly Evans, the landlord's wife, told her.

There was no answer to Erin's knock, but she thought she
could hear noises inside. Still having her key, Erin let herself
in. The sight of Nevin made her blood run cold. The bed
was moving as he shook with fever.

'Oh, God!' she whispered, experiencing the urge to turn
and run from this terrible infection. But Nevin had nobody
to care for him except her, so she'd have to stay.

With some urgency she shouted down to Molly, who came
scurrying from her room to stand in the gloomy hall at the
bottom of the stairs.

'Nevin's sick. He's caught the flu.'

The woman began to back away, her hand against her
mouth. 'I'm not going near him.'

'I'm not asking you to. I'll look after him. Have you got
a telephone?'

'No, but the priest from St Patrick's does, where Nevin
goes to mass on Sunday.'

The woman fetched a piece of paper and wrote down Jean
Baily's telephone number, and a message to be relayed to
her father.

> Take Colby and go to the country without me. I've been
> in contact with the influenza infection and don't want
> to pass it on to him. I intend to look after Nevin until
> he's better.

'Ask the doctor to visit when he can,' she told Molly, 'and
leave us some fresh water on the landing every day.'

The woman also took the precaution of having a man come
in and spray the house with disinfectant.

The doctor shook his head and drew Erin aside. 'The hospitals are crowded and I don't think he'll survive this with those weak lungs of his. He'll be better off being nursed here. All you can do is keep him as comfortable as possible and encourage him to take liquids. I'll call again tomorrow.'

So began Erin's vigil over the desperately ill Nevin, who hardly recognized her. All she could do was bathe his over-heated body, and try and spoon liquids into him, something he resisted by feverishly pushing her hand away.

'Don't you dare die on me, Nevin O'Connor,' she said fiercely, when he asked for a priest in his ramblings. But she sent for the priest anyway, who performed the Catholic rites required to ease Nevin's soul into heaven, should God call him.

After the door closed behind the priest, Nevin quieted. His eyes opened. The priest had brought about a miracle and Nevin will recover, Erin thought. She opened the letter the landlady had left on the stair for him. 'Here's a letter from your mammy. I'll read it to you.'

She'd been wrong. Although Nevin seemed to recognize her, his eyes were liquid with fever and the heat from his burning body reached out to her. His lips were blue-tinged, as if his lungs couldn't cope with the effort of breathing.

'Sing "Danny Boy" to me first, Erin,' he requested.

So she softly sang to him, and his eyes were far away and a faint smile appeared on his face. When the last note faded he closed his eyes and gave a bit of a sigh, saying so wearily that she could hardly hear him, 'Sure, but Ireland's a pretty sight, so green and misty. Remember when we were children and—'

And that was the ending to Nevin O'Connor's short life, the memory he'd wanted to share, left unsaid.

Anger filled her and she said out loud to God, 'Would it have hurt to have given him another second or two so he could have shared it with me?'

The doctor came, looking weary, to confirm the absence of life. 'I'll send someone to pick his body up. Do you have the money to give him a decent burial, or will I leave it to the parish?'

'I'll pay for it.'

'Are you a relative? I'll need someone to fill out the forms.'

'I'm a friend from childhood. Nevin was like a brother to me, and was part of our theatre act. His folks are in America. I can do the forms and inform them of his death.'

The doctor nodded and took out the necessary forms.

After he'd gone, Erin opened the letter from Nevin's mother.

Dear Son,

Life is terribly hard here in America. Your father has gone away to look for work, but we haven't heard from him for several weeks.

Although I miss you something awful, son, please don't come here. We haven't got room for you. We all live in the one room, and can barely afford enough to eat.

As for our Annie's death. She was no longer a daughter of ours. The girl got what she deserved, for she brought shame down on the family, that she did.

It was terrible news our Liam dying in the war. Would you get in touch with the army and see if he was owed any wages. If so, send them on as soon as possible. Thank you for the money. You're a loyal son. I pray to God on my knees every day that you keep well and keep sending it, as we're sorely in need.

From your loving Mammy.

Erin's eyes filled with tears. Poor, dear Nevin had been supporting his family. No wonder he'd never had any money to spare.

He looked so peaceful now. She washed and dressed him, so when the undertaker came for his body he'd be in his best clothes, with his hands clutching the bowler hat he'd been so proud of.

'You look like a proper gent,' she said, and kissed his cheek before the undertaker screwed the lid shut.

He was buried like that, a simple headstone ordered with birth and death dates, too short a span for such a fine lad. She had inscribed on it, *Nevin O'Connor. Violinist.* She had also asked the stonemason to chip a shamrock into the stone.

Afterwards, Erin wrote to Nevin's mother, informing her of her son's death and sending her some money. She told him she'd sold Nevin's violin to pay for his burial. It was a lie though, she couldn't bear to part with the battered old thing. She signed the letter 'Chauncy Green, care of the Empire Theatre', knowing Chauncy wouldn't object when she told him.

Erin returned to Imperial Mansions and allowed herself the luxury of copious tears while she mourned for her friend and partner. But she knew it wouldn't bring Nevin back, or the thousands of other who were dying. She spent the next month in self-imposed quarantine, except for necessary outings, just in case she'd picked up the infection. She didn't want to pass it on to anybody.

She then telephoned her father, eager for news of her son.

Jean Baily answered, laughing when she said, 'Colby's well. He's in the garden with Charles, *helping* him weed the borders. The pair of them adore each other. Catherine's coming down next week. Charles is sending the car up for them.'

Jean was calling her father by his first name, Erin thought and grinned, wondering if their relationship was growing into something more.

But Jean was still speaking. 'Dorothea Sanders has wed Lord Templeton, and they've gone to his country estate to escape the influenza outbreak. No doubt she'll soon get bored and return to the city. Your father has been dreadfully worried about you, though.'

'I spoke to him just a week ago, to say I was all right.'

'Why don't you come down with Catherine . . . surprise him? The weather is perfect. You'll love it here, and the rest will do you good before you have to go back to work.'

'Who's that on the phone?' she heard her father's voice in the background say.

'Just the butcher.'

'Oh, I though it might be Erin. Let me know if she calls, and ask the butcher if he's got any of those delicious pork sausages we had last week.'

'I most certainly will.' Jean gave a soft chuckle, saying, 'You will be able to deliver on Saturday, won't you? It's for Mr Colby's birthday dinner.'

197

Erin smiled at that. There was something special about having a father who cared about you, even though it had come late in her life . . . and it was his birthday. When better to surprise him? 'I most certainly will.'

Erin had only seen Catherine once since the backstage party. She looked smart in a blue gown with a little fur cape set about her shoulders.

They smiled at each other as Jonathan placed Erin's luggage in the car. Then the girls hugged. 'You look wonderful,' Erin whispered against her ear. 'Being engaged suits you.'

Catherine blushed. 'You don't think he's too old for me, do you?'

The man was handsome, but his greying hair placed him in his late forties. Erin frowned. 'What's more important is, do *you* think he's too old?'

Catherine shrugged. 'Sometimes. Jonathan's very nice, though. Mother thinks he's a good catch since he's very clever. He's taken over management of the firm. Eventually, it will belong to me, so if we're married it will make things easier.'

And more convenient for Jonathan, Erin couldn't help thinking.

The kiss Jonathan planted on Catherine's forehead was brief and passionless before he settled her into the car. When he turned to Erin there was something else in his eyes. His mouth brushed over her hand and he caught her eye as he straightened, saying quietly, so Catherine couldn't hear, 'Perhaps we could have dinner together, sometime?'

'I don't think that would be a good idea,' she said and joined Catherine.

In the mirror, she saw Jonathan staring after the car as it drove away, a frown between his brow. He wasn't a man who liked to be turned down, she thought.

Catherine turned to her and laughed. 'The last time we were together in a car, you were driving.'

'If you can call it that, for the car was all over the road, and you were throwing your leg braces at Patrick Maguire. Didn't they give him a good clout, though?'

'Mr Flatterly sent Kell's car home, you know. It's in the garage. Mother wants rid of it. But Uncle Charles has told her she can't get rid of anything, because the company and property became Kell's after Father died. Mother and I were left some money, of course.'

Erin's heart flared into life at the mention of Kell's name and, although the thought caused her much pain, she said, 'Kell is dead, Catherine.'

'Not officially. They say we have to wait until the war is over and all the men accounted for, to be certain. I miss him so much. He was my rock. I could always lean on him when I was unsure of myself.'

Erin gave her a hug. 'You can lean on me instead.'

'There's something I want to ask you, Erin.'

Sensing what it was, Erin slid her a glance. 'You've heard about my son, haven't you?'

'Then it's true?'

When Erin nodded, Catherine fell quiet.

'There's a sour look on your face. What are you thinking?'

'I'm disappointed. You see, I always looked up to you.'

'Even though I was the bastard of Callacrea?'

Catherine winced. 'I never held that against you, and now I know the circumstances it doesn't seem to matter, anyway. After all, it's Uncle Charles we're talking about.'

'No doubt he got me on my mother the same way any other man would have. Does knowing I have Charles Colby for a father make a difference to how you feel about my background?'

'He loved your mother, you see, and would have married her if he'd been free.'

'What if he hadn't loved her? What if she'd loved him, and he'd just used her? Would that have made me less in your eyes?'

'Don't, Erin. I can't bear to think of it.'

'Then you shouldn't have started it. You're condemning me along with my child, and without even knowing the circumstances. My son is my heartbeat. I'd die for him.'

'If Uncle Charles accepts him, then so do I.'

'Do you indeed? That's terribly patronizing. Did anyone ever tell you that you're a bloody snob?'

Catherine looked affronted at first, then wounded. 'No . . . no, they didn't. I'm not, am I?'

'Sure, you are. And a hypocrite, as well, because you say one thing to my face and mean something else.'

'You're supposed to be my friend, Erin.'

'I was your maid. Because I rescued you, it doesn't mean I'm your friend, *Miss Catherine*. I'd have rescued a dog under the same circumstances. Friends support each other. They stick together through thick and thin, defend and protect each other. They don't call each other names. My partner, Nevin O'Connor, was my best friend. It was the worst thing in the world when I lost him.'

'I suppose Nevin was the father of your child. I apologize. I'm sorry.'

'He certainly was not,' Erin said angrily. 'You can keep your apology. It's none of your damned business, anyway. Don't talk to me for the rest of the way.' Folding her arms, Erin moved to the opposite side of the car and stared fiery-eyed out of the window, unable to remember when her dander had been raised so much.

There was silence for a while, then Catherine said in a snuffly sort of way, 'You don't have to go all fierce on me. I'm sorry, Erin. Don't let's quarrel.'

'We've already quarrelled. Don't think your tears will move me, and I've asked you not to talk to me.'

Catherine sniffed. 'I wouldn't dream of talking to you now you're being so mean. I haven't got a handkerchief on me though, and my nose is dripping on to my fur.'

Remembering a fox she'd seen as a child, Erin scolded, 'I expect that mangy fox skin was trotting around Callacrea having a grand old time before somebody put a bullet through its head.'

'I doubt it. It's mink. Minks don't trot, they slink like weasels.'

Handing over her handkerchief, Erin grinned at Catherine. 'Since when did you learn to stand up for yourself, clever britches?'

When a muffled giggle came from the other side of the car, Erin hit Catherine with a cushion and began to sing. '*There's a tear in your eye—*'

'—*And I'm wondering why,*' Catherine sang in return.

Soon, they were singing at the top of their voices, and the chauffeur joined in on the chorus in a gruff baritone. 'Irish Eyes' had never been rendered in so sprightly a manner.

The singing continued as they cleared the outskirts of London. It was a glorious day, the sky bluer than Erin had seen it for a long time. The car purred through a summer landscape; the breeze shook the canopy of summer leaves. The fields were worked into a summer patchwork quilt. Wheat made patterns of ripe undulating gold. Poppies flamed. Primroses, marigolds and dandelions dotted the meadows with yellows, and the whole blurred into a glorious riot of colour as they raced past.

Erin hadn't set foot outside of London since she'd first arrived there. Used to the streets, the alleys and the buildings embracing each other in the smoky air, the countryside came as a delightful surprise.

They stopped for a picnic lunch in the New Forest, pulling off the road and setting a little table. There was cold chicken, asparagus and tomatoes, with crusty rolls and crisp red apples.

They were just finishing their wine when some small ponies appeared and wandered towards them.

'You wouldn't think there was a war on,' Erin said. 'This seems a world away.'

Her palm flattened, Catherine fed the core of her apple to a whiskery pony. 'They say it will be over by Christmas.'

'I hope someone will think it was worth the loss of life.'

Erin had begun to pack things back into the picnic basket when Catherine put an arm round her. 'Nothing will be worth the loss of Kell.'

'No, nothing will be worth that. They gave him a white feather, you know.'

'Who did?'

'Some women outside the theatre Kell took me to in Dublin. They were demonstrating, and one told him he was a coward for not being in the army. They gave him a white feather and he signed up. I wonder how many other young men those women sent to their deaths.'

Catherine's eyes searched her face. 'How did Kell react to being given a white feather?'

'He was surprised at first, I think, that anyone would have thought him a coward. He signed up straight away. There was a sweet sadness about him, but also resignation, as if he was determined to do his duty and was trying hard to be brave.'

A picture of Kell, his hair tossed by the wind, his dark eyes alight with laughter, came instantly to Erin's mind. She closed her eyes, hanging on to the memory for a second, seeing him through the eyes of a sixteen-year-old girl on the brink of womanhood – one who'd always adored him.

'He looked so proud in his uniform,' Erin continued. 'He had his photo taken and asked the photographer to send me a copy. He would have sent one to your parents, as well.'

'It was probably destroyed in the fire. I'd love one for myself, do you still have it?'

Erin knew she'd never part with it, but would keep it for Colby. 'I imagine the photographer in Dublin would be able to supply you with a copy.'

'Oh, how simple. Why didn't I think of it? Kell would have used our usual photographer, I imagine. I shall ring Mr Flatterly and ask him to make enquiries. Did I mention that Olivia Winslow's fiancé lost his life? He had only been in the flying corps for five weeks when his plane was hit by machine-gun fire. It crashed and burst into flames. They got him out, but he only lived for a few days. A blessing really, Olivia said, though she was terribly upset. She said it's the last time she'll become involved with someone young enough to go off and fight, and will look for someone older.'

While Catherine prattled on about her war work, Erin gazed out of the window at the countryside.

If Kell came home now he'd be a different man than the one who had departed, changed by his experiences, she thought. She could only imagine what those experiences had been. She was different herself now, more adult, less naïve.

'War would have changed Kell, you know?' she said absent-mindedly.

'Yes. There's something sad about returned soldiers, isn't there?'

'Yes. Their eyes are hollow and inward looking. It's as if they're seeing their souls for the first time, and are shocked because they've found something they don't quite like in themselves, but can't come to terms with it.'

Tears filled Catherine's eyes. 'I'd rather remember my brother as he was, I think. It would be awful if he came home badly maimed, or burnt, like Olivia Winslow's fiancé.'

'Is that more awful than being dead, I wonder. He'd still be the same Kell inside.'

'You know very well I didn't mean that.'

'I know.'

They walked silently back to the car together. As they settled themselves, Catherine said in a small voice, 'I'm selfish to think only of my own feelings.'

'You've always been one to avoid facing unpleasant truths.'

Catherine's mouth pulled into a wry line. 'If you've got any more faults to point out, do let me hear them now.'

'Perhaps we should examine why you're engaged to Jonathan Granger, a man more than twice your age. Do you love him?'

Sweetly, Catherine countered with, 'Will you tell me the circumstances of your son's birth if I answer your question? It's infuriating being kept in the dark – as if you don't trust me.'

Giving a faint smile, Erin nodded.

'Well then, I do love Jonathan, in my own way. He's a good friend to me. He's the only person who makes me feel as though I exist, except for you and Uncle Charles. I can relax in his company. He looks after me and holds an important position in the company. I'm quite pleased that he considers me a suitable stepmother for his daughter, too. And my mother approves of him. Being engaged to Jonathan stops her pressuring me to find a suitable man and settle down.'

'In other words, he's a substitute for your father. You'll be acting like a middle-aged woman the week after you marry him.'

Her eyes flew open. 'That's a perfectly horrid suggestion to make.'

Erin shrugged. 'Your Jonathan asked me out to dinner after he put you into the car.'

'He was just being kind. I expect he was going to turn it into some surprise for me.'

'He was being an opportunist. There are dozens of men like him hanging around the stage door, most of them married. You deserve better than him, Catherine.'

'You're hardly in a position to advise me about marriage, Erin. Oh, why do we keep arguing? There, I've told you what you wanted to know. Now . . . I believe you were going to tell me who fathered your child?'

Erin stared at the back of the chauffeur's head, trying not to smile. 'No, Catherine, you only wanted to know the circumstances of his birth.'

She ignored Catherine's black look, knowing that the identity of Colby's father would soon be revealed to Catherine, for they'd just crossed the border into Dorset.

'The simple truth is I fell in love with a man who went off to war. I received news that he'd died. Colby is the result of that love.'

'What about his family?'

'His mother didn't want to know about it.'

'How dreadful of her. Did the man know he had a child?'

Erin shook her head. 'I wish he had, since Colby looks so much like him. I know he would have been proud of his son. Now, can we talk about something else?'

Catherine squeezed her hand. 'You're quite sure you can't bring yourself to trust me with his name?'

Catherine's face was so earnest that Erin was hard put not to laugh. When she set eyes on Colby, her reaction was going to be interesting.

'Let's sing something again, shall we?' she said, and soon the car was filled with the sound of voices again.

They were laughing as they pulled up in front of a large thatched cottage with a garden full of flowery delights, and a porch rambled all over by fragrant white and red roses.

How pretty it was, how fresh and clean the air smelled. And how quiet it was, except for the drone of bees and the sound of a child's laughter.

'Colby,' she whispered and was out the car and hurrying to the back garden, where the sound had come from. She stood still at the sight of the man and the child, absorbing the scene. Kell's old dog, Wolf, lay on his side in the sun.

Her father had given him a home. His tail flopped up and down in greeting and he gave a small huff.

Her father turned to her, and smiled before stooping to speak to Colby.

Colby's eyes shone brightly, and his mouth curved joyfully when he saw her. 'Mamma,' he whispered, then louder into a scream of delight, 'Mamma!' and he came running over the lawn to be scooped up into her arms, hugged tightly and covered in her kisses.

She inhaled his baby smell and her lips caressed the soft curves of his cheeks. The few weeks they'd been apart seemed like months. 'I've missed you so much, you little wretch.'

There was intake of breath when she turned to face her friend. 'Meet my son, Colby. Does this answer your question?'

'Kell,' Catherine whispered. 'He looks like Kell . . . he's Kell's son, isn't he?'

Erin nodded and said, 'Are you still disappointed in me?' Catherine burst into tears. 'Oh, Erin,' she said when she'd recovered. 'How perfectly lovely the world is, sometimes.'

Sixteen

Erin revelled in the summer spent with her father. The days were long and lazy, the company perfect, and she found herself enjoying the privileged life she'd once envied.

Once Catherine had got over her shock about Colby, she found great pleasure in the company of her nephew and took countless photographs of him. She plied Erin with questions about Kell. 'When did you fall in love with my brother?' she asked.

'The first moment I met him, I think. Though I didn't know it at the time.'

'Was that when my mother was playing lady of the manor and we dropped in for tea? She hated doing those duty visits.'

'And we hated being on the receiving end. My mother said I had to be on my best behaviour. The cake she baked took our whole week's supply of flour. Not only that. The seam had split under the armpit of my dress and I was frightened to lift my arm up in the air in case someone noticed it.'

'Would it of mattered if we had?'

'Of course. I was conscious of the fact that we were poor. It would have brought shame down on my mammy's head if somebody had mentioned it and considered her a bad mother.'

Catherine began to laugh. 'Over a split seam? That's ridiculous.'

'Is it? After she died I found her purse. There was a halfpenny in it. I kept it, to remind myself of what poverty was like. Kell was with me that day . . . he didn't laugh.'

The laughter died abruptly, and it was as if the brightness had fled from the room. Catherine said, 'I'm sorry, Erin. I didn't think.'

Erin gave her friend a hug, wishing she could take back what she'd just said. 'It's me who should be sorry. It's not your fault we were poor, and I shouldn't be pricking your conscience about it.'

'No, you shouldn't. I'm not going to apologize for the life I was born into. My father gave generously to charity, and he provided paid employment for many people. When you were in need he gave you a job and a roof over your head. Have you ever wondered what would have happened to you if he hadn't?'

'Many times. I expect I would have ended up starving on the streets of Dublin.'

Catherine stared down at her hands. 'Uncle Charles would never have allowed that to happen, you know. I overheard him talking to my father, and he asked that you be kept on in Callacrea House, when the other servants were being laid off. And he insisted that the cook be kept on to keep you company, because she had nowhere else to go. He told Father that he'd pay your salaries, though I didn't know why at the time.'

'Didn't you think it odd?'

'No, because Uncle Charles is a dear, who wouldn't say a bad word about anyone. He cared about people and hated to see anyone hurt.'

Erin gazed out into the garden, where her father was sprawled on the grass. Colby was crawling all over him, trying to snatch his hat off of his head. How lovely a man he was, and how she wished he'd brought her up.

Jean Baily, dressed in a lacy blouse and plain blue skirt, was seated in a chair nearby. There was a book open in her hands but she wasn't reading it, just watching the two romping males with a smile on her face.

Love for them all welled up in her and warmed her heart. 'This is the best summer I've ever spent. I've been so lucky, and I'm thankful for that. And for you as a friend, dear Catherine.'

The sun was slanting through the window on to an occasional table. Erin rose to her feet as the clock chimed three. 'I'll prepare the tea tray.'

Catherine picked up the camera she'd brought with her,

pulling open the front to reveal the concertinaed interior. 'I rather want to take some photographs to put in my album. Stand by the window, Erin, so the light's on your face. Take one of those flowers from the vase and hold it to your nose.'

Erin laughed as she did as she was told, slanting her eyes towards Catherine. The sudden flash startled her.

Smiling happily, Catherine said, 'That was a good shot. I'm going to develop these myself when I get back to London. I'm taking lessons from a real photographer. I'm going to record our lives.'

Erin's eyes fell reflectively on Colby and she murmured, 'While the promise of what might have been is still burning bright in us. Do memories retain their clarity when we've grown old, do you think? Do they mock us with their eternal youthfulness?'

Catherine laid a hand over Erin's. 'You'll always remember Kell, you have part of him in Colby.'

Erin smiled as Colby gazed at his grandfather with a big grin. He'd managed to get the hat, and was in the process of fitting it on his own head. When it fell down over his eyes, nose and mouth, he began to giggle. There was an air of expectation about him.

'Boo!' her father said, lifting the brim up, and Colby staggered backward and fell over, laughing uproariously.

'I'm beginning to think the pair of them are children instead of a generation apart,' Erin said laughing. 'Yes, I do have part of Kell in Colby, and my son is more than a promise. Thank you for helping me put things in perspective, Catherine. You should consider taking up photography as a career.'

Summer became a glorious autumn. The trees were alive with colour and the fallen leaves crunched underfoot. They gathered chestnuts and roasted them in the embers of the fire.

In October they celebrated Erin's birthday with cake and champagne. After Jean lit the nineteen candles, Charles rapped on the table with a spoon. His eyes were shining, his voice low with the emotion he felt, as he lifted his glass.

'To my daughter, Erin, who has brought love and laughter into my life. I wish you success in your endeavours, and a life filled with joy.'

Tears choked Erin's throat.

'Blow the candles out and make a wish, my dear,' he said. So she did, her silently expressed first wish a plea for something she couldn't possibly have. Then she said, 'I've come a long way from Callacrea. It would be a waste of a wish if I asked for the support and friendship of the people who are nearest and dearest to me, for I already have it.' She gazed around at them, her heart so full the words found it difficult to launch themselves from her mouth. 'I'll wish for this dreadful war to end soon, so sons and fathers can return home to be reunited with their loved ones . . . if not in body, then in spirit. And I wish you weren't returning to London, Catherine. It's been lovely seeing you.'

'I can't say I'm looking forward to rattling around in that empty house by myself again. It's full of ghosts.'

'You could move into Imperial Mansions if you wanted to,' Jean said. 'We have room for another.'

Catherine grinned at them both. 'That would be wonderful.'

Much as she'd loved being in the country, Catherine had her war work to do. She was enjoying the contact with the public, though the flu epidemic had scared many of the other women away. The lines at the soup kitchen had lengthened too.

The gaunt, strained faces of the women and children, the plight of the soldiers, back from the war, wounded and unable to find employment, bothered her. She recorded it all as best she could with her camera. Catherine had never experienced poverty, and probably never would, but she now knew what it did to people and was pleased for Erin that she'd been able to rise above it and earn a living from her wonderful talent.

She had left a key to the family house with Jonathan, so he could check on the mail. Not that she was expecting any herself, but the house bills came regularly and were dealt with by Jonathan in her mother's absence – though she doubted if the new Lady Templeton would ever move back in.

She was dropped off at the house late in the afternoon, the day after Erin's birthday. Placing her bag in the hall, she hurried to the local grocer's to purchase some essential items, intending to have an omelette for supper.

Catherine had just returned, and she smiled when she spotted Jonathan's briefcase in the hall. She was about to call out his name out when she heard Olivia Winslow's voice.

'I thought I heard a noise. What if Catherine has come back from the country early?'

Catherine's eyes flew open when Jonathan answered her. 'Don't be a silly goose. Catherine's the dependant type, she doesn't do anything without telephoning me first.'

'You will tell her about us soon, won't you?'

'Of course, as soon as I hear about that position with your father's firm.'

Olivia gave a heartfelt groan. 'You know, I hate deceiving poor Catherine. She's so trusting and sweet, like a puppy dog.'

Catherine's cheeks began to burn.

'So do I, darling, but she adores me, and will be terribly hurt.'

She strangled a laugh. So, she adored him, did she? 'Past tense, Jonathan,' she muttered.

'But, darling, if this was all brought out into the open and we were engaged to be married, the job would be yours. You should have proposed to me in the first place.'

'How could I when you were engaged to that flyer chap? Your father won't be home from the country for another month. We'll tell people then, otherwise I'd lose the position I've got in the meantime. Being dismissed would go against me. Dorothea's a vindictive woman when she can't get her own way.'

'But why should she dismiss you?'

'She doesn't think Catherine will attract a husband, and wants the girl off her hands. I had a pressing gambling debt to pay, and she gave me the money to clear the debt. The arrangement was that I get a further amount when Catherine and I are married. Dorothea will demand the money back when she finds out, and now I'm in no position to repay it.'

Catherine's cheeks flamed. How dare her mother do such a horrible thing to her. And to think she'd defended Jonathan to Erin. But Olivia was speaking again and Catherine felt no guilt about eavesdropping on the conversation.

'Let her ask for it back, then. I've got more money than we'll ever need. I can pay all your debts.'

'Darling, that's generous of you. I'll think about it, if it will help solve the problem of our relationship. In the meantime, come to bed. I can spare an hour, but want to get home to have dinner with Sabrina. She's been difficult since I mentioned sending her to boarding school.'

Catherine was surprised to discover that she wasn't all that upset by what was going on between the pair. She was more distressed that she was being deceived. In fact, she felt a sense of relief.

She opened her mother's bureau. Pulling out a piece of paper she wrote Jonathan a letter, reminding him she was a director of the company he worked for. She requested he leave the house key on the hall table, and suggested he tendered his resignation in writing – further, that he appoint his second-in-command to the manager's chair before he worked out his notice, because she'd hate to embarrass him by being forced to do it for him.

When sighs and cries of pleasure reached her ears she felt a bit guilty about not revealing her presence in the first place. She was furious to think that Jonathan would take advantage of their relationship and his position in the company. But to use her home to pleasure himself and his woman was disgusting as far as she was concerned.

Gathering up her bag, Catherine let herself out and slammed the door behind her. Snatching the engagement ring from her finger, she dropped it down the nearest drain.

Erin's birthday wish came true a month later.

At eleven a.m. on the eleventh day of November, in the Forest of Compiègne, an armistice had just been signed. On the battlefield the mouths of the guns ceased their thunder, and there was an unnerving silence. A steady stream of soldiers started making their way towards the French ports.

In the prison camp, Kell was suddenly jerked out of sleep by his arm being shaken.

'What's going on?' he said, his voice sounding loud in the face of the silence all around them. 'Why has it gone quiet?'

The soldier who'd shaken him had a huge grin on his face. 'The war's over, sir. We have to make our way to headquarters.'

'The hell it is?' Kell didn't know whether to laugh or cry. Luck had been on his side. He had received good treatment in the hospital and was whole again. He felt strange, as if the war had turned him into someone different. The first thing that came into his head was the thought of soaking in a warm bath. He smiled then. What an exquisite luxury that would be.

Cheering had broken out. As his fellow prisoners surrounded him, he fished in his pack and brought out a half bottle of brandy one of his captors had given him for his birthday.

He took a swig of the fiery liquid, then handed the bottle to one of his companions. 'Here, share this between you. I was saving it for Christmas, but there's a better reason to celebrate now, it seems. You've earned it.'

Because Kell was long-serving, and had an essential business he needed to get back to, he was lucky enough to be one of the first to be handed his ticket home.

He spent the next two months in a chateau, celebrating Christmas there with a prayer service, where the chaplain gave thanks for their survival.

Kell remembered Danny Robinson, and he shed some tears for the brave lad. What a bloody waste of life! He indulged in a moment of anger and, although he was thankful he'd been spared, he couldn't help but think: Why him and not me?

He could find no answer to the question.

He built up his health as best he could, but food was still scarce and his body was covered in sores. The tension of the past couple of years was still coiled tightly inside him and he didn't know how to release it. Kell thought he might spring apart if he let it go, and disintegrate into a thousand scattered pieces.

He'd seen hundreds of men suffering from the war, their eyes staring, bodies jerking and muttering to themselves. Shell-shock they called it, though some called it cowardice. The thought of losing control scared him. Sometimes, he was so tired he could barely keep his eyes open, but his sleep was beset by dreams that jerked him awake.

Kell composed a letter to his mother and Catherine, telling them he'd be home in February. In London, his letters joined several others on the hall floor.

There was a crowd waiting when the ship docked. People hugged each other all around him. Wives and children reunited with their husbands and fathers. . . and sweethearts. He remembered Erin Maguire, her eyes so blue and pretty, and her hair a fall of midnight. He wished she was there to hug him tight.

But why should she be? he thought, shouldering his way through the crowd after searching in vain for a sight of his sister and mother. Three years was a long time.

He sighed, perhaps his letters hadn't arrived. Services were uncertain as countries struggled to gain some normality. They would be for some time to come, he expected. He gave a faint smile as he thought of the surprise he'd give them.

But nobody answered his knock at the door, and the place had an air of neglect about it. Going round to the back he forced open the kitchen window and climbed inside. He directed his voice into the emptiness. 'Catherine? Mother?'

Dust sheets covered the furniture. The clocks had stopped. Letters were scattered across the hall rug, including his own. He picked them up, placed them on the table. The stairs creaked under his tread.

Kell's room was familiar. His shaving mug, brush and comb were laid neatly by the mirror, his pyjamas were folded on the chair. A photograph that Catherine had taken at Callacrea House stood on the dresser. He was sitting on the step, laughing. The frame was draped with black fabric.

Something hit him in the guts as he gazed at it. Running downstairs, he opened the writing bureau his mother usually used. He found the official letter straight away, filed neatly.

He began to laugh, and laughed until tears began to course down his cheeks. 'I'm dead,' he shouted out. 'I'm bloody dead, and nobody thought to tell me.'

He went to the telephone and jiggled the rest up and down. That was dead too. For a moment, Kell was tempted to go to the office. But he was too tired and too dirty, and he was hungry.

Turning on the gas, he lit the pilot light and began to fill the bath. The fire was already laid in the study. He put a match to that, too.

His investigation of the larder yielded a tin of caviar, some plain biscuits and a tin of peas. He ate all three without tasting them and when the kettle boiled he made some tea. Although it was stale, it tasted good with condensed milk to add to it.

Later, he lay up to his chin in water, as hot as his body could stand. Steam filled the air and rivulets ran down the walls. When he was clean, Kell put on his pyjamas, then went to his bedroom. The bed wasn't made, and the room was cold. It had began to drizzle outside.

He went to Catherine's room, feminine with its lacy curtains and flowered bedspread. At least it had sheets and a thick eiderdown. Crawling under them he curled up on his side – and found himself facing a photograph in a frame on the bedside table. It was one of himself when he'd been a toddler. He was sitting on the grass with his Uncle Charles, with the Dorset cottage in the background. He'd never seen it before.

There was something odd about the photograph, but he couldn't quite think what.

When he woke up the next morning he knew exactly what was wrong with it. Charles had only bought the cottage ten years previously, intending to do it up in time for his retirement. He reached out, picked the photograph up and brought it closer. Charles Colby looked to be the same age as when Kell had last seen him. The photograph was recent.

There was a woman's shadow on the grass. So who did the child belong to? Had Catherine married? Surely not, she'd only been seventeen when he'd left. He frowned. Catherine was old enough to have a child and the family resemblance was strong. His mother? Kell smiled at the thought. She'd hate having a child to look after at her age, and he wasn't quite sure if it would be possible anyway, since she must be nearing fifty.

He placed the frame back on the table. He felt stronger now he'd had a good rest. He rose, took another leisurely bath, treated his sores with the Vinolin creme he found in the bathroom cupboard, then shaved the whiskers from his chin. He threw open his wardrobe. Thank goodness his clothes hadn't been thrown away, though they hung on him now.

He found some oats and made a porridge of sorts with boiling water and the condensed milk. Not knowing quite what to do with himself, he decided to go to the office.

The office and showroom of the Sanders' Gas Appliance Company was a good walk. The streets and pavements were wet from the rain and there wasn't much traffic. The place was locked. As he ambled back home he passed a church. Hymns were being sung. He felt disorientated. It must be Sunday.

Charles Colby's door opened a crack to his knock. A woman he'd never seen before gazed at him. 'Mr Colby has gone to the country for a week. Can I take a message, sir?'

'Yes . . . if you would. Just tell him that Kell Sanders called.'

'Yes, sir.'

The smell of something cooking wafted out to him. Kell's mouth watered. 'You couldn't spare something to eat, I suppose.'

The woman's eyes widened and the door began to close.

'I'm not a beggar, Charles Colby is my uncle,' he shouted against the panel. But the door remained closed against him.

Erin was rehearsing. The Empire Theatre was to open with a spring revue in April. The show was named, *Our Brave Gentlemen (A tribute to our heroes)*.

Chauncy was tearing his hair out, as he always did in the lead up to a new show. 'I can't find a fiddler to replace Nevin.'

'There will never be another Nevin and I don't want anyone else. I can play my harp, and the orchestra can do the rest.'

'But you were billed as The Shamrocks.'

'The new playbills haven't been printed yet, have they? Change it to The Shamrock.'

'That sounds daft. What about The Irish Shamrock?'

She grinned and teased, 'Sure, but doesn't everyone knows the shamrock is as Irish as Mulligan stew.' Erin remembered something Kell had said to the shop assistant in Dublin all those years ago. 'I'd rather be a bird than a shamrock. What about The Irish Nightingale?'

'The Irish Nightingale, it is then.' He took her face between her hands and kissed her forehead. 'It's good to see you again, luvvy. I hear you turned down an offer from the Gaiety.'

'I'd rather work for the devil I know than the devil I don't know. You gave Nevin and me a chance when we were down. Now you need me, and I'm glad to repay that debt.'

'You could become famous at the Gaiety, Erin.'

'And wouldn't that be grand, if fame was what I was after. I just want to sing on the stage, that's all.' She laughed. 'I think I enjoy showing off.'

'You know how much depends on the opening show, don't you, sweetheart? I've sunk everything I've got into it. The new costumes cost a fortune. If it fails you'll be out of work again.'

She smiled. 'Now don't you be getting yourself heart-scalded in advance. The show will be a success, and I'll be asking you for a raise afterwards.'

They watched a row of girls come on stage. Dressed in red soldier's uniforms, they wore short tartan kilts and caps with a feather.

A drummer offstage began to rat-a-tat, the dancers to tap their feet in perfect unison. Then the wail of the bagpipes came from the orchestra pit. The sound of feet tapping grew softer and the girls assumed a pose when an awkward-looking, gravelly-voiced baritone with fierce eyes and flaming red hair walked on stage and began to sing 'Scotland the Brave'.

'He can't sing very well,' she whispered. 'What's his name?'

'Red MacDonald,' Chauncy answered. 'He's the under-study to the real singer and is just learning the routine. I doubt if we'll need to use him.'

It was a good routine, despite the Scotsman's voice. The revue was coming together beautifully. Chauncy had a winner on his hands as far as she could see.

Usually, her father's car would pick her up and deliver her home. But he and Jean had taken Colby with them to the country for a week.

'I'll be all right,' she'd told them. 'Patrick Maguire will be long gone by now.'

But Patrick was not long gone. He was living off the earnings of a prostitute, housed not far from the theatre.

When Erin left the theatre for home that night her mind was full of the coming show, so her normal caution was abandoned. Patrick slid out of the shadows of a doorway and followed after her.

He caught up with her just before she turned into a brightly lit street and dragged her into an alley that ran down behind a row of shops, a hand clasped over her mouth.

'When I let you go, if you scream, I'll shoot you,' he warned. 'Do you understand?'

When she nodded he released her, but she was backed into a corner and couldn't escape. The pistol he held filled her with dread. Patrick would use it, she had no doubt – and he'd use it as soon as he got what he wanted from her. She was in great peril.

'I need money. I have to get away to America, the polis have got wind of me.'

'I haven't got much. The theatre has been closed. Nevin died of the flu and I had to use my savings to bury him.'

Snatching her bag he began to rifle through it. While he was distracted, Erin pushed him backwards and began to run. A shot whistled over her head. As she turned into the street she gave a sigh of relief when she saw a bus coming. She made it to the stop on time and scrambled on to the platform, as Patrick came into the street and began to make a run for the bus. She shouted to the clippie, 'Quick, get moving, that man attacked me and has stolen my bag. He has a gun.'

The bus took off with mind-numbing slowness, its engine rumbling like an old tractor. Patrick gained on them for a while, but he seemed to run out of wind and dropped back.

'Thank you, you saved my life,' Erin said to the clippie, trembling all over as she was dropped off at the end of her street. The bus was about to go off in the opposite direction.

'Make sure you phone the police, dearie,' the clippie shouted, as the bus juddered off. 'Scum like him should be locked up and the key thrown away.'

Locked up? Erin recalled the words after Catherine had let her into the flat and she'd told her friend of her lucky escape. Erin paled as fear stabbed at her. She whispered,

217

'The keys to this place are in my bag, and so is the address. What if he comes here after us?'

Catherine looked as though she might be sick. 'You'd better ring the police right now, and tell them what happened. They might send somebody over to protect us.'

'You do it, Catherine. I can't stop shaking.'

Within half an hour Erin was being interviewed by a constable and another man. Catherine made them some coffee.

The second man, of medium build, neatly dressed and well-spoken, introduced himself as Andrew Jameison. The constable wrote down Erin's statement.

'Are you a detective from New Scotland Yard?' Catherine asked.

His eyes came up to hers, an astute grey. 'I am.'

'Well, I do hope you catch Patrick Maguire, soon. He was an accessory to the murder of my father. I think he'll murder us too if he can, since he has a gun. We were witnesses to the crime, you see.'

Andrew Jameison looked sympathetic. 'I know. I assure you, we're doing our very best to catch him. We knew he was in London and we have somebody working on it. I'll leave the constable here for tonight so you feel safer, though I doubt if Maguire will risk coming here.'

'That's what we thought at Callacrea House,' Erin said soberly. 'But my stepfather, Dermot Maguire, and his sons, Michael and Patrick, did come. And Lord Sanders was killed.'

'You should think about getting the lock changed, and have a sturdy bolt attached to the door on the inside. I'll send a locksmith over tomorrow, with your permission.'

Catherine exchanged a glance with Erin, then said, 'We thought we might go and stay at the family house until he's caught. But Miss Maguire has to go to the theatre to rehearse, and it's further away. He knows where she works, you see.'

'It's certainly an awkward situation. This flat has only the one entrance, and it has a doorman. It's much safer than a house. You should stay here.' Andrew Jameison suddenly smiled. 'The theatre is covered, but I understand that you didn't have your usual car waiting for you tonight, Miss Maguire?'

How the devil had he known that? 'My father went to the country.'

'Next time you have to walk, let Chauncy know and you'll be provided with an escort. Until Maguire is apprehended, the pair of you should stay out of harm's way as much as possible.'

Smoothly, he handed Catherine his card. 'I'd be happy to personally escort you myself if you need to go out, Miss Sanders. Please call me.'

Catherine's cheeks dimpled and she gave him a dazzling smile that transformed her. 'Tomorrow, I have to go home to check that everything's all right and pick up the mail. I want to develop some photographs too. Perhaps you'd accompany me.'

'It would be my pleasure,' the man said, obviously willing to be dazzled. 'Would ten o'clock suit you?'

'It's just perfect,' said Catherine.

Erin grinned.

'You forward hussy,' she whispered in Catherine's ear after Andrew had departed.

'I'm smitten. Do you believe in love at first sight?' she said dreamily.

'He might be married.'

Raising an eyebrow, Catherine turned to the policeman. 'Is Andrew Jameison a married man, constable?'

'No, Miss Sanders.'

'Tell me all about him, would you?'

'Rumour has it that he worked for the War Office before he came to us. Hush-hush stuff. He's a very clever young man. Cambridge, I believe.'

'I wonder if he knew Kell,' Catherine said wistfully.

Seventeen

The first thing Catherine noticed was that the letters had been placed neatly on the hall table.

'Somebody's been in here,' she whispered to her companion.

Andrew Jameison took a gun from under his jacket and they silently searched the lower floor, noting the dishes on the draining board in the kitchen.

There was a creak from upstairs. 'Stay here,' he said and was gone, running silently up the stairs like a cat.

Catherine held her breath. Where was he?

Then came the sound of a door banging back against the wall, a loud curse and Andrew shouting in a voice loaded with menace. 'This is the police. Stay where you are!'

'I'm hardly in a position to move, old man, since I'm up to my ears in a bath of water. Am I to take it I'm under arrest?'

Catherine's eyes flew open with shock and she gave a little squeak of excitement.

'State your name?' Andrew said.

'Kell Sanders. Lower that blunderbuss, there's a good chap. I think this might be a case of mistaken identity.'

'*Kell!* It's my brother, Kell. Don't you dare shoot him,' Catherine cried out as she scrambled up the stairs and dashed through the door, knocking Andrew sideways, just as he was placing his weapon back in its holster.

'Good job the safety catch was on,' Kell drawled. Reaching out for the towel he pulled it over himself and grinned in a rather abashed manner at her. 'I'm not used to entertaining young ladies in the bathroom, even if you are my sister. Perhaps you and your bloodthirsty companion would allow me a little privacy.'

Catherine blushed and averted her eyes. 'I'm sorry, Kell.

I didn't think . . . Oh, Kell . . . you're alive . . . how absolutely wonderful.' She burst into tears.

'Exactly my sentiments, sis. Now, lose yourself while I make myself decent. Make some tea if you would, then you can bring me up to date with what's going on.'

'I warn you, I'm likely to hug you to death first,' she said tearfully as she left.

'Not too hard, I hope,' Kell said almost to himself as she clattered off down the stairs, thinking ruefully of his hollowed stomach and protruding ribs. 'I might break.'

The man lingered, holding out his hand. 'I feel the need to apologize. I'm Andrew Jameison.'

'Catherine's boyfriend?'

Jameison raised an eyebrow. 'Not yet. I'm just looking after her.'

'You seem to be good at it, and you handled that pistol like an expert. Who did you say you worked for?'

'I didn't, but I'm attached to New Scotland Yard.'

'Special Branch, at a guess.' Kell rose from the water. 'You frightened the hell out of me when you burst in, you know. Pass over that dry towel, would you? Why are you looking after Catherine? Is she being threatened?

'You've heard of Patrick Maguire?'

'Yes, of course I have. I've known him since we were children. Isn't he implicated in my father's death?'

Andrew nodded. 'Amongst other crimes. He's trying to raise the money to get out of the country.'

'And you think he might approach Catherine?'

'It's possible, since she's an easy target and was witness to your father's murder. Much as I'd like it, I can't be with her all the time. She'll be safer if she leaves London until he's caught. If you know Patrick Maguire, you'll have heard of his stepsister, Erin Maguire.'

Kell couldn't stop a smile touching his lips. Good Lord, how that girl kept appearing in his life. She was like a warm secret he nursed. 'Erin used to be our maid in Ireland. What of her?'

'Her stepbrother has been in touch with her, demanding money. Would you say Miss Maguire was reliable?'

'Totally. Her step-family treated her very shabbily, you

221

know.' Hadn't he done the same? 'She wouldn't willingly help Patrick, not under any circumstances.'

'Good. I'll take your word for it. Do you have somewhere safe to take your sister?'

Kell nodded. 'Consider it done. We'll go to my uncle's cottage in Dorset. I was going down there anyway, in case Catherine was staying with him. My car is in the garage and it started when I tried it, after a bit of fiddling. I'll be leaving at midday.'

'I'll go down and tell your sister while you get dressed.'

Within two hours Catherine and Kell were on their way. She'd decided not to tell Kell or Erin about the other until she'd taken advice from her uncle. And she'd sworn Andrew to silence about it as she'd handed him a note for Erin.

'You will look after her, won't you, Andrew,' she'd said. 'And yourself, please. Take care.' And she'd gently touched a finger to his face.

His glance had held hers for a meaningful moment. 'I do hope we shall see each other again, Catherine.'

'Of course we shall. If I'm not back before, I shall definitely be back for the opening of Erin's new show in April. You're invited as my guest, and you have my uncle's telephone number, so I hope you'll call me.'

She smiled to herself, sure that he would, and snuggled down in the car. Kell had insisted that she wear a leather helmet and jacket to guard against the cold and she'd found one of her mother's fur coats to wear over the top. There had been enough of her clothing left in the house to fill the small bag at her feet. And she wouldn't need anything formal.

She intended to ask her uncle to inform her mother of Kell's survival when they got there, though she'd brought Kell up to date with her mother's remarriage. 'She's Lady Templeton now.'

'She married Harold Templeton? I'll be damned!'

'You soon will be if you don't eat soon. I nearly had a fit when I saw you!'

'So did I when you came crashing through the door,' he said with a grin. 'That boyfriend of yours came as a surprise. I've got a feeling I know his face from Cambridge, though we were in different colleges.' He slid her a sideways glance.

'You've grown into a lovely woman in my absence. No wonder that policeman couldn't keep his eyes off of you.'

'Andrew isn't my boyfriend. Goodness, I only met him yesterday. He's rather nice though, and I hope to see him again.' Catherine touched her hands against her heated cheeks and said in a flustered manner, 'Why are you teasing me about a man I've only just met? I made up my mind not to marry after my fiancé took up with Olivia Winslow.'

'Olivia Winslow! Who is this man who lacks such taste in women?'

'Jonathan Granger.'

Kell whistled. 'He works in the company office, doesn't he? He's bright enough, but always struck me as being rather underhand. He's too old for you, I'd say.'

'Oh, I allowed myself to be manoeuvred into it, and he used me to gain promotion. I sacked him a few weeks ago, then promoted his second-in-command to the manager's chair.'

Kell looked shocked. '*You* sacked him?'

'I am a director of the company, and somebody had to. Women have been doing men's work for ages now.' She giggled. 'The company is surviving without him, and he's taken employment with Olivia's father. You know how crusty he can be. Jonathan has to start at the bottom, apparently. They're to be married on Saturday, but I've declined the invitation to attend.'

'I should think so. You'll be better off with the policeman.'

'We'll change the subject, shall we?' she said firmly. 'We must stop for lunch at the inn at Lymington. They serve a lovely steak and kidney pie there.'

He grinned at the thought of having a solid meal inside him. 'Whatever you say, sis. Have you seen Erin Maguire lately? Is she well?'

She shot him a glance. 'I see her often, Kell. Erin is on the stage and is doing marvellously well for herself. The public adores her. We'll go and watch her perform when we get back to London.'

'Yes . . . I'm so glad she was successful. She was such an adorable little creature.'

Noting the wistfulness in his voice, Catherine said,

223

'Dearest, Kell. You'll never know how much you were missed by us all. I shall telephone Uncle Charles when we get to the inn. He can break the news to Mother, we're not on speaking terms at the moment.' She leaned over and kissed his cheek. 'This has been the best day in my life and I love you, my darling brother. I was so sad when that letter arrived and I thought we'd lost you.'

'I'm just glad I had some family to come home to. The news of Father's death was a shock, or rather, the nature of it was. You must tell me about it when things have settled down a bit, if you can bring yourself to. Some experiences need to be left alone.'

'Was the war dreadful?' she asked quietly.

His mouth tightened. 'I think I'd rather look to the future than look back on the past.'

To which remark Catherine fell silent. Kell didn't know the half of it yet, and part of his past was at the cottage, waiting for him.

Charles Colby had an ear-to-ear smile when they turned up, and although they hugged and slapped each other's back in a manly way, their eyes were moist.

'Let's get inside. I'm frozen after that car ride,' Catherine said.

The cottage was warm and the fire leapt and crackled in the gate.

From the kitchen came the smell of roasting lamb. Kell was surprised to see their housekeeper there. Wolf got up from the mat to greet him, as though he'd never been away.

'Mrs Baily? How lovely to see you.'

'And you, Mr Kell. I'd prayed for your safe return, though we had all given up hope.' She exchanged a glance with his uncle. 'You'd better tell them both right away, Charles.'

'Jean and I were married at the local registry office yesterday,' Charles said. 'Jean is Mrs Colby now.'

After the flurry of congratulations, Catherine took Jean aside. 'Where's Colby?'

'Having his afternoon nap. He'll be awake soon.'

'Then Uncle Charles had better tell Kell about him before he wakes.'

Kell was mystified when his uncle took him into the conservatory. 'I'm sorry if it's a bit chilly out here, my boy, but there's something you need to be told.' He cleared his throat. 'Do you remember my daughter, Erin?'

Fear mixed with guilt stabbed painfully at him, and he fingered the shamrock hanging around his neck. 'Of course I do. She was such a lovely, decent girl, and so sweet. Nothing bad has happened to her, has it? I couldn't bear it if she'd died. You see . . . she made me laugh with her funny ways. She had nobody, and she needed to be loved, so much. I'm afraid I took advantage of that, and I'm sorry for that . . . but I did love her.'

'Do you still love her?'

Kell shrugged and pushed a hand through his hair. It was nice not to feel lice crawling though his scalp. 'I honestly don't know. I think of her now and again with fondness, but war tends to dampen a man's appetite.' His eyes met his uncle's. 'You're taking a devil of a time to get to the point. What exactly is it?'

'Erin gave birth to a son who is the very image of you, Kell. His name is Colby Kell Sanders Maguire. I have acknowledged Erin as my daughter, and Colby as my grandson.'

Kell's breath left his body as his uncle's words rang in his ears. Only Erin could have dreamed up a name like that, he thought. He would have shouted with laughter if he hadn't been struck dumb. Sinking into the nearest wicker chair he allowed the news to sink in. He'd taken his pleasure from Erin, not giving much thought to what the outcome might be.

He couldn't see this as a problem though, but as a gift. A grin slid across his face. 'A son! Damn it, I'm proud. I must make arrangements to support him.'

'Oh, my grandson has support. Me and his mother. And Dorothea met Colby for the first time a couple of days ago, when they came to witness our wedding. Though I haven't told Erin that yet. Despite everything, your mother was quite taken with her grandson. As he's unmistakably your son, she's willing to meet with Erin to try and make amends.'

Just then a knock came at the door and Catherine poked her head around. 'Have you told him yet, Uncle?'

Charles nodded.

Her eyes searched Kell's face, and when she seemed satisfied with what she saw there, she said, 'We'll be in the sitting room when you're ready. You *are* ready, aren't you? Colby's existence isn't his fault, you know, and he shouldn't be penalized for the circumstance of his birth.'

Kell rose to his feet, a smile on his face, eagerness tugging at him.

The sitting room was how he'd always remembered it, an expanse of polished wooden floor, the comfortable armchairs, shabbier now. The fire in the grate had a blackened beam for a mantelpiece, covered in twinkling brasses.

The small boy was sprawled on the carpet playing with the wooden train that had once been his. It could have been himself, so Kell had the strangest feeling that he was a ghost looking down on the past. Had he died in the war, after all?

'Colby?' he whispered, smiling again at the absurdity of the name.

The boy looked up. Eyes dark and liquid stared at him in surprise for a moment, then with a little cry of alarm, he rose to his feet and sped to Catherine's side, scrambling into her lap, as if it were a place of safety.

She soothed him softly. 'It's all right, Colby. This is your daddy, come home from the war.'

Kell took the armchair next to Catherine, to allow the boy to get used to him. After looking at him for a while, Colby pointed to a photograph in a frame and whispered, 'Mummy!'

Erin's face was suffused with light, a flower was held to her nose. Her eyes were alight with laughter and were slanted towards the photographer. Kell's breath caught in his throat as he picked it up to examine it. How exquisite a woman she'd become. His throat thickened. 'Did you take this, Catherine?'

She nodded. 'Erin and I are good friends. We live together in Jean's flat, though I imagine Jean will live with Uncle Charles from now on.'

'And Colby?'

'He lives with us. Erin won't let him out of her sight for long, except this Patrick Maguire business has cropped up and she feels he'll be safer in the country at the moment.'

'Why isn't Erin here as well?'

'She's rehearsing for a new show. It opens in April.'

Kell couldn't stop his smile from coming. 'So she made it on to the stage.'

'Oh yes, and she's very talented. She had a partner, but he died from the flu. Nevin O'Connor. He used to play the violin, and his father was our foreman after Maguire went to prison. They used to sing on the streets to support themselves until they were discovered.'

'I think I remember Nevin.' He placed the photograph back on the table. 'She's beautiful. Is she still bossy?'

'Yes . . . and she makes me laugh. Oh, Kell, Erin has been so brave. She saved my life, then Mother turned her away and she had such a struggle to survive in London by herself, even though Jean tried to help her. Then Colby came along and she had another mouth to feed. Erin was just getting on her feet again when the theatre closed. And Nevin died. I didn't know about Colby's existence for a long time. Mother knew, but she didn't let on. They might have died from starvation, but Erin always found a way to support them all. She has such pluck.'

'That's my girl,' he said softly.

She placed a hand on his arm. 'Is she still your girl, Kell? I'd hate to see her hurt. You see, although she puts on a brave face. I think she has always loved you.'

'I rather think she might be, Catherine. But I won't know until I see her again.'

Colby climbed down from Catherine's knee, picked up the train and brought it to him. 'Choo-choo train.'

'Yes, it is, you funny little chap. Will you sit on my knee now?'

The boy stuck his finger in his mouth, grinning while he shook his head. There was something of Erin in that grin, and a challenge. Kell laughed as he swept him up. 'I think we might phone your mother, and let her know I'm still alive, don't you? What's the number, please, Catherine.'

'Best if I do it,' she said. 'It will need breaking to her gently.'

But Kell wasn't in the mood to listen.

*   *   *

Erin was halfway out of the door when the telephone rang. She waved to her police escort, who'd arrived to take her safely to the theatre. 'I'll be down in a minute.'

'Hello, Erin Maguire speaking,' she said.

There was silence at the other end, then somebody whispered, 'Hello, Erin.'

The hairs on the back of her neck stood on end at the sound of the voice. It was a cruel joke to impersonate her dead sweetheart. 'Who are you?' she managed to say.

'It's me . . . Kell. Don't hang up, Erin. I know you think I'm dead, but I'm at the cottage with Catherine and . . . *our* son.'

'You have my son.' Panic filled her. 'It's Patrick, isn't it? You've kidnapped him. If you harm one hair on his head I'll hunt you down and kill you, just see if I don't.'

'No . . . no . . . listen to me . . . I'm not Patrick Maguire—'

Catherine's voice came on, calm and strong. 'Erin, listen. It's me, Catherine. It's true. Kell is alive and he's come home. He was taken prisoner. Isn't that the most wonderful news? There's nothing for you to worry about, really. You must catch the first train down tomorrow, one of us will meet you at Wool station. And don't forget to tell Andrew where you're going, so he can make sure you get on the train safely.'

Patrick Maguire had gained entrance to the theatre by simply walking through the stage door with a crowd of hopefuls who were auditioning for the remaining act in the show.

While their names were being taken by a woman, Patrick heaved a basket of clothes to his shoulder and walked straight past them. He found a dark corner and hid behind some scenery. It was a busy place. A crowd of long-legged chorus girls walked past, chattering and laughing, leaving an aroma of perfume and perspiration behind. People greeted each other.

There was the sound of a piano, of tap-dancing, singing. A man shouted instructions and banged with a stick on the stage. Scenery was cranked around. Somebody swore.

After a while he heard Erin's voice. 'I have to go down to the cottage tomorrow, Chauncy. I'll be taking the early train down to Wool, and will be away for a couple of days. Red will take me to Waterloo station. I hope me taking time off won't cause too much trouble.'

'It won't be. We're working out the lighting for your songs tomorrow, but I can use one of the dancers for that. And I've got to work in that new act somewhere. Take the rest of the day off – the week if you like. We'll be rehearsing in earnest the week after, so I'll expect you back then. I wouldn't do this for anyone else, though.'

'Thanks, Chauncy.'

Slipping from his hiding place, Patrick picked up the same basket and followed her as she picked her way through the backstage jumble to a narrow corridor containing a row of doors. She went into the one with her name on.

Patrick was just about to put down the box and follow her in, when a powerful-looking man with red hair came from the opposite direction and knocked on the door, calling out, 'It's Red.'

'I won't be a moment.'

Patrick wasn't fast enough to pull back into the shadows and the man stared hard at him. 'I haven't seen you before. What are you doing hanging around the women's dressing rooms?'

'I'm new. I was looking for Chauncy's office. I have to take this to him.'

'Go to the end of the corridor, turn right and go down a flight of stairs. What's your name?'

'Stanley Wilson.'

The man stood there and watched him walk off. It wasn't worth the risk of going after her now, Patrick thought. He'd catch the same train as her tomorrow.

Andrew Jameison received a call from Red MacDonald later that day.

'I'm almost certain Maguire was at the theatre today, boss. Although it was too dark to see his face clearly, he had an Irish accent and gave me a false name. When I went back to the theatre, Chauncy told me that nobody called Stanley Wilson is on his books. We did an unobtrusive search of the theatre, but there was no sign of him.'

229

'I'll post an armed constable in the lobby of Imperial Mansions to keep an eye on the comings and goings tonight. Even though the locks have been changed we can't take any risks.'

'Miss Maguire intends to go to the country tomorrow. She's taking the early train from Waterloo. From what I gather she was talking about it earlier with Chauncy. Maguire may have overheard because he followed her to the dressing room shortly after. Luckily, I got there about the same time.'

'Thanks, Red. We can't take any chances with her. I expect I'll travel down with her. Deliver her to the station and see her on the train if you would. I'll take over from there.'

'He knows my face, so he might smell a rat.'

Andrew grinned. 'Use your imagination. Kiss her goodbye, or something. You're on first-name terms, so Maguire will think you're sweethearts.'

Red laughed. 'My pleasure, boss. She's a feisty piece of goods though. I just hope she doesn't slap me for my trouble.'

'If you're an entertainer I'll eat my hat, Red MacDonald,' Erin said when they got to the station. 'You work with Andrew Jameison, don't you?'

He smiled at her. 'It's that obvious?'

'Well, you tend to hang around the theatre without doing anything much. You can't sing very well and you have a gun in a holster under your jacket. You look lovely in a kilt, though,' she teased.

'Thank you, Erin.'

'I saw Andrew getting on the train with another man as we came on to the platform. Am I in danger?'

'It's possible. Just sit down and go about your business, lass. And put the rug over your knees so you don't get too cold.' He placed her case on the overhead rack, and opened the window. 'I'll talk to you from the platform until the train leaves. We've got to make it look as though I'm seeing you off.'

A shabby-looking woman and man got into the last carriage. The man had a beard, wore a hat pulled down over his eyes and a voluminous mackintosh, even though it wasn't raining. The beard reminded her of a false one that a villain would wear in pantomime. The woman hung her head out of the window as the whistle blew, and gazed along the train. Other people were doing the same. The woman waved to someone. 'Everything seems sinister to me now,' she told Red.

'Try not to worry about anything, even this. My wife's going to kill me if she finds out, but it's part of the act, so here goes, and try to respond.' Red leaned forward and kissed her on the lips.

'You cheeky devil, but you kiss nicely,' Erin said to him afterwards as he walked alongside the moving train, smiling self-consciously and looking rather red in the face. She blew him a kiss as they began to pick up speed, noticing he studiously avoided looking at the windows of the end carriage.

She settled down with a book on her lap, not reading it, and trying not to feel nervous. She thought about Kell as she gazed out through the window and watched the winter landscape passing by. Soon it would be spring and the grass would be full of daffodils. She was not the same girl Kell had left behind. Would he still like her after all this time?'

When they reached Southampton she bought herself a buttered bun and a cup of tea, seating herself in the steamy cafe to eat it. There was no sign of Andrew Jameison amongst the teeming passengers on the platform.

The shabby woman and her bearded companion got into the same carriage she occupied, but further down. There was only one other passenger in her compartment. A man who looked like a travelling salesman, and smelled of mothballs. He slept until they reached Bournemouth, then woke with a start to glance at his watch and mutter, 'Late, as usual.' He clicked his teeth as he hefted his case from the rack and departed.

For the next leg of the journey Erin had the compartment all to herself. The wheels clacked rhythmically over the rails and the rapid huff-huff-huff of the engine lulled her to sleep. Her head rested against the corner and the rug was wrapped around her legs, for the heater didn't work.

A woman strolled down the corridor, glanced in at her, then strolled back up again and knocked at the lavatory door.

A few seconds later the bearded man came out of the cubicle and casually headed down the corridor. His way was

231

blocked when somebody stepped out from a compartment in front of him. As he reached for his gun, Patrick Maguire's hands were grabbed and secured with handcuffs behind him.

'Fecking polis,' he spat out, beginning to struggle, and the beard slid down around his neck.

He received a punch in the midriff for his trouble. Andrew Jameison pushed his captive into the nearest compartment and lowered the blinds. 'Get the woman,' he said to his companion.

When Erin woke it was to find Andrew Jameison seated opposite her. Her eyes widened in alarm.

'We're coming into Poole Station, Miss Maguire, where I'll be getting off. I want to put your mind at rest before I do. Patrick Maguire has been captured and will be removed from the train shortly.' He rose to his feet, tall and confident. 'Give my regards to Miss Sanders. Perhaps you'd tell her I'm looking forward to seeing her again.'

Erin rose to her feet too, all the tension draining from her now Patrick was no longer a danger. But she couldn't help asking, 'What will happen to him?'

Andrew shrugged. 'He'll be sentenced for his crimes in the appropriate manner under the law. The man's a coward who doesn't deserve any sympathy. You've been very brave. May I?' He leaned forward to kiss her on the cheek. 'Good luck, my dear.' Then they were rounding the bend into the station, and he was gone.

Erin watched from the corridor as Patrick Maguire and his companion were shoved into the back of a police van by a couple of constables. When the door closed on them, Erin knew it was the last time she'd see her stepbrother.

'Good riddance to bad rubbish,' she muttered as the train moved off. Butterflies attacked her stomach as she realized she was very near her destination. Looking in the dingy mirror over the seat she tidied her hair.

As they pulled into the station her heart gave a giant leap when she saw Kell waiting on the platform. Colby was with him, perched on his father's arm and clinging tightly to his neck as, with some alarm, he watched the engine puff steam.

How thin Kell looked, she thought. His face was so pale and gaunt that his eyes appeared large and bruised. His suffering showed and her heart ached for him.

She was the only passenger to alight from the train, and she carried the travel rug strapped to her small suitcase. She wanted to run to him, but couldn't, her knees were trembling too much.

Kell smiled when he saw her coming, a smile that broadened when Colby pointed a finger and shouted out, 'Mummy, hurrah!'

Her son was beginning to sound quite the toff under the influence of his grandfather, Erin thought, grinning to herself.

Then she and Kell were suddenly only a foot apart, and she didn't know what to say, except, 'Sure, but no self-respecting crow would pick your bones clean, Kell Sanders.'

His eyes were dark against hers, trembling with tears, so she knew the vulnerability of him. His smile was as she remembered it, warming her as he reached out to gently touch her cheek. 'You've grown into a beautiful woman. It's so good to see you again, Irish.'

'Enough of your blarney,' she said, falling in love with him all over again. 'The last time I listened to it I found myself in trouble. Give me a hug, so I know I'm not dreaming. Or pinch me, if you'd rather.'

'I wouldn't rather.' When he laughed and drew her against him, his chin resting on the top of her head, Erin knew everything would be as it should, and she was content to wait.

Welcome home, my dearest love, she thought.

Eighteen

It was April. The people were in the mood to be entertained. The Empire Theatre was packed to the rafters for the opening night. The audience stood around the sides of the theatre and at the back.

From where she stood, Erin could see her father's box, and the one next to it, hired by Lord Templeton for the occasion. Dorothea was in diamonds and furs, and sparkled like a chandelier. Erin could see Kell sitting there, handsome in his evening suit. She blew him an imaginary kiss.

The opening act had gone down a treat, and the dancers came rushing off, exhilarated by the prolonged applause, to change for their next number. There was an air of expectation in the audience.

'Now, the little lady we've all been waiting for. Miss Erin Maguire, the Irish Nightingale,' Chauncy said, and kissed her as he came offstage, whispering in her ear, 'Kill them in the aisles, Erin.'

The stage was dimmed, except for a spotlight on Nevin's violin, which was mounted on a stand. She walked on to a wave of applause then, waiting for it to die down, said, 'Many of you will remember my former partner, the talented Nevin O'Connor. He can't be with us tonight, or any other night.' She paused for a moment, then said as the violinist in the pit picked up his bow, 'I miss you, Nevin my darlin', and this song is especially for you.' She sang 'Danny Boy', nearly choking on the words as she recalled his passing. When she finished, there wasn't a dry eye in the house, including her own.

After that she sung 'Black is the Colour' in memory of her mother, accompanying herself on the harp.

She went off to thunderous applause and cries of encore.

Chauncy held up his hands for quiet, but it was a long time coming. 'Erin will be back to perform soon. In the meantime, we have many fine acts to entertain you with.'

It was the best show Chancy had ever put on, and the audience appreciated every moment.

As a finale, Erin donned the blue dress Kell had bought her and secured the bow at the back of her head. She told the audience, 'I'm going to sing the very first song I ever performed on stage in a theatre,' and she glanced at the dark interior of the box. 'It's dedicated to a very special returned soldier. One of England's finest heroes.'

> Mellow the moonlight to shine is beginning.
> Close by the window young Eileen is spinning . . .

When she'd finished, without waiting for the applause to abate she began to sing a stomping Irish jig. The spotlight moved on to the legs of one of the female dancers, who began the finale with traditional Irish dancing, That led to the chorus line and soon everyone was filing on stage to take the first of many bows. Finally it was all over, except for the national anthem.

Erin's dressing room was filled with flowers. Soon it was filled with well-wishers, too. Kell shooed them away and closed the door.

'You were more than wonderful, Erin. You were perfection.'

Tears came to her eyes, 'So many sad memories in those songs, Kell. It was good to get them out, but painful.'

He gazed at her, his eyes dark and lustrous. He'd gained a little weight over the past few weeks and looked healthier. 'There were many good memories, as well, and between us we could create more. Will you marry me, my darling Erin?'

'Do you love me, Kell?'

He pulled her into his arms. 'I've always loved you. Now I love you in a much deeper, truer way. When I was in France I questioned what I was fighting for. As soon as I saw my son, I knew. As soon as I set eyes on you again, I knew I loved you without any doubt. I always will.'

235

'What will your mother say? She doesn't think I'm good enough for you.'

'I've told her I can't live without you, so she'll congratulate us if you accept, and will welcome you as her daughter-in-law without reservation. She adores her grandson.'

'There's never been anyone else for me but you, Kell.' Erin told him. 'I'm like my mammy, who loved only one man all her life. You promised to come back and you asked me to wait, and I did.'

'It was unfair of me to ask that of you. And unrealistic to expect such a promise to be kept, but you were too young to know it then. I took advantage of what you felt for me. But I do love you, Erin, and I want to be a father to our son.'

She kissed him then, with all the love she felt for him. 'Sure, I'll marry you, Kell Sanders. Someone's got to look after you.'

He took her by the hand and led her out to where her friends and family waited. 'Erin has accepted my proposal of marriage,' he told them simply.

A cheer went up.

Being with those close to her, their faces shining with the pleasure they felt, Erin was filled with love. Mammy darling, she thought, I wish you were here to share this moment with me. 'Tis a lovely father you provided me with, and a fine man I've got for myself. You gave me a life when I was born, and promised nothing more. But life has given me much more than a promise.

Slipping her hand into Kell's, she shared with him the best wishes of their friends and family for their future together.